Praise for Debra Webb

"...a fast-moving, sensual blend of mystery and
suspense, with multiple story lines, an unusual hero
and heroine, and an ending that escapes the trap of
being too pat. I thoroughly enjoyed it."
—*New York Times* bestselling author Linda Howard
on *Striking Distance*

"Debra Webb delivers page-turning,
gripping suspense, and edgy, dark characters
to keep readers hanging on."
—*Romantic Times* on *Her Hidden Truth*

"...more daring than some authors would risk."
—*All About Romance* on *Striking Distance*

"Debra Webb's fast-paced thriller
will make you shiver in passion and fear."
—*Romantic Times* on *Personal Protector*

"...a hot hand with action, suspense, and last—
but not least—a steamy relationship."
—*New York Times* bestselling author Linda Howard
on *Safe By His Side*

Dear Reader,

You're about to read a Silhouette Bombshell novel and enter a world full of excitement, suspense and women who stand strong in the face of danger and do what it takes to triumph over the toughest adversaries. And don't forget a touch of thrilling romance to sweeten the deal. Our bombshells always get their men, good *and* bad!

Debra Webb kicks off the month with *Silent Weapon,* the innovative story of Merri Walters, a deaf woman who goes undercover in a ruthless criminal's mansion and reads his chilling plans right off his lips!

Hold on to your hats for *Payback,* by Harper Allen, the latest in the Athena Force continuity. Assassin Dawn O'Shaughnessy is out to take down the secret lab that created her and then betrayed her—but she's got to complete one last mission for them, or her superhealing genes will self-destruct before she gets payback....

Step into the lush and dangerous world of *The Orchid Hunter,* by Sandra K. Moore. Think "botanist" and "excitement" don't match? Think again, as this fearless heroine's search for a rare orchid turns into a dangerous battle of wills in the steamy rain forest.

And don't miss the twist and turns as a gutsy genius races to break a deadly code, trap a slippery terrorist and steal back the trust of her former CIA mentor, in *Calculated Risk,* by Stephanie Doyle!

Strong, sexy, suspenseful...that's Silhouette Bombshell! Please send your comments to me, c/o Silhouette Books, 233 Broadway Suite 1001, New York, NY 10279.

Sincerely,

Natashya Wilson
Associate Senior Editor, Silhouette Bombshell

Please address questions and book requests to:
Silhouette Reader Service
U.S.: 3010 Walden Ave., P.O. Box 1325, Buffalo, NY 14269
Canadian: P.O. Box 609, Fort Erie, Ont. L2A 5X3

DEBRA WEBB

SILENT WEAPON

Silhouette®
BOMBSHELL™
Published by Silhouette Books
America's Publisher of Contemporary Romance

SILHOUETTE BOOKS

ISBN 0-373-51347-X

SILENT WEAPON

Copyright © 2005 by Debra Webb

This edition published by arrangement with Harlequin Books S.A.

www.SilhouetteBombshell.com

Printed in U.S.A.

DEBRA WEBB

was born in Scottsboro, Alabama, to parents who taught her that anything is possible if you want it bad enough. She began writing at age nine. Eventually, she met and married the man of her dreams and tried some other occupations, including selling vacuum cleaners, working in a factory, a day-care center, a hospital and a department store. When her husband joined the military, they moved to Berlin, Germany, and Debra became a secretary in the commanding general's office. By 1985 they were back in the States, and finally moved to Tennessee, to a small town where everyone knows everyone else. With the support of her husband and two beautiful daughters, Debra took up writing again, looking to mystery and movies for inspiration. In 1998, her dream of writing for Harlequin came true. You can write to Debra with your comments at P.O. Box 64, Huntland, Tennessee 37345 or visit her Web site at www.debrawebb.com to find out exciting news about her next book.

This book is dedicated to a very special lady
who has struggled hard to overcome her own
physical impairments. Not once in her life has she
allowed being physically challenged to prevent her from
reaching for her goals. With all my love, respect and
admiration, this one goes to Erica Nicole Webb Jeffrey,
my oldest daughter. Never stop dreaming
and keep reaching for those goals.

Chapter 1

Sometimes I think I hear the roar of the wind blowing, but I've figured out that it's more likely the rush of blood in my ears when my heart pounds...like now.

I watched the two men hunkered over their beers. I could scarcely see the face of the new arrival at the table, but the other man's—the man I'd followed to this Lower Broad Street honky-tonk—was quite clear even in the low lighting of the smoke-filled bar. He looked furious. But combined with that fury was something else...something like panic.

A smile curled the corners of my lips. It's foolish, I know, but I couldn't help feeling a little empowered by his trepidation. Imagine, me—Merri Walters—striking fear in the heart of a murderer.

My whole family would be absolutely horrified at the idea of my walking into a place like this alone. The slightly run-down bar, nestled in the midst of numerous other more prominent establishments like Tootsie's Orchid Lounge, was located in Nashville's famous honkytonk central, slap in the center of downtown. It just wasn't considered proper for a young woman to be out and about in such places without an escort or a friend, at least to my mother's old-fashioned way of thinking. But then, I've always been different.

How else could the only girl in a houseful of boys survive? Whatever obstacles life threw in my path, I always worked extra hard to overcome them. Not that I fancied myself some sort of martyr or heroine, but even I had to admit that I had proved my relentless determination in the past two years. Whether my family was prepared to admit it or not, there were things I wanted to do in life, and taking extreme measures was the only way I knew how to make the point clear.

That's why I had to do this. Come here. To a bar not listed in the prestigious brochures offered by the Chamber of Commerce or among the suggested places to visit in Music City, tailing a man whose identity I'd discovered in a cold-case file in the Metro Police Department's historical archives.

That's what I do for a living now. I file the records of closed cases as well as cold cases deemed unsolvable by the powers that be. Each all-inclusive record is filed first by the date of the crime, then in alphabetical order by either the victim's last name or the moniker used to refer to the case, like Church Street Strangler or Eastside Robberies. Occasionally I retrieve a complete record for a detective who has discovered new evidence and decided to reopen the case. But this isn't one of those kinds of cases.

This is *my* case. I stumbled across it by accident. My predecessor had misfiled the record. According to the lady who trained me, the previous archivist had grown bored with her work years before she'd retired at age seventy. At first I'd been somewhat bored as well, until I decided to familiarize myself with the workings of Metro detectives. Just something to pass the time since my co-worker spent her every free moment studying for the bar exam. Conversation is seriously limited by a co-worker that fiercely focused on her future.

At fifty-one Helen Golden had decided she wanted a new career. Seven years later she was ready to take the plunge. I loved working with her, had deep respect and admiration for what she was doing. Hey, the woman was facing the bar exam as well as turning sixty in only two years. Maybe her example had prompted my own decision as I sought to learn more about the investigators for whom I filed and protected records.

There were the meticulous, detail-oriented detectives whose reports were methodical to the point that I wanted to scream *get on with it already*. And then there were the guys who investigated by the seat-of-their-pants method and who utilized one primary tool—gut instinct.

That was my preferred method, I decided after reading more than a dozen case files.

Forcing my errant attention back to the matter at hand, I surveyed the two men I'd followed into this saloon. The first, my primary suspect, stood tall—well over six feet—and was broad-shouldered. He had thinning hair about the color of the brown fur of a guinea pig I once owned. The beady eyes were dark brown or black as well. His square face with its perpetual glower and heavy lines made him look about fifty, though I knew from the file that he was only forty-one. He had a criminal record a mile long, petty stuff mostly except for two charges of felony assault. The one murder charge hadn't stuck. That's why I was here. After reading the file, I'd known, as had the detective in charge of the case, one Steven Barlow, that this guy was guilty, but the good detective hadn't been able to prove it.

Proving it was, admittedly, the tricky part. Charges couldn't be filed nor could juries be swayed by gut instinct alone. Unfortunately, in situations like this one, the police can only go so far. Their hands are tied to an extent by the civil rights of the suspect. A cop can't listen in on a suspect or search his property without a warrant approved by a judge. A cop can't lie or otherwise mislead a suspect beyond a certain point for fear of having the case thrown out on a technicality like coercion. In my unofficial research I had decided that it was vastly unfair to expect a cop to collar a slippery bad guy when he couldn't do anything underhanded.

That's the beauty of my plan. You see, I'm not a cop. I'm just an overzealous file clerk taking her week of paid vacation after her first full year on the job. There are no rules governing how I conduct my investigation. I'm limited only by the fact that I cannot arrest or shoot the slimeball. But I can set him up to get caught, which is exactly what I intend to do.

I watched intently as the two men spoke quietly but fiercely about what needed to be done. The first man, the one I'd followed, whose name is Brett Sawyer, used his hands occasionally as he spoke, making frantic gestures to punctuate his words. It hadn't taken a psychology degree to figure out what buttons to push to set this guy off—though I'd taken a few psych courses in preparation for my former career.

Until two years ago I was an elementary school teacher. But that person no longer existed. I tuned out that line of thinking and zeroed in more fully on the two men under surveillance.

I have to move the body tonight, Sawyer growled. His mouth twisted savagely as he flung the words at the other man.

…mistake.

I only caught the last word Sawyer's companion uttered. Dammit. I needed the entire conversation, but moving to a different table was out of the question. Sawyer had looked straight at me when I came in and sat down, but he hadn't looked again. Not even when the waitress came by and took my order. I had to keep it that way. His suspicion was the dead last thing I wanted to arouse.

I'm telling you she knows too damned much to be yanking my chain! Sawyer muttered fiercely. *Details. She knows frigging details no one else could know!* The vein in his forehead throbbed viciously, as if it might pop at any moment.

My heart skipped a beat. I knew with complete certainty that the *she* he mentioned was me. But he didn't know my identity…only my voice. My heart kicked into a faster rhythm. My ploy had worked. Sawyer thought I knew everything. And I did, to a degree. I had the case file, which included evidentiary information not released to the media, as well as Metro's top homicide detective's gut instincts and hunches.

I bit back a smile. No getting cocky just yet. Stay calm. Pay attention. I couldn't get carried away with my own ingenuity right now. The two men seated only a few feet away had committed at least one heinous murder. If I screwed up—got caught—I could very well be their next victim. The thought made me shudder.

So, I sipped my beer and glanced at the newspaper in my hands. I had it propped so that I could look beyond the top of the pages while appearing to stare directly at the headlines. I'd gotten pretty good at this kind of maneuver. Maybe I'd finally found my niche. Good thing, too. With thirty looming only a couple of months away, I had begun to worry that I might never figure out what to do with the rest of my life.

This could be my new calling.

The unidentified companion said something else I didn't get. Double damn.

I'm not taking the risk, Sawyer said. *I'm moving the body tonight with or without your help.* He chugged the last of his beer before slamming the mug down on the table hard enough to make the other man's glass wobble.

The companion's hands came up in a calming gesture. *All right. All right.* He glanced covertly from side to side. *...time...*

Desperation slid through my veins. I couldn't afford to miss the time and place specifics. But I couldn't get a fix on the second guy. Not good.

Ten, Sawyer said. *We'll meet there and do this thing. We should have taken care of this a year ago, then maybe someone wouldn't be blackmailing me.*

Your problem—the second man said as he glanced in my direction. Goose bumps poured over my skin—*is that you slept with a player.*

Shock rumbled through me on the heels of that statement. He thought...oh, God. Sawyer thought the female calling him was some woman he'd had a relationship with. Dread curdled in my stomach. Oh, Jesus. I hadn't anticipated that. What if he hurt the woman? It would be my fault. Surely fate wouldn't play that kind of cruel joke on me. I was trying to do something good here.

The companion pushed up from his chair, jerking my attention back to him. Six-one or -two, I estimated. Black hair, peppered with gray. Blue or gray eyes. Dressed expensively. I hadn't seen his face in any of the pictures in the case file or newspaper clippings, making him an unknown factor. He paused to say something I missed completely and then walked away. Sawyer stared after him a moment before motioning for the waitress to bring him another beer.

My pulse rocketed into overdrive. What if the guy who'd left intended to take care of Sawyer's old girlfriend? A cold, harsh reality sent the air rushing out of my lungs. I'd made a terrible mistake playing amateur sleuth. I'd unintentionally put someone's life in jeopardy.

A new epiphany washed over me, obliterating all the self-confidence I'd walked in here brandishing like a shiny sword. I would never be able to do this alone.

I needed help.

I didn't have the location for tonight. I only knew that the two men planned to meet at ten o'clock and move the body, which meant constant surveillance. I couldn't risk letting Sawyer out of my sight from now until then. Not to mention that if he planned to harm the woman he suspected of blackmailing him, I had to watch every move he made in order to keep her safe. But what if his friend took care of her? I shuddered at the idea. But I couldn't afford to borrow trouble.

Sawyer hadn't mentioned the woman's name. The guy in the fancy designer suit didn't look like the type to do anybody's dirty work. Those two facts made me feel a little better. Okay. There was nothing I could do about the other guy, anyway. My only recourse was to keep Sawyer in my sights and call for backup when the time came.

Another wave of uncertainty hit me, making my gut clench. How the hell was I going to persuade Metro PD to go along with my cockamamy plan? Even I recognized how seriously nonsensical it sounded.

I didn't personally know the detective who had initially worked this one. I knew Barlow was the best, but that's all. He would likely think I was some sort of weirdo with a major case of cop envy. But, it appeared that was a risk I would have to take.

Sawyer stood, then tossed a few bills onto the table.

My heart lunged into my throat. When he turned his back and took two steps toward the door, I shouldered out of my attention-drawing red sweater and left it on the back of my chair. I had already placed money on the table. I abandoned the newspaper and quickly looped my hair into a ponytail before exiting the joint. If Sawyer noticed me now he wouldn't remember a woman with her hair pulled back—sunglasses, I quickly shoved them into place—and a navy T-shirt.

I got into my car, parked several spaces away from his in a side lot. Thankfully, another vehicle, a gray four-door Saab, pulled up behind his Ford SUV while he waited for an opportunity to merge into Broad Street traffic. At six o'clock the last of the evening rush-hour traffic had peaked and started to lighten almost imperceptibly. I idled up behind the sedan in my little compact Jetta and waited.

My cell phone vibrated and I answered it, my attention divided between the display and Sawyer's big black SUV.

Merri, where are you? Did you forget about dinner tonight?

I read the words and cringed. "Sorry, Mom," I said, hoping the traffic noise wouldn't be picked up by the phone's speaker. "I completely forgot." I grappled for an acceptable excuse as the SUV took a left. The Saab made an easy right, but I still had to get out without causing an accident or incurring undue drama, like the blowing of horns. In the meantime I couldn't lose sight of the SUV.

Where are you? appeared on the small screen.

Uh-oh. Overprotective mom radar had reared its head.

"I'm meeting friends for dinner. I'm really sorry. I hope you don't mind."

Now or never. I nosed out onto the street in hopes the herd slowing for the changing traffic signal would give me a break. To my supreme relief it worked. No one made a fuss about letting me out.

Well, I suppose that's all right, spilled onto the screen next. I didn't have to hear my mother's voice to know that she was disappointed that I would be missing yet another family dinner. The Walters were big on get-togethers.

A new kind of relief surged through me. I had hoped the friends thing would work. My entire family worried that I didn't get out enough. How could my mother fault me for doing what she constantly nagged me to do?

Also, I had managed to get within four cars of the black SUV I feared I had already lost. Thank God.

"I'll call you tomorrow," I offered. "Maybe we can have lunch." I needed my full attention on driving.

My patient mother agreed to the date and let the conversation go at that. I closed my phone and tucked it back into my pocket, all the while hoping I would still be breathing come tomorrow.

I stuffed all the uncertainty and fear back into a little compartment in some outer recess of my mind and focused on the street and my target. I could do this. I had to do this. I couldn't pretend my inconsequential job—my insignificant life—was enough anymore.

I needed to do *this*.

Sawyer drove all the way across town, then left Nashville proper behind. I found it more and more difficult to keep a prudent distance between our vehicles. As many movies as I had watched with cops doing just this sort of thing, I hadn't realized how hard it might actually be. When he turned into the entrance of Spring Hill Cemetery I almost panicked.

What was I supposed to do now?

Think!

Don't stop. Keep going.

Somehow managing to hold it together, I drove on past the cemetery and parked on the side of the road near a copse of trees. It wouldn't get dark for at least another hour. I told myself again that I could do this. Then I made my way through the woods to the cemetery fence.

Easy enough. I could see him quite well from here, especially with the aid of my handy-dandy binoculars. I steadied myself and zoomed in on my prey.

Sawyer stopped and stood over a grave on the far side of the cemetery. The headstones in this area looked newer than the others. I concluded that the graves here represented the most recent burials, though all were old enough to have a nice green coat of grass blanketing them. If I remembered correctly, this cemetery was something of a historical landmark. I found it hard to imagine any of Sawyer's friends being buried here.

Did you do this to me? Sawyer demanded. The perpetual glower he wore had morphed into a savage scowl and was directed at the grave at his feet. Since the back of the tombstone faced my position I couldn't see anything but the surname, Bradshaw. Sawyer's tendency to constantly survey his surroundings allowed me to follow his words. *Celeste, you stupid, coldhearted bitch, I'll hunt down every friend you had. Every freakin' relative until I find out who you told. I'll kill all of 'em. Do you hear me?* He smirked. *Maybe not. It's probably hard to hear over all that cracklin' in hell.*

Celeste? Who was Celeste Bradshaw? Think. My heart pounding hard enough to jar my insides, I squatted amid the bushes near the fence I used for camouflage and tried my level best not to react to the words. The woman was dead, for God's sake. How could he do this? I gave myself a mental shake. What was I saying? He was a murderer. Nothing he did should surprise me, but somehow it did. At least I didn't have to worry about him trying to hurt the woman. She was already dead. Surely I could bring him down before he got around to her friends and relatives. A massive weight suddenly settled on my shoulders. I made a mental note as to the location of the grave for future reference, assuming I had a future.

I'd almost made a horrible mistake. I hadn't even considered the possibility that he might blame someone for what he assumed was a leak of information. Maybe this cop business wasn't for me after all. I hadn't thought out all the variables.

Too late to be backing out now.

He snatched a gun from under his jacket and fired three times into the ground—into her grave. I jerked with each shot, imagining the accompanying explosions and the path of the piercing bullets plowing into the protective vault that entombed the dead woman's coffin.

Casting one last sour look downward, Sawyer did an about-face and started to walk away, then hesitated abruptly.

My heart all but stalled in my chest.

I held my breath…held perfectly still as he scrutinized the shrubbery that concealed me. Reason told me that I was too far away and hidden too well for him to see me. But I couldn't be certain. For what felt like an eternity, he stared directly at my position as if some sixth sense had warned him that I was there.

Please, God. Oh, please don't let him find me.

Just when I thought my chest would burst from holding my breath, he walked away. Ten full seconds passed before I could move. I quickly retraced my steps and climbed into the relative safety of my Jetta.

Thank God. Thank God.

I watched in the rearview mirror as his SUV tore out onto the highway, and it took every ounce of courage I possessed to execute a U-turn and follow him.

I stayed as far back as possible while still keeping him in sight. As we moved back into the city limits, tailing him grew easier with other vehicles to use as camouflage, allowing me to get closer. If anything about this could be called easy. I suddenly felt ill-equipped all over again for the task I'd set out to accomplish. Where was all that confidence I'd woken up with this morning?

Sawyer returned to his office, presumably to resume the business of overseeing his numerous legitimate working assets. I waited in my car a safe distance away but well within sight of the exit and his SUV.

Three years ago he had purchased more than a dozen convenience stores for the sole purpose of cashing in on the lottery cow. He also owned a number of apartment buildings, which probably contributed to his motive for killing a man. The guy had stood in the way of a major deal and Sawyer had eliminated the problem, though no one, not even the detective assigned to his case, had been able to prove it.

First and foremost, no body had ever been recovered. That was the essential element of the defense's entire case. Without the body, every meager speck of evidence the D.A.'s office had was circumstantial. The charges had ended up being dismissed when the state couldn't come up with the body or irrefutable proof. Sawyer had walked away a free man. For more than two years he hadn't made a single mistake. Probably never would have.

With my two psych classes under my belt and my innate sense of people, I had taken a shot in the dark. I'd used the oldest trick in the book. I'd pasted letters together on a plain white page of paper to form the words that would shake Sawyer's carefully constructed little world. The message was simple: I know where you hid the body.

I had nothing to lose. If I was wrong about Sawyer, then he would simply get a good laugh out of my meaningless threats and that would be that. But, if he *had* murdered his competition and disposed of the body as I believed, he would worry, maybe just a little, as to whether or not I was telling the truth.

When I didn't get the desired reaction immediately, I sent more letters. Gave the details only someone who knew what he'd done would know. Or, in my case, someone who'd reviewed the case file and, for instance, knew that he'd taken exactly $657 from the missing person's middle desk drawer. The crime-scene report also reported that enough blood had been found on the carpet of the victim's office that he couldn't possibly have survived the attack, but there wasn't a damned thing that indicated a murder weapon or anything else. No body, just a bunch of coagulated blood.

But Detective Steven Barlow had a theory. No letter opener had been found in the victim's desk. None of his employees or associates could actually say whether or not he'd possessed one. When the pocketknife Sawyer carried was found clean of any sort of residue connected to the crime, Barlow had suggested that he'd used a letter opener. Barlow was convinced that Sawyer hadn't gone to the victim's office to kill him. The murder had transpired during the ensuing argument. None of which he could prove.

I, on the other hand, had nothing to lose by using Barlow's conjecture as a ploy to prod a reaction out of Sawyer. So I sent more cut-and-paste letters. I mentioned tiny little facts no one should know. I also asked questions like, What'd you spend the $657 on? Where did you hide the letter opener? It was a shot in the dark. A play on Barlow's hunch. But it had worked.

Sawyer was seriously worried.

Tonight at ten o'clock he intended to make a drastic move to protect himself.

I'd sent the first letter in time for Sawyer to receive it the day my vacation started. By Wednesday, when he hadn't reacted, I sent another from the post office that delivered in his neighborhood. That way I could be sure it would be delivered the next morning. On Thursday I broke down and made a call from a phone booth. The whispered message was simple: *I know what you did.*

By Friday, I had my reaction.

After all, my vacation was only for one week.

Now all I had to do was stay on his tail until I had the location. Well, there was that one other little detail. I needed backup. Someone who could take him down when he made his move. Even I wasn't fool enough to believe I could do that part alone.

With two brothers who are cops and two more who are firemen, I could call one or all of them, but that would be a mistake. Protecting me would be their one and only concern. I needed someone who could look at this objectively with an eye toward capturing a killer.

I knew exactly who to call.

Chapter 2

My voice deserted me when he answered my call. I stared at the name flickering on the screen.

Steven Barlow.

Barlow, thirty-five years old. Metro cop for four years, homicide detective for the last nine. Degree in criminology. Barlow was considered one of the top investigators in Metro's homicide division. He had served as lead investigator—the one who'd tried to nail Sawyer three years ago. I hadn't personally had the pleasure of meeting Barlow, but I had seen him in the hallowed halls of the city's police headquarters. He was tall, maybe six-one or -two, and wore his black hair regulation short. But the blue eyes proved his most disturbing asset. He hadn't ever really looked at me, but our gazes bumped into each other's once or twice in passing.

Though it was rumored he carried a heavier caseload than any other investigator in Metro, and his collar record certainly backed up his unparalleled reputation, he always looked calm, unhurried and more confident than any man I'd ever known. His entire demeanor screamed of relaxed confidence.

Hello.

The new word on the screen carried the same effect as a dash of cold water on my face.

"Brett Sawyer is a murderer," I said carefully. "I can prove it. At ten o'clock tonight he's going to move the body you've been looking for. Stay close to your phone and I'll call you with the location."

I started to disconnect but more words tumbled across the screen before I could depress the necessary button.

Who the hell is this?

That was the one drawback to using my cell phone. As soon as he checked his caller ID, he would know exactly who I was. But there was nothing I could do about that. I couldn't risk going to a properly equipped phone booth. I had to keep Sawyer in my sights. Couldn't move until he did.

"Just stay by the phone," I repeated before severing the connection. I sure wasn't going to ask him for his cell number, though it would have been handier. His home phone number was listed in the personnel directory. That would just have to work…as long as he didn't leave home.

I couldn't worry about that right now.

Two more hours. Besides, during that time I felt certain Detective Steven Barlow would track down my home address, the make and license plate number of my car, and my place of employment. If I was exceedingly lucky he wouldn't get around to calling any member of my family before 10:00 p.m. rolled around. Not that any of them could possibly guess in a million years where I was just now, but I didn't want my mom or dad, or even my brothers, worrying unnecessarily.

I could do this. Yes, I had my moments of doubt, like back in the cemetery, but for the most part I was cool with the way this appeared to be going down. Sawyer had made his contact and a rendezvous time had been set. All I had to do now was stay close, wait and not get caught. It was entirely possible that a man like Sawyer had people watching him for security purposes. In fact, it was more than simply possible. It was probable. I could be under surveillance myself at this very moment, but I doubted it since no one had approached my car. Maybe Sawyer wasn't as smart as he considered himself to be. Just maybe he thought he had gotten away with murder so he had nothing to worry about.

I felt my phone vibrate, and my breath caught. My heart squeezed once in my throat before slipping back down into my chest. I cursed. Getting this jumpy wasn't a smart idea. Get a grip, Merri. It's way too early to be this antsy. My next thought evaporated as my gaze focused on the caller ID.

Barlow.

What the hell did he think he was doing? Any distraction could be dangerous. But I had to answer... didn't I? I needed him. If he chalked up my call to some crank playing jokes...I couldn't take the chance.

"Hello," I said quietly.

Why did you call me with that ominous message, Miss Walters?

I stared at the screen as my heart bumped madly against my sternum. What the hell did I say to that? Worse, why hadn't I thought of this very scenario? Not only would he have my name after checking his ID unit, he would have my cell number. I knew that...I just hadn't considered he would call back. So many, many possibilities. Obviously too many for a mere file clerk to have anticipated.

I know who you are. I just can't figure out what you hope to accomplish with this hoax.

Fear blasted through me. Hoax? Oh, my God. That was the last thing I needed. If I couldn't make him believe me, he might not come when I need him. There had to be a way to convince him. But how? What could I say that would prove anything? Quoting my knowledge of his old case would prove nothing. I didn't actually have any evidence to back up what I knew would happen tonight. I'd launched this unofficial investigation on a hunch. The only proof of anything I possessed was my word as to what I had seen play out in that bar tonight. I had waited all week for Sawyer to react to the trap I had set. Quite honestly, I'd begun to believe I might have made a mistake.

Then he'd made his move. My conclusions on the case had been right. I had to see this through…couldn't let anything go wrong now.

I swallowed my trepidation and said the only thing I knew to say, "Detective Barlow, this is no hoax." I moistened my lips and plunged onward. "I've read the case file a dozen times over. You know I'm right about Sawyer…you knew it three years ago, you just couldn't prove it. I can help you do that now. Tonight." I sucked in a deep breath. "Just stay by your phone and I'll call you with a location as soon as possible. After that there won't be much time. You must come as soon as I call."

Silence radiated across the line. The ability to hear wasn't necessary. The absence of words on the screen screamed loudly of his hesitation. He still wasn't convinced.

How did you get the file on Sawyer?

Oh, no. I wasn't going to do his legwork for him. "I'll let you figure that one out on your own. Right now I have to go." I had already allowed my attention to be splintered by the conversation for too long.

Where are you?

I ended the call. I felt reasonably sure that the detective didn't have the ability to do an impromptu trace on my call from his home, but I couldn't be certain he hadn't put in an order for someone else to do so before he placed his call to me. Triangulating my position could very well be entirely within Metro's ability. I had watched enough TV crime dramas to feel fairly confident with that assessment. Why take the chance?

It was almost dark now. The sun barely glimmered above the horizon. Long shadows crept across the quiet street and lights glowed from a number of the windows of the high-rises along this block on the fringes of the business district. Seven cars besides mine lined the deserted street. Not nearly as many as I would have liked. At this hour most of the workers employed in the offices had long ago left for home, but a few remained to finish up necessary projects or to earn brownie points toward a promotion.

The building that housed Sawyer's offices stood only four stories but looked as new as any of the others. According to the directory posted outside the main entrance, the lobby and a conference room were on the first floor. The entire top floor housed Sawyer's suite of offices, and the floors in between, his worker bees. I didn't know how long he would work tonight, but I needed to be prepared to move when the time came for him to make his appointment. I couldn't let anything sidetrack me.

As if he'd picked up on the presence of unfriendly forces in the area, Sawyer exited the main entrance

and strolled over to his SUV, which he'd parked in the
small lot that fronted his building. His was the only
building on the block that had its own private parking
lot. That lot stood empty save for Sawyer's SUV. He
opened the driver's-side door and rummaged around inside but his movements lacked real purpose. He seemed
to be buying time. He closed the door and moved
around the vehicle as if inspecting the exterior in the
fading light. My heart rate kicked into a faster rhythm.
What the hell was he doing? His gaze abruptly cut to
the vehicles lining the curb on the far side of the
street…including mine.

I slid down in my seat until I could scarcely see
through the very bottom of the car window where it met
the upholstery of the door. My breath stalled in my
lungs as I waited to see what he would do next.

I didn't have to wait long. He started across the lot,
headed straight for this side of the street. What if he
walked up to my car? Demanded to know who I was and
what I was doing?

Not for a second did I dare take my eyes off him.
Above the dash I saw him pause at one of the cars
parked farther up, four vehicles past my position.
Every mistake I had made in my calculations of how
this little operation would go down flashed before my
eyes. I hadn't considered that he might have extra security, though I hadn't seen hide or hair of anyone as
of yet. Or that Barlow would give me any grief when
I told him I'd solved his case for him. I also hadn't

given any thought to what I would do if a moment like this transpired.

If Sawyer moved toward my vehicle…what would I do?

My fingers itched to reach toward the ignition and turn the key. With nothing parked behind me, I could throw the transmission into Reverse and barrel all the way down the block before executing a quick turn to get the hell out of here. But if I did that, he would know. The whole operation would be blown and then my efforts would be for nothing.

And Barlow would know what I had done. Not to mention that Sawyer would likely get my license plate number as I rushed away and he would not rest until he tracked me down. My new career, such as it is, would be over, but far worse, my life likely would be as well.

So, I forced myself to remain perfectly still. To keep my breathing slow and steady. To stay as calm as anyone could in this situation.

The top of his head disappeared from my line of vision and I felt my insides go cold. Was he moving toward my car now? Keeping low so I wouldn't see him? I balled my fingers into fists and fought the need to run.

I resisted the near overwhelming urge to close my eyes and wait for death to descend. Good thing, too, because a gray sedan suddenly drove past my position. Sawyer was behind the wheel. He didn't even look in my direction.

Profound relief washed over me. As difficult as it

was, I waited three more seconds before I eased back up in the seat and started my car. By the time I backed up and turned around he had stopped at the end of the block to wait for the traffic signal to change. In my peripheral vision I noted that one of the parked cars was missing. Why did he keep a car parked on the street when he had a lot in front of his building?

The answer was simple, I realized. He, unlike me, had contingency plans.

Though it was dark now I didn't turn on my headlights. I rolled slowly forward, giving the signal time to change so that he would be focused on moving through the intersection rather than on what came up behind him. As he pulled out onto the main street, I followed. He merged into traffic on the cross street, which facilitated my ability to tail him and allowed me to turn on my headlights. This new vehicle he drove was a late model, four doors. Much harder to keep in sight since it blended in with the other vehicles rather than rising above them as the SUV had done.

I felt damned proud that I'd managed to keep my head about me during that last minute or so. If I'd ducked down too far in my seat or closed my eyes, I would never have seen him leave. I would still be parked on that street in front of his office wondering where he'd disappeared to. I prayed my good luck and my nerve would hold out for another hour and forty-five minutes.

* * *

Steven Barlow had worked murder cases for too long to talk about. He shook his head as he allowed his mind to traverse the files and faces of his professional past. That was never a good idea. Too many ugly reminders of the evil that men and women alike could do.

With hard work he managed to bring the killer to justice most of the time. Hardly ever failed, to be quite honest. But three years ago, he had. Failed, that is.

Brett Sawyer had gotten away with murder and Steven knew in his gut the man was guilty as sin. But he hadn't been able to prove it. Whether Sawyer was that smart or just damned lucky, he still couldn't say. And it really didn't matter. All that mattered was that the bastard had gotten away with it.

Steven plowed his fingers through his hair and stared at the phone on the table next to his couch. What the hell was Merrilee Walters doing? How did she think she could pull this off? Not that Steven considered himself infallible, but at least he had the gold shield that gave him license to track down killers. This woman was a file clerk, for Christ's sake!

Worry gnawed at his gut. Did the woman have a death wish? He put in a call to dispatch and had all calls to his home forwarded to his cell phone in the event he had to leave the house any minute now. Then he requested a trace on Merrilee's cellular. Just to be sure he got her, he put out a silent APB on her car. He didn't want her name going out over the airwaves just in case anyone who owed Sawyer was listening and…

"Just in case she's nuts," he muttered.

After the initial call it had taken a moment, but he'd remembered the woman. She worked in the archives. Cute. Flaming red hair. Pretty green eyes. Shy.

She'd never spoken to him, nor had he to her.

But then, his social life pretty much sucked. He stared at the bowl of popcorn on the coffee table that he'd been devouring before her call. Hell, it was Saturday night, and since he wasn't hot on the trail of some killer, he sat at home, alone, watching a made-for-television movie.

Refusing to be disgusted with his own choices, Steven hauled himself up from the couch and followed his instincts. Might as well get dressed for business.

That old sixth sense—cop sense—was telling him to get ready. Merrilee Walters had gotten herself into a whole shitload of trouble, and if he didn't do something about it she would most likely end up dead.

No way in hell was he going to let Sawyer get away with murder again. Even if the victim had brought it on herself.

Steven shook his head again. What the hell was this little file clerk up to?

Chapter 3

That's the problem with being deaf. You can't hear a damned thing. My impairment is commonly called *profound* loss. You don't hear anything at all. I hadn't heard Sawyer open the car door or slam it shut. Hadn't heard the engine start or anything else.

I've learned to live with the lack of that crucial sense. What else could I do? But it had been devastating at first. Even now a slice of pain went through me at the memory. A few months before my twenty-eighth birthday I'd suffered a typical sinus infection. Nothing major, the usual nuisance. But the infection wasn't just any old bug, it was a rare strain that would evolve and spread and do serious damage before the doctors, including the best ENT to be found in the whole state, could recognize and stop it. In the end, I survived, but my hearing was gone. A mixed hearing loss, functional as well as neurological.

What on earth did a twenty-seven-year-old woman do when she suddenly found herself deaf? Who wanted an elementary school teacher who didn't know how to be deaf? One who no longer knew how to teach without the ability to hear? Needless to say, the school board did the only thing they could, they gave me a disability pension. And my fiancé, the very one I was supposed to wed in a mere three months, walked away from our relationship with no real explanation. I could only deduce that, as a songwriter, he felt that the woman with whom he would share the rest of his life needed to be able to hear and appreciate his music.

So, here I was, two years later, venturing out on my very first unsafe limb. Diving into my very first adventure as a handicapped woman.

I hated the term, but I couldn't deny its accuracy.

I moved into the right lane, two cars behind Sawyer. That was another thing, I could still drive. Deaf people are actually very good drivers. According to statistics, deaf people have fewer accidents than those who can hear. Maybe because we become more visually observant. Makes sense to me.

Speaking of visual observance, I had no idea where Sawyer was headed. It seemed to be a little early for getting into position for his ten o'clock rendezvous.

Oh, hell. Something else I hadn't considered. If the location was out of town, that would increase the time necessary for Barlow to arrive once I made the call. Definitely not a good thing.

I bit down on my bottom lip and toyed with the idea of getting Barlow back on the horn and telling him the entire truth right that second. But what if I did and Sawyer had connections in the police department? I hoped that wasn't the case, but I couldn't take the risk. I had to let this play out and hope Barlow would come through for me.

Whether or not this operation worked was in large part up to me. Just me. For the first time in two years I felt like I might actually accomplish something meaningful. I couldn't give up too soon…couldn't screw up, either. I had to make this happen. Had to prove I could do more with my life again than sit around waiting for a disability check to arrive or simply filing papers.

I shook off the old, familiar panic that attempted to creep up my spine. I would not let fear hold me back. I'd almost done that two years ago. I refused to go backward.

My family had rallied around me. Would have taken care of me the rest of my life with no questions asked. But merely existing was not enough for me. I needed more. I needed to do something that mattered. Something beneficial to society as a whole. I'd had that as an elementary teacher. I loved my teaching work…loved the children. Not a single day passed in my former career that I didn't feel as if my small part genuinely mattered in the grander scheme of things. Sitting at home as a deaf, disabled woman almost drove me crazy at first, before I'd convinced my family I had to contribute to society somehow.

One year later, after intensive counseling and training, I felt ready to face the world again. The counseling had helped me get past feeling sorry for myself. Unfortunately, even I wasn't above that pathetic pitfall. The training had taught me how to function without one of my senses.

I could sign, but it wasn't my favorite way to communicate. I was well into my twenty-eighth year by then. Speaking had been my primary means of communication for far too long to change. I could still speak, I just couldn't hear. One of the instructors at the academy for the hearing impaired had offered a solution I could live with. Lip reading. So I started to study the art. It's more than merely watching the lips…the whole face is involved, and like science, it is by no means exact.

I grew very good at it. Very, very good. Within months I could read lips and respond in a conversation with scarcely a delay. Most strangers I encountered these days didn't even realize I was deaf. So far, being deaf hasn't affected the way I speak. I did have to study new ways to modulate my speech. I learned the difference in how it feels to speak in a normal tone versus a raised voice or shouting. I paid particular attention to the tension in my throat muscles and to the reaction of others. Once you started to pay attention and respond more to your visual world, it was amazing how much you could read on a person's face. Like most things in life, everything was in the details.

Likewise, I could tell the tone in which a person was speaking by the expressions on his or her face and other subtle mannerisms. Once in a great while I meet the proverbial poker face. Then I have no choice but to interpret his tone by his words. I don't like the loss of control that comes with those rare situations. That was just another reason I hated talking on the phone. For one thing, I had no way of knowing who was speaking. I could assume, based on the number I dialed, who might answer, but I couldn't know for sure. Caller ID helped, at least I knew the name that went along with the number from which a call is made to me. Having no power over that aspect of my life was disturbing when I let myself dwell upon it—which wasn't often.

Sawyer took a left too quickly for me to react. I had no choice but to drive to the next turn and hope I could catch up with him on the first cross street.

I didn't draw in another breath until I saw his car move beneath a streetlight halfway up the next block. I followed.

"Thank God," I muttered.

With less traffic on this side street there was only one car between us, which made me a little nervous. He slowed for a turn. That turn, a right, left nothing between us. I managed to click off my headlights in the nick of time. No way was I taking the risk of being spotted. He would be watching for a tail. He couldn't be so stupid as to go forward with this plan and not be aware of his surroundings. He would be on the lookout for trouble.

Ten more minutes passed before Sawyer made another turn, again to the right. I recognized the area. Residential. Low rent. My heart pounded with anticipation, my palms were sweating. I kept swiping one or the other on my jeans to keep a firm grip on the steering wheel.

Thirty minutes later, with a full hour to go until the appointed time, he had driven around and around, seemingly in circles, before moving back onto the street he'd originally turned onto. What was this guy doing? My phone had vibrated twice more since the last call from Barlow but I ignored it. Couldn't take my eyes off my target.

Sawyer took another right and picked up some speed. The addition of some light traffic allowed me to turn my headlights back on. We left the city limits behind, but there were still plenty of houses and the occasional convenience store. Still, the farther from Nashville proper we ventured the more worried I got. I should call Barlow. No, not yet. I didn't even know where we were going…I couldn't do that.

Sawyer hooked a left. I turned off my headlights once more, praying I wouldn't run over anyone or anything. I wasn't familiar with this area. No streetlights. Wooded. One or two houses, then nothing. Once in a while a field would interrupt the expanse of forest. Without traffic for camouflage I had no choice but to remain dark.

He turned right onto a road that disappeared into the

trees. Talk about utterly lost. Maybe in the daylight I would have recognized the area. I waited a second or two before following the same route. His taillights disappeared around a bend in the road. Narrow, tree-lined. Gave new meaning to the term *rural*.

My pulse skittered, but I'd come too far to back out now. I made the turn…this one the "no way back" kind, because this road was one lane at best. If Sawyer turned around or backed up I would be in serious trouble. I watched him make another left, his taillights bobbing, onto yet another road—a constricted path, actually, I decided when I reached it. I blinked in surprise when I saw the interior light of his car come on. He had stopped and was getting out fifty or sixty yards from the last turn he'd made. I saw this only by virtue of that interior light. He was too far away for me to see anything clearly.

I didn't dare move a muscle, though he was plenty far away enough not to hear the engine of my Jetta, which according to my brothers ran as smoothly and quietly as the salesman had insisted it did.

Sawyer shoved his car door closed. The interior light went out. With the trees blocking the moon, it was black as pitch this deep in the woods. I had long ago turned off my headlights so there was no chance of him seeing me if he turned around…as long as he didn't hear me. I prayed my brothers were right about the noiseless operation of my little four-cylinder.

Okay. I had two choices. I could sit right here until he got back into his car and risk him seeing me when he started the engine, turned on his lights and began to back up, or I could roll forward, away from the road onto which he'd turned, and risk him hearing the sound of my tires bearing down on whatever lay beneath them. As best I could tell, it was a dirt road, but I had no way of anticipating if there was any gravel involved or how much racket would accompany my forward movement.

The one thing I knew for certain was that I couldn't just sit here. He was nearly two hundred feet away....

Screw it. I had to do something. I relaxed my right foot from the brake pedal ever so slightly and allowed the Jetta to roll forward away from the intersecting road where he'd turned off. I had to conceal my position before he'd accomplished whatever he'd come here to do. Might as well be now. Since I couldn't turn on my lights and no longer had his to follow, I had to assume the road before me continued on. I couldn't be sure any more than I could be about the one he'd taken. For all I knew that road could take him back to the main drag we'd left some minutes ago. Too many variables. Something else I should have thought of.

I parked about twenty yards away and shut off the engine, then took a deep, bolstering breath and got out. I eased the door closed and walked back to the road he'd taken. Moving cautiously to ensure I didn't give away my presence and because I couldn't see a damned thing, I slowly maneuvered closer to where he'd left his sedan. I looked around in hopes of spotting him. Nothing. Just blackness.

Damn. If he—

The bob of a flashlight abruptly caught my attention. He'd walked deep into the woods. I hesitated just long enough to consider that at this time of year there could be snakes or any number of other critters roaming around. Then I contemplated whether or not I actually needed to see what he was doing out there. I knew the location. I could always come back in the daylight.

Deeming that the best course of action, I backed into the tree line on the other side of his car, just far enough to be hidden when he returned. The warm, mossy smell of the forest settled over me but did nothing to soothe my jangling nerves.

At least thirty minutes passed before Sawyer emerged from the woods. My legs had grown cramped and the phone in my pocket had vibrated again. I saw the jog of the flashlight he carried seconds before he came up behind his vehicle. My eyes had adjusted to the darkness to the point that I could vaguely make out his form.

He popped open the trunk; the light inside blinked to life and cast a dim glow over him. My eyes widened as my brain assimilated what I saw. I clamped my hand over my mouth and swallowed the cry that rocketed into my throat.

It wasn't until Sawyer had dumped the load he was carrying into the trunk and something had fallen to the ground that I truly understood what he'd gone into those woods to get.

The body—or what was left of it.

The object that had fallen, in the brief instant I'd

seen it, looked roundish…kind of white in color. My throat closed on a scream.

The load had looked like a big old filthy sheet, bundled up in such a way as to keep whatever it contained from falling out of either end, but it hadn't worked. I shuddered violently.

He reached down and picked up the part he'd dropped. Bile burned at the back of my mouth as I watched him toss the skull into the trunk of his sedan. He dusted at the dirt on his shirt, then slammed the trunk closed on his cargo.

He'd gotten into his car and backed halfway down to the intersecting road before my trembling legs responded to my brain's command. I had to move. Had to get to my car. I couldn't lose him now.

I traveled through the woods at a dead run, ignoring the slap of knee-deep undergrowth and the occasional jar of slamming into a small tree or large bush. I no longer cared about the snakes or other night creatures that might be there. I couldn't fail. I had to do this. Get to my car…follow him. My future depended upon my accomplishing this mission every bit as much as justice was counting on me.

He backed out onto the road, right where my car would have been had I not moved it, and started forward. With him out of the way I stumbled into the clearing the narrow road made and ran harder still. I reached my car and scrambled behind the wheel at the same time that his taillights disappeared around the bend. He was headed back to the main road.

I twisted the ignition and shoved my foot onto the gas pedal. When I had executed a three-point turn I barreled after him. Headlights off, I slowed enough to approach the bend cautiously…just in case. Moved through the curve just as he pulled out onto the paved highway.

Muscle-quivering relief surged through me. All I had to do now was stay on his tail until he reached his destination, where his ten o'clock appointment would surely be waiting.

Sawyer drove back to Nashville.

It wasn't until he made the turn onto a street I recognized that I understood where he was going.

The Green Hills area.

When he continued on this street I knew exactly where he was going. The construction site of a new shopping mall.

The image of the man he'd met earlier this evening suddenly morphed into recognition. That's why he'd looked familiar to me. He was Reginald Carlyle, the man who owned or had developed almost every mall in this town, among others. What did he have to do with Sawyer and the murder?

Then it hit me.

Sawyer had bought up several old buildings. Nothing one would consider a big deal. Definitely not anything worth killing for, though he clearly had done just that. When I thought about where the properties he'd purchase were located, it all made sense. If Sawyer was doing business with this big developer, a mall or some other huge venture was planned for the properties he had acquired. Maybe would have been built already had they not been waiting for the stench of a murder charge to settle.

I parked my car behind a massive Dumpster loaded with discarded pieces of lumber and got out, then moved as close as I dared to where Sawyer had parked his car. Close enough to see that Carlyle had not arrived. Sawyer got out of the sedan and retrieved his damning cargo. He carried the remains to a spot about fifteen feet from his car and dumped it. I couldn't make out the significance of his choosing that spot. At least not until he'd strode across the parking lot and climbed into a dump truck. Wait…not a dump truck…a cement truck.

Oh, no.

I fished out my phone. Should have done this already. I punched in Barlow's number. My nerves twisted with trepidation as I waited through ring after ring. Damn him! I'd told him not to leave the phone. His home number was the only one I knew. When he'd spoken his name in greeting and it appeared on the screen I whispered my location and told him if he wanted that body to come as fast as he could. I closed the phone and shoved it back into my pocket.

Sawyer had backed the truck to the location where he'd dumped the body. The drum or whatever it was called on the back of the truck was turning, keeping the cement properly mixed. Jesus Christ. Even I knew what that meant. Someone had delivered that load of cement to him tonight. Had left the truck ready for his use. The only way the cement would have remained usable was if it were fairly fresh and the drum kept turning.

I surveyed what I could see of the construction site from my position just to make sure whoever had brought the truck wasn't still hanging around. I prayed Barlow would get here soon. From his home he should be able to make the trip in twenty minutes if he drove really fast.

Please let him drive fast.

I didn't know if he would bother calling in any uniforms since he wasn't sure about me and what I was up to.

Just then, another sedan parked next to Sawyer's, jerking my attention back there. I suddenly prayed as hard as I could that Barlow had called for backup. Maybe I should…my thought process halted abruptly as a figure exited the second car.

Carlyle.

A feeling of determination settled over me. I couldn't let these two get away with murder.

Sawyer and Carlyle stood next to the cement truck for a bit. It looked as if they were arguing. The lights that had been added for site security provided enough illumination that I could see Carlyle's frantic waves of exasperation or anger. Sawyer pointed a finger at his companion and shook it, his face contorted with fury. Nope, these two definitely weren't happy campers.

My fingers tightened around my phone and I wondered if I should just go ahead and call 911.

There really wasn't any choice. I couldn't risk that Barlow wouldn't get here in time. My fingers tightened on my phone.

Harsh fingers suddenly clasped around my mouth and I was hauled up against an unyielding body. My chest constricted with terror as the reality meshed fully in my mind. My phone slipped from my fingers. The cold steel barrel of a pistol bored into my temple. I could feel lips moving against my ear as whoever held me uttered words I could not hear.

I wondered briefly if I should bother fighting him—and it was definitely a him. I could feel the hard male contours of his body. I braced myself for making a move for his weak spot, but he suddenly released me.

I bolted but he manacled my arm with brute strength before I could get out of his reach. I whipped around to look into the face of my captor.

Barlow.

"What the hell are you doing?" I whispered, feeling that the sound was hoarse, with my heart straining against my throat as it was.

He frowned. *I…stay quiet. Backup…on…way.*

I struggled to catch his words, but in the dark and with him glancing around I missed parts. I managed to draw in a much-needed breath. Told myself to calm down. I considered what I'd gotten of his words and decided he wanted me to be quiet and that backup was on its way. I nodded, then pointed to the two men still arguing in the distance. "Sawyer dumped the body down there. I think he's—"

I get the idea.

Barlow had moved closer, giving me a better view of his face. I felt glad for that, but at the same time uneasy with his nearness. I managed a nod of understanding. Obviously he'd been here long enough to figure out what was going on. But how was that possible? How could he have gotten here so quickly?

"How long have you been here?" I asked. I wasn't sure I kept my voice as quiet as I should have. Obviously I didn't since he held a finger to his mouth.

I put out an APB on your car. A cruiser spotted you thirty minutes ago and gave me your location. He followed you until I got into position.

Just something else I hadn't planned for. Damn. Maybe I wasn't cut out for this work after all.

He moved closer still. *I just have to know one thing. How the hell did a file clerk...*

Reading his lips wasn't difficult this close, but he turned his head to check on our two suspects and I missed that last part.

I tapped his shoulder and he turned back to me. "You have to look directly at me when you speak," I told him.

Another of those weary frowns furrowed his brow. *What?*

"I'm deaf, Detective. I have to be able to *see* what you're saying."

For three fierce beats he simply stared at me.

You're kidding me, right?

Chapter 4

Who would have thought that finding out I was deaf would be news bad enough to overshadow bringing a murderer to justice?

I slammed the file drawer shut and huffed an impatient breath. The look on Detective Steven Barlow's face would stay with me for the rest of my life. Disbelief, shock even. He'd figured out in no time flat that I was a mere file clerk in Metro's historical archives, but his source had evidently forgotten to mention that I was deaf. He'd kept his back turned to me a good portion of the time while I was being interrogated. Only allowed me to see what he wanted me to hear, in a manner of speaking. But I was no fool. I gathered from his tense body language that he did not like what I had done.

Go figure. I helped pluck a murderer off the street—one he had failed to nail—and he had the audacity to be furious with me! Men, I would never get them. Especially cops and firemen. And I'd grown up in a houseful of guys who turned out to be one or the other.

I opened the next drawer, inserted the file and slammed the drawer back into its niche. Just because I was a woman didn't mean I wasn't as capable as any man. And just because I was deaf didn't mean I was helpless! I hated it when people looked at me that way.

Gentle fingers took hold of my chin and guided my face to the right, drawing me back to the here and now. My dear friend and co-worker, Helen Golden, smiled at me and said, *Honey, I know you had a rough night last night but don't take it out on the file cabinets.* She smoothed a loving hand over the beige metal to emphasize her point. *It's our job to preserve the past. It's what we do for the future.* She arched a skeptical eyebrow. *Even if some of us aren't satisfied being a mere historical archivist.*

"Not you, too," I grouched. *Was everyone around me against me?*

My co-worker looked stung. *I have plans, too.*

I sighed. She was right. By this time next year she would be working at some fancy-shmancy law firm. "I'm sorry, Helen, but I had to do this." She, of all people, should understand.

Helen folded her arms over her chest and tried to look annoyed, but she failed miserably. *Do you know that the chief—the chief of detectives, mind you—called me into his office this morning to question me about what you've been up to? Why, I've worked at Metro for twenty years and not once have I ever been summoned to his office.*

Okay, maybe she was a little irritated at that. How could everything have gone so wrong? I hadn't meant for it to be this way. The murderer had been caught redhanded with the body—well, there was still the small technicality of identifying the remains. It had been two years, it wasn't like they were visibly identifiable. But I knew. My letters and that call were what had prompted the bad guys into action.

Sawyer and Carlyle were both being detained as individuals of interest for questioning. The two men's overpriced lawyers were pitching a hissy-fit, but this time the law was on the side of the police. They not only had human remains but had caught Sawyer and Carlyle preparing to bury said remains beneath eighty yards of cement. The cement-company driver had been brought in for questioning as well. As I had suspected, he'd merely followed orders, delivering a truck with the requested amount of cement at the time and to the place designated. Money talked. No good businessman quizzed a well-paying client.

Faring no better than the suspects, I had spent the better part of the day yesterday being interrogated by Barlow as well as Chief Nathan Kent, the chief of detectives Helen spoke of. Both detectives appeared to be furious that I had taken this mission upon myself.

I explained over and over how the case had been mis-filed and I'd ended up reading it out of curiosity. The plan had come to me in a blast of inspiration that I couldn't explain. I had been searching for some way to fulfill myself. To feel as if I was once more contributing to society. I hoped that if I proved successful in bringing Sawyer to justice I might be able to move into a position with Metro that would serve two purposes—self-fulfillment as well as community service. But that scenario appeared to have bombed big time. The whole ordeal had turned out way different than I had antici-pated.

What's worse, you read a cold-case file and tracked down the real killer. Helen shook her head from side to side, a resigned expression dragging her usually smil-ing features into a frown. *And I can't even tell anyone.* Helen's bosom heaved with what was no doubt a put-upon sigh, but then her eyes glittered mischievously. *I hate secrets. What fun is knowing something so excit-ing and not being able to tell anyone?* She turned back to her own filing.

That was another thing. Not that I had done this for the glory, but I had hoped to prove to the world that being deaf didn't have to mean giving up a noteworthy life. There would be other deaf folks who could bene-fit from my story. But that wasn't going to happen, ei-ther. Chief Kent had put a gag order on all those involved with Saturday night's bust. Well, at least, the ones who knew how the events had transpired, including me.

I couldn't tell a soul. Of course, my family knew and was fit to be tied. It would have helped tremendously if Chief Kent had kept them out of this. But his concern for my condition and overall safety had preempted that possibility. Sarah Walters, my best friend and sister-in-law, was Chief Kent's secretary and probably the sole reason I'd been hired in the first place. If I had my guess, keeping my job after this would likely be more associated with Chief Kent wanting to keep his indispensable secretary happy than with the fact that I had helped solve an old homicide case.

Going home to my small bungalow on Greenview had been wishful thinking last night. My parents had shown up at Chief Kent's office and insisted I stay the night at their home. The chief hadn't helped matters by suggesting that it might be a good idea just in case some of Sawyer's men got wind of my involvement.

Wasn't that just the perfect ending to the perfectly hideous day? Going home with my parents like a naughty child. Not that I didn't love my parents, but I was twenty-nine years old, for Christ's sake. I was out on my own and a fiercely independent woman for nearly a decade before the loss of my hearing. I wasn't supposed to be going backward. I need to be my own person…to contribute to the betterment of mankind…at least to some sort of independent future for myself. I might be deaf, but I'm not an invalid! Why couldn't I get that through their heads? I had to do what I had to do.

It was the Irish genes I'd inherited from my mother's

side. We both sported the telltale red hair, though hers required a box of Clairol now and then. My mother had absolutely no room to talk about being bullheaded. No one, and I do mean no one, could be more stubborn than my sweetheart of a mother. Why couldn't she see that I merely needed the same control over my own destiny?

I trudged back to my desk and grabbed up another armful of files. Oh, well. At least I still had my job. That was something. A smile tickled the corners of my lips. As frightening as parts of my vacation had been, I had to admit, I had loved the thrill of the chase. My blood heated and goose bumps pebbled my skin with the memories. Maybe I *could* be a cop. There were laws that protected the rights of the physically impaired so they couldn't be discriminated against. I should look into that avenue. Who said I had to spend the rest of my life in the dungeon beneath Metro filing old cases for the various working divisions? I wanted more.

Depositing one file after the other into its appropriate drawer envelope, I lost track of time by mulling over the weekend's events. Detective Barlow was kind of cute, even thoroughly furious as he'd been on Saturday night. I couldn't help thinking of the way he'd hauled me up against his body to keep me still and quiet. Add strong and well muscled in addition to cute.

I pushed those foolish thoughts aside. He was probably married, anyway. Besides, after two years I had pretty much figured out that guys didn't go for deaf chicks. I hadn't had one offer for dinner or a movie, much less anything else, since losing my hearing. That first year, I had to admit, might have had something to do with my life-is-over attitude. But for the past year there hadn't been a legitimate excuse for being ignored. My outward appearance hadn't really changed that much. If anything I was thinner. I'd never been drop-dead gorgeous by any means, but I was attractive. At five-six I was average height. I kept in shape with Pilates as well as a two-mile run three times a week. I'd been told I had nice green eyes. I should at least get an occasional offer for dinner and a movie!

I shrugged off the depressing thoughts and finished the stack of files. Some contained new, quickly resolved cases that held hardly any reports or other evidentiary documents, while others held new information to be added to thicker files on older cases. The unsolved cases were designated a bit differently than the ones closed after having been solved. Occasionally a review would be done to determine if more could be done to help solve an old case. But that didn't happen often. There just wasn't enough time or manpower. Law enforcement was like teaching, there was never enough funding to go the full distance.

When I would have turned to walk back to my desk, a quick tap on my shoulder warned me that someone had moved up behind me. I'd been too caught up in thought to notice. At times I could feel the change in my environment when someone came close, but I had to be paying really close attention to be aware of the subtle difference. Clearly this was not one of those times.

Sarah, my sister-in-law, gifted me with a weary smile. *How's it going?* she asked.

Sarah, of all people, knew how difficult things were for me right now. She and I had been best friends all through high school. We both played in the school band. To this day I hated the sound of a flute. I rolled my eyes at my own slip. The last time I'd heard it, I'd still hated it. Sarah said the same about a clarinet. The truth was neither of us had cared for playing a musical instrument. Being in the band had been a means to an end. It meant we went on all the district play-off trips with the football players without having to don one of those cutesy cheerleader outfits and stand on our heads. What more could a teenage girl want?

I shrugged in answer to her question. "Is my name mud upstairs?" I felt certain she had heard any rumblings going on in her boss's office.

She dragged me over to the side, a little farther away from where Helen conscientiously worked. Sarah held my gaze a moment before she said, *Chief Kent is having a closed-door session with Detective Barlow and Chief Adcock right now.* She chewed her bottom lip for a moment. *I believe they're talking about you.*

Uh-oh. That didn't sound too good. I knew Chief Adcock was the chief of Homicide. Then again, I supposed it made sense, since the case I'd solved fell under his jurisdiction. I'd seen him at some point over the weekend.

"Am I in big trouble?" Translation: bigger than I already knew.

Sarah did the shrugging this time. *All I know is Barlow doesn't look pleased. Whatever the chief has decided, Barlow doesn't like it.*

A frown wiggled its way across my brow. Why would Barlow care what happened to me? I mean, it wasn't like we really knew each other. He should be grateful I'd solved this case for him. But I knew he wasn't. I'd skirted the law, which, technically, I had not been obliged to follow to the letter since I'm not a cop, and I'd risked my life without being smart enough to tell anyone what I'd uncovered. If I had been killed—I cringed inwardly at the thought—no one would ever have known what I'd accomplished. I could see that quite clearly now. Funny thing, I hadn't thought about that once while absorbed in the heat of the hunt.

"Is he angry that I got Sawyer when he couldn't? Do you suppose he doesn't like that I made him look bad despite the upside that a murderer has been apprehended?"

Sarah thought about that for a bit, leaving me with the need to distract myself or burst with anticipation. I studied the delicate features of her face. Sometimes her beauty caught me off guard. Long, silky blond hair, serene gray eyes, a face that demanded any man breathing take a second look, and a willowy figure to boot. I'd known her forever. My brother was really lucky. Michael was two years older than me. A fireman in the Brentwood area where he and Sarah lived. The two were planning to start a family this year. Sarah would make a terrific mother. Not once had she ever let her beauty go to her head.

I don't know Detective Barlow that well, she said. *But he doesn't strike me as the type to let his ego get in the way of the job. I'm really not sure what's going on.*

Her lips formed the words cautiously, her face un-committed to a particular emotion. If she'd looked overly concerned I would have been worried. Since she didn't, I felt relatively relieved. Relaxed but guarded, if that makes sense.

She draped her arm around my shoulders and gave me a squeeze. *I should get back to the office. I'll let you know if I hear anything.* She smiled. *See you tonight.*

Oh, God. How could I have forgotten about that? My folks had insisted that another family dinner was in order tonight. Since Saturdays or Sundays were gener-ally the days we had family get-togethers, I could only assume the worst. This meeting would be about me, same as the one going on upstairs. The one difference was the chief only held the power to make my profes-sional life miserable. My family, well…they held seri-ous power over my entire existence.

The Walters family home stands proudly in a quiet, genuinely middle-class neighborhood on the fringes of Nashville's west side. The houses that line the streets of the neighborhood are the signature architecture of the seventies. Think *Brady Bunch* tri-level. Four or five bedrooms, three bathrooms and always, always a den for the family as well as a formal living room for entertaining.

Not that the Walters family entertains on a regular basis, but holidays and birthdays are big deals in a clan this size. Especially when you take into account the uncles, aunts and cousins. Good thing they all have the big *Brady Bunch* kitchen and dining room, too.

I moved around the table placing the silverware next to each china plate. Blue Willow, the same pattern my mother had used for my entire life. At family get-togethers, each member always had his or her chore. The men were currently slaving—think the loosest definition found in Webster's of the word—over the barbecue grill while the women scurried to set the table and place the cold side items on the buffet.

All four of my brothers are married, but none has kids as of yet, much to the dismay of my folks. Since my hearing loss and the subsequent exit of my fiancé, the pressure has been off me to produce offspring.

I surveyed the table to make sure I hadn't missed anything and couldn't help thinking that the scene belonged on the set of *Cheaper by the Dozen*. All four of my brothers were lugheads when it came to the overprotective sibling genes. Not once in school did anyone dare to pick on me. Not the boys, for fear of being pounded. Not even the girls, for fear that their brothers would be pounded or, in the absence of a male sibling, for worry of being blackballed in the dating arena. In order to remain popular among the star athletes one had to stay on the good side of the whole team.

Boy, did I have a surprise waiting for me when I

went off to college. For the first time in my entire life
I'd had to stand up for myself without big-brother
backup. I guess that's when I realized what I'd been
missing all that time. I didn't want to be the sweet little overprotected girl who never got into trouble and
who never, ever took a chance. Needless to say, I made
up for lost time in a big way. The only thing conserva-
tive about my higher-learning experience had been my
major, elementary education. I dated a different guy
every week and basically had a blast. Not that I'd been
promiscuous. The fact was I'd only slept with two guys
my entire college career.

Life had calmed down when I'd settled into teaching
and my work had given me the sense of accomplishment
I needed. Why couldn't anyone see that I needed that
feeling again? It was so simple…such a small thing.

Someone tapped my shoulder and I found Lola, my
next-to-oldest brother's wife, waiting patiently for my
gaze to settle on her lips.

*Food's ready but first we have a family meeting in the
den.* She looked about as pleased regarding the prospect
as I did.

I nodded, then followed her down the hall to the den.
Everyone else was already there. I took my seat. That's
another thing about big families. Everyone has an assigned seat. The concept cuts down on the quarreling
over who sits where—it especially did back when we
were kids.

Martin, my oldest sibling, started off the conversation. Usually the opening words were issued by my father. That he'd deferred to the senior member of Metro's police force in the family set me on edge. This was no typical family meeting. This was about me and my little undercover escapade.

Merri, you know how much we all love you.

Uh-oh. Now I was really worried. In my experience, whenever a family meeting started off with those words it usually meant I was grounded for at least a week. But I was almost thirty…grounding was not likely on the agenda.

I nodded, well aware that everyone in the room expected me to respond in some way.

What you did this past week, however heroic, was very foolish.

Anger flushed my cheeks. "We've already been over this," I said pointedly. "I don't want to talk about it anymore." I glanced at Sarah in hopes of getting some support.

She moistened her lips, looked from me to Martin. *The chief has already counseled her firmly about it,* she offered. She managed a smile for my benefit. *I don't think we have to worry about our Merri getting into anything over her head like this again.*

As much as I appreciated Sarah's bolstering words, she was wrong. They were all wrong. I looked from one concerned face to the next. How did I make them see that I had to do something more? Being a file clerk, or historical archivist, as Helen would say, simply was not enough.

"Mom, Dad—" I met the gaze of each as I spoke "—as much as I understand and appreciate your concern, you have to understand my position. I have aspirations." I searched my father's eyes. The eyes of a man who had risen from untrained office assistant to the top CPA in his firm while raising a family. Funny, I mused, momentarily distracted by the idea. Not a single child he'd spawned had gone into his line of "safe" work. Why was it so unthinkable that I would want to do more? "There's no point in discussing the subject further, because you already know how I feel." We'd had this talk hundreds of times since the onset of my disability.

But the risk you took this time was out of character even for you, Merri. This from my mom.

That was true. I couldn't really explain where that had come from. As fiercely independent as I'd been since my college days, I'd never been foolhardy. But when I'd read the case file on Sawyer I just couldn't help myself. The files I'd read previously had set me on fire…had fueled a yearning inside me like I'd never before experienced. I loved trying to figure out who the bad guy was…trying to solve the puzzle. What was so bad about that?

I started to say as much, but my father stopped me with an uplifted hand. I held my tongue and let him speak. To this day, not a single Walters kid back-talked.

We've discussed what happened at length.

A sinking feeling, disappointment or something on that order, tugged at my stomach. We'd talked as a family once last night. When had they talked at length? Why hadn't I been included in the discussion, especially considering I was the subject?

Merri, my father went on, the worry in his eyes only adding to the hurt starting to well inside me, *we feel that perhaps additional counseling is in order. The catastrophic changes in your life these past two years are enough to make anyone behave erratically. We want you to be happy, but we also want you to be safe.*

I felt utterly betrayed. I surveyed the people I knew with complete certainty loved me and couldn't help feeling that they'd let me down. They just didn't understand how much I needed their complete understanding right now.

Very little of what was said after that penetrated the haze of disappointment. Each of my brothers took his turn telling me how I had to be extra careful, couldn't look out for myself the way I used to. Even Sarah remained quiet, rather than suggesting otherwise.

Nothing I did or said would matter, so I didn't bother arguing. I let them talk, get it all out on the table. But none of it would change my mind.

For the first time in my life I truly felt alone. After a lifetime of having my family's full support, it was one hell of a letdown. But I couldn't judge them too harshly. Every single one of them had my best interests at heart. They all loved me…they just didn't get it.

We ate dinner in relative silence. Occasionally someone would bring up the winner of some sporting event or a late-breaking news story they'd heard. The atmosphere in the room had gone from solemn determination to walking-on-eggshells tension.

I had caused this. My entire family was worried and uncomfortable and it was my fault. How could my plan have gone so awry? I thought I was doing the right thing.

Would it be this way from now on? Could they ever accept that I still had hopes and dreams despite my inability to hear? I couldn't spend the rest of my life pretending I was happy and avoiding any semblance of the unsafe. I knew that about myself if I knew nothing else. The tricky part would be making them see that I could do more. Being deaf didn't have to be the end of my life. It could be the beginning.

Maybe my impairment would actually empower me. Sitting here now I watched my family eat and chat, all looking healthy and happy. Unless I looked directly at their lips I had no idea what any of them said. I heard absolutely nothing. Silence. There were times when I thought I heard things, but the doctors had explained that having spent so many years in the world of the hearing, I might mistake knowing for hearing. I knew what a fork scraping against a plate sounded like. Therefore, when I watched someone eating, sometimes I thought I heard the sound when actually what I perceived as hearing was a memory.

I couldn't help wondering if that was what gave me the ability to focus so intently on solving a case. I didn't have to tune out noise or my surroundings, that was already done.

I could be very good at investigating cases. I wasn't sure being a detective was right for me, but something on that order. Maybe a profiler of some sort.

My family, as much as I loved each and every one of them, would just have to get over it.

I drove home that night still preoccupied by my father's words. They thought I needed more counseling. Well that wasn't going to happen. I didn't need to talk over my problems with a shrink. I needed to get on with my life. No need to pay two hundred bucks an hour to hear what I already knew.

Too tired to bother with the garage, I parked in the driveway and took my time trudging up the front steps. Sleep would be good about now. I felt exhausted since I hadn't actually gotten very much sleep Saturday or Sunday night. I'd been far too keyed up. I glanced across the street and noted the car parked there. The chief had mentioned there would be someone watching my house for the next few days…just in case. That was likely standard procedure and not due to my inability to hear.

Thankful I'd left the porch light on, I shoved the key into the lock, but before I could twist it, a hand settled on my arm. A squeal escaped me as I whirled to face the possible threat.

Steven Barlow.

I pressed my hand to my throat and fought to catch my breath. "What're you doing here?" Damn. He'd scared me to death. Boy, was I glad my folks hadn't been here to witness that.

I didn't get a chance to talk to you today.

I felt my cheeks heat with embarrassment as he looked me up and down, thoroughly assessing me before allowing his gaze to settle back on mine. Why was it he made me so nervous? So ill at ease in my own skin?

Finding my voice, I asked archly, "Was there something else we failed to go over?" We'd talked plenty already, and none of it had been pleasant. He stood firmly on the side of my family…I should be careful…taking risks was not smart.

He shook his head. *I think we covered most everything.* He looked away for a moment as if he didn't want me to see whatever was in his eyes. Eventually that piercing blue gaze fixed back on mine. *I didn't come here to give you a hard time, Miss Walters.*

Oddly, at that moment, when I should have been mad as hell, I couldn't help wondering what his voice sounded like. It was silly, I know. But I couldn't help it. Deep and husky or low and smooth as silk? Did he have any sort of accent? I didn't know if he'd grown up in the south. I really didn't know much of anything about him.

I forced my attention back on the conversation. "Then why did you come here, Detective Barlow?"

I wanted to tell you in person that we've moved ahead with formal charges against both Sawyer and Carlyle. He searched my eyes again, looking for a reaction maybe. I'm sure he saw my unrepentant glee. *And, the truth is, we couldn't have done this without you.*

A little shock radiated through me. Well, what do you know? Someone was finally admitting that I did good.

I beat back a smug smile. "Thank you, Detective. I appreciate your saying so."

He nodded. *Keeping your name out of the papers has nothing to do with blowing our own horn or trying to take credit for what you did,* he went on. *We're simply attempting to protect you from any fallout. There's no way for us to know all of Sawyer's or Carlyle's connections.*

I had no doubt about that. "I understand."

He set his hands on his hips, pushing the lapels of his elegant navy suit aside. He was the only detective I knew who dressed so well. His white shirt looked freshly starched, though I felt certain he'd been wearing it all day. The navy-and-gray-striped tie completed the classy look.

You took far too many risks, Miss Walters, despite the good that you did. I hope you'll keep that in mind in the future.

I wasn't sure what he expected me to say to that so I didn't say anything at all. I was sick to death of hearing about the risks I'd taken. Life was a risk. Walking out your front door in the morning was a risk. Driving down the street was a risk. Nothing about this life was certain. I felt I'd learned that better than most.

When I didn't immediately respond he looked away

for a moment, then said, *Good night, Miss Walters,* and walked away.

He got into his nondescript black sedan, which he'd parked behind mine, and drove away.

I stood on my porch for a long while after that, just thinking. He was right. So was my family. I had taken several huge risks in the past few days. But the risks had been necessary to get the job done. I was no naive kid. I had been willing to take them. Why was it they added up to nothing? Didn't count?

What was it going to take to make people realize that I couldn't just fade into the background? I would never be happy simply existing.

There had to be more.

I wouldn't accept any other scenario.

Maybe I was in over my head, but that's exactly where I wanted to be.

Chapter 5

Tuesday afternoon at quarter past four I tugged my purse strap onto my shoulder and waved a goodbye to Helen, whose shift didn't end until five. Today had been busier than usual and I was ready to call it a day. Still, I didn't exactly look forward to going home. At least being busy had kept my mind off last night's family meeting. No one at work had mentioned the incident, not even Helen. I had a feeling Chief Kent had made sure all who knew about my undercover stint were reminded not to discuss the episode. I hadn't heard a single peep from a soul.

A couple of the detectives who dropped by the counter to check out a case file had studied me a little closer than usual, but that could have been my imagination.

At the elevator I stabbed the call button and the doors slid open immediately. To my surprise Sarah waited in the car. She smiled.

I was just coming to get you.

I hated the way my guard went up immediately. This was Sarah, my lifelong friend…my brother's wife. I shouldn't feel ill at ease with her just because she was also the boss's secretary. But somehow I did.

"What's up?" I managed an answering smile. My fingers twisted around the strap of my purse in anticipation of the worst.

She flared her hands and adopted a "dunno" expression. *Chief Kent would like you to sit in on an impromptu meeting with the other chiefs.*

The somersault in my chest knocked the breath right out of my lungs. "Okay." I sucked in a mouthful of oxygen and joined her in the elevator. Looking as cool as a cucumber, Sarah leaned forward and pressed the button for floor six. My stomach dropped to my feet with the upward momentum of the car. Lord, what now? Had the chief decided he couldn't keep me around after all? Maybe he'd decided I could be the poster child for things not to do while employed by Metro.

I tried my best to keep my composure from slipping. I didn't want to look scared or even nervous, for that matter. There was nothing I could do to change the outcome of the meeting except maybe beg for a second chance. Surely I could find another job. I had an excellent record with the exception of this one deviation.

That had to count for something. Then again, I supposed I should have thought of that before I launched my Merri Walters amateur sleuth persona.

On the sixth floor we stepped off the elevator onto plush carpeting. Unlike my work area in the basement, the walls up here were dressed in a warm coat of paint the color of sand. Reserved but elegant paintings, each highlighted by its own personal spotlight, adorned the walls. In the center of the reception area and at the end of the corridor on the left as well as the right, a lavishly detailed wood table supported a massive, lush bouquet of flowers.

Sarah made a polite comment to the receptionist and then led me toward the corridor to the right and the main conference room, a place I'd never before had any reason to visit.

She hesitated before opening the door and squeezed my arm. *You're going to be fine, Merri.*

I nodded, uncertain of my voice. I wasn't as worried about being fine as in *not in serious trouble,* I abruptly realized. I was worried about being unemployed and having no one to blame but myself.

Sarah pushed open the door and waited for me to step inside. When I'd ventured into the unknown territory, she gave me one last reassuring smile then stepped back into the corridor, closing the door behind her. I drew in a steadying breath and turned my attention to the room at large. The seven men seated around the oval conference table stood and Chief Kent introduced me before stating the name of each man in the room. Somehow I managed to keep my smile in place and my knees from giving way as I alternately watched his lips and met the expectant gazes of those he introduced.

Please join us, Miss Walters. Chief Kent gestured to a chair directly across from his. *We have a lot of ground to cover.*

The man closest to me pushed in my chair after I'd taken my seat. When he had settled back into his, the meeting began.

For the next forty-five minutes I watched the men around the table discuss issues ranging from budget cuts to changes in the political atmosphere of Nashville. Not once did any of them ask me a question or direct any comment to me. To say I felt out of place would be a mammoth understatement. I felt like the token female in a hard-core men's club. I truly had no idea why I was here.

When the meeting concluded the room cleared without much fanfare. A few nods were tossed my way but nothing else. About the same time I decided this was my cue to leave as well, Chief Kent asked me to stay.

I waited near the seat I'd kept warm for nearly an hour, mulling over yet again the fundamental question of why I had been asked to attend this meeting. I considered that surely if his intent had been to fire me he wouldn't have had me sit in on this meeting. It didn't make sense to fire an employee after exposing her to the worries and whims of all one's chiefs. Adcock and Kent, on the other side of the room with their backs turned to me, continued a private conversation.

I resisted the urge to shift from foot to foot, tried to remain patient. I couldn't understand why I'd been asked to stay if the conversation didn't include me. Just then the door opened and I glanced fully in that direction to identify who had entered the room. My jaw dropped and an entirely new kind of tension trickled through me.

Detective Steven Barlow.

So maybe I'd counted my chickens before they hatched. The weekend's incident was the only reason I could think for having Barlow show up for a meeting with the chiefs that involved me.

Let's take our seats, Chief Kent suggested when Detective Barlow had moved around to the end of the polished conference table.

My knees bent of their own accord, lowering me into my chair. Chief Kent resumed his seat directly across from me while Chief Adcock, the chief of Homicide, sat to his left. Barlow didn't offer to move closer. Instead, he remained at the very end of the oval mahogany table designed to seat sixteen. That shouldn't have made me uneasy, but it did. Truth was, he made me uneasy period.

Miss Walters, Chief Kent began, *I'm sure you're aware that this weekend's events have been discussed in-depth by Chief Adcock and myself during the past forty-eight hours.*

"Yes, sir." I swallowed against the lump of uncer-

tainty welling in my throat. How could I not have fore-
seen all this negative attention? I had foolishly assumed
that everyone would be so thrilled I'd solved the case
that I would be a hero…or at least admired and respected on some level. Man oh man, talk about failed
expectations.

*Chief Adcock and I have considered at length how
you managed this enormous feat. We're intrigued with
your somewhat raw investigative talent.*

*Having said that…*Chief Adcock picked up the ball
next. *We asked you to sit in on this meeting as a sort of test.*

A test? I wasn't sure I understood. I glanced in Barlow's direction but he kept his gaze focused straight
ahead, not really looking at anyone in the room. My un-
easiness scooted up a notch.

"I'm not quite following," I admitted, looking from
one chief to the other.

Barlow didn't react, but the two chiefs exchanged a
look. After a moment Kent took the lead.

*We'd like you to tell us as best you can, considering
you had no advance notice of what was expected of you,
what this meeting was about. Try to recall as many of
the comments made by the various attendees as you can.*

I have to admit, that was about the last thing I expected him to say. But, if this little test would help me
keep my job, I was definitely game. With that in mind,
I did as requested. Taking my time, paying particular
care not to leave anything out, I related everything I remembered about the meeting.

When I'd finished I said as much.

For several seconds no one in the room spoke or moved. I worried then that maybe my voice had shaken more than I'd realized or that I'd left out something pertinent.

Had I failed the test? It was difficult to gauge since I didn't really know what precise milestones or standards were included in the test.

I felt relatively confident about how much of the meeting I had recalled, but that didn't mean I'd recited what they wanted to hear. Was I supposed to have made some sort of final conclusions or assessments? I didn't think so.

Excuse us a moment, Miss Walters, Chief Kent said. He and Chief Adcock stood and moved to the far side of the room, turning their backs to me once more, ensuring I didn't eavesdrop on their conversation.

I glanced at Detective Barlow, but he didn't meet my gaze. The tension twisting inside me mounted. What was up with this? I resisted the urge to squirm in my seat. I did smooth my skirt, before clasping my hands in my lap. I wondered briefly if Sarah waited for me outside. Then I speculated as to whether or not she'd called my folks and relayed the latest in the saga of Merri Walters's doomed career moves.

I looked up when the two chiefs approached the table once more. I guessed now I would learn my fate.

Miss Walters, Chief Kent said as he sat down, *we have a rather unorthodox offer to make you.*

When the chief's gaze shot to his right, to Detective Barlow, I turned in that direction as well.

I want it on the record, Barlow said without even a glance at me, *that I object to this so-called unorthodox offer.* His expression alone made it quite clear that he disagreed with whatever Chief Kent was about to propose.

Anticipation seared through my veins. What was going on here?

Your objection is noted, Adcock said. He did so rather pointedly, if the irritation lining his face was any measure.

A moment passed before Kent spoke again. *If you choose not to accept this offer it will in no way affect your present position, Miss Walters.*

He definitely had my attention now.

I moistened my lips and asked, "What sort of offer?" I felt my heart start to beat harder as I waited for him to explain. I couldn't help hoping that somehow my unofficial investigation had actually put me in line for something more than filing records in the basement. If that proved the case, I had to say the two chiefs had taken the long way getting around to it.

I don't know if you're familiar with the Raby case, Chief Kent said, *but Arthur Raby was one of the most highly respected pillars of this community until his death just over one year ago. In his life he served as a city councilman, deputy mayor and champion of numerous noble causes. No one loved this city more than Arthur Raby. I considered him one of my closest friends and confidants.*

I remembered the name. Raby was shot down by an

unknown assassin. His murder was thought to have been connected to his bucking a huge development planned by some corporation on the outskirts of Nashville. Raby had been working for years to help set up a new rent-to-own, so to speak, low-income housing development. The corporation, in contrast, wanted to build a golf course and high-end housing development. The hope was to begin to turn the south side of Nashville into another Franklin or Brentwood. I hadn't kept up with the progress of either development after the initial flurry of news related to Raby's murder, but I was pretty sure the golf course and mansions had won out over the proposed low-income housing. Seemed like people in the development business liked killing the competition. But this particular case was way bigger than Sawyer and Carlyle. Strip malls and apartment buildings were peanuts compared to the plans Arthur Raby had fought to derail. Bottom line: big-time real estate could be murder.

We, Chief Adcock said, drawing my attention back to the two men seated across the table from me, *were unable to pursue the case as we would have liked since the Federal Bureau of Investigations had jurisdiction.*

That surprised me, but I did vaguely recall some noise in the papers about increasing tension between Metro and the bureau. In all honesty I had been deep in the throes of my own problems and hadn't been more than superficially aware of anything else.

"Why was the bureau involved in the first place?" I

asked. I hated to admit I didn't know why, but I was, after all, just a civilian—one who'd taken little note of the problems of the world during that time frame of personal devastation.

Are you familiar with the name Luther Hammond? This from Kent.

"No, sir." Okay, I was sounding dumber by the moment. I wondered if they would change their mind about an offer of any sort considering how little I appeared to know about the subject. I also considered whether or not I might be better off if they did change their mind. I chucked the concept and forced my mind back on the matter at hand.

Attention shifted down to Barlow's end of the table. I settled my gaze on his well-formed lips. I blinked, wondered why I would in a million years notice that just now. This definitely was not the time.

Luther Hammond is a thug of the highest order, Barlow said. He glanced at Chief Kent but I didn't turn to the chief quickly enough to catch whatever he said.

I shifted my gaze back to Barlow in time to follow his next words.

When you encounter the word mob *you surely understand the implications?*

The question was intended for me, I realized. I nodded stiffly. It wasn't quite clear to me whether or not he'd intended to be condescending. His expression didn't give away his emotions, but his words made me feel just a little more uncomfortable.

Luther Hammond is the mob in this city. Again he said the words with no readable emotion.

I blinked, startled. Nashville had a mob? Since when? I've lived here all my life.

His reach includes every imaginable evil from drugs to prostitution to cheating on his taxes and everything in between. He strong-arms politicians and cuts down anyone who gets in his way.

Something akin to fear shimmered through me. The tummy-twisting sensation you feel when something goes bump in the middle of the night and you can't remember if you locked the door or some accessible window before collapsing into bed. How could such a monster be operating in my hometown without my knowledge? Was I that far out of touch? A part of me wanted to ask what this had to do with my recent actions or, for that matter, with me, but that twinge of fear kept my lips tightly sealed. I had a disturbing feeling I was about to find out.

He's a killer, Barlow added. *He killed Arthur Raby and got away with it just as he gets away with the rest of his dirty deeds.* This time I could see the fury burning in those piercing blue eyes. Detective Barlow hated Luther Hammond and that hatred went way deep. I braced against the shiver that realization elicited.

So far I'd made only two connections to the case I'd been involved in and this one, murder and real estate. I, as all those present well knew, was no expert in either.

"How does he get away with it?" I asked before I had

the good sense to stop myself. I felt reasonably sure I was supposed to be playing the part of listener in this.

Barlow's gaze shifted from me to Chief Kent, clueing me in to who was speaking next.

Because we haven't been able to come up with enough evidence to stop him. Kent appeared to consider his next words carefully before continuing. *Initially the bureau kept us out of their case. But we've gotten past that and now we have an opportunity to get in with our own agenda.*

Hammond's security is extremely tight, Chief Adcock said. *We've tried repeatedly to get to him. But he's too smart for the usual methods. No amount of surveillance has touched him. His people stay on the cutting edge of technology. We haven't been able to even get close.* Like Chief Kent and Barlow, until the last, Adcock kept his expression carefully schooled. I paid close attention as he continued.

The opportunity Chief Kent spoke of is a position within Hammond's household staff. For several years now Hammond has used the same cleaning service. The service comes in twice a week and does the heavy cleaning, but Hammond requires a live-in maid as well. The duties are fairly minimal. Keep the small details straight, putting books back on their shelves, make the beds daily. No kitchen duty, he added hastily. *The chef has his own assistant who takes care of those chores.*

We've nurtured a contact within the cleaning service. Kent took up the story from there. *This contact is willing to place an undercover operative in the position.*

Sounded like a tremendous step in the right direction. I just couldn't figure out what it had to do with me.

As Chief Adcock mentioned, the traditional methods of surveillance don't work on Hammond. He knows all our tricks. Kent fell silent a moment as if he needed to assess my reaction thus far before he went on. *We need something he won't expect. We need you, Miss Walters.*

For a moment I waited for him to say more, certain I'd misunderstood somehow. Abruptly I realized it was my turn to speak. "Me?" I'm sure the single syllable came out more a squeak than a word.

With your...impairment, Chief Adcock explained, *Hammond would never suspect you of listening in, if you get my meaning. He wouldn't consider a woman such as yourself a threat.*

He had a point there. If Luther Hammond was half the monster the men in this room thought him to be, I doubted anything about me would threaten him in any way.

If you choose to accept this assignment, Miss Walters, Chief Kent said, *you will be working directly with Detective Barlow.*

Okay, now I was lost. "I don't understand," I confessed. How could I possibly help Detective Barlow? I knew nothing about Hammond or this case. Yes, I could see that the man would never in a million years feel threatened by me, but I couldn't see how that fit into my accepting the assignment to work with Detective Barlow. Most likely anything I would be involved with would be behind the scenes. I had definitely learned the hard way that I lacked the necessary experience to do field work.

The chiefs swapped another of those unreadable looks. Chief Kent took a stab at clarification. *We would like to place you inside Hammond's home, as his new maid. Our hope would be that your phenomenal lip-reading ability would prove useful in gathering intelligence on Hammond's ongoing operations.*

I felt my eyes go wide at the same time my heart stumbled a couple of times before flopping back into a recognizable rhythm. Me? Go undercover in the home of a mobster?

I realize we're asking a great deal of you, Miss Walters. Adcock looked contrite and I realized then I'd uttered my questions out loud. *This kind of sacrifice is far above and beyond the call of duty. But, to be quite frank, we're desperate to bring down Hammond and his empire.*

Forcing my mind past the obvious, that I was untrained and completely inept in the field, I asked, "What's to keep him from discovering my true identity?" Hey, I'd watched enough movies to know what happened to undercover operatives whose covers were blown. That was the part of the movie where I turned my head.

We've set up a new background for you, Adcock explained. *Since your work here as well as your life has been rather low-key, at least until recently, and we believe we have that incident under wraps, there is nothing to connect you to anything other than the cover we've arranged. If Hammond runs a background check on you, he'll find that you've been employed by the cleaning service since you reentered the work force just over one year after the onset of your impairment.*

Chief Kent hastened to add, *All you have to do is watch Hammond and his associates in your capacity as the live-in maid. Detective Barlow will arrange ways for you to pass along whatever you learn.*

I told myself this was the break I'd been looking for. The opportunity to do more. But other confusing thoughts kept muddying my ability to grasp the concept. "How long would this assignment last?" That was a legitimate question. I congratulated myself for being able to at least come off as reasonable.

There's no way to answer that question, Adcock admitted. *You could be there days, possibly weeks.*

I frowned. "What about my family? What do I tell them?" Now, there was a problem that wouldn't be that easily resolved. My folks are intensely overprotective. I couldn't just drop off the family radar with no explanation, and accepting this kind of assignment would not be acceptable.

Miss Walters, Chief Kent said, *if you accept this assignment no one can know. Your cover has to be protected at all costs. Your family and friends will need to believe you're away for job-related training.*

That could work. Lying to my family wasn't something I felt comfortable with, but this wasn't exactly lying, I told myself. Excitement began to inch up my spine. This was it. My opportunity to prove I could do more, make a difference. If I made this happen, how could Metro not consider me for a real investigative position? Considering how desperate the chiefs were, I felt certain I could finagle whatever training I needed for an investigative-profiler-type career move.

I now fully comprehended the test. The chiefs had wanted to ascertain how much of the various comments made during the meeting I could gather and recall. Clearly I had made an impression.

The whole setup sounded simple enough. "When do I start?" I looked from one chief to the other. Their attention shifted to Barlow. I snapped my gaze in his direction. Jesus, I'd almost forgotten about him in all the excitement. A smile quirked my lips. I couldn't believe it! My plan had worked, gotten the right attention. I, Merrilee Walters, was going to be an undercover investigator on a very important case.

Just so you understand, Miss Walters, Barlow said, his face impassive as usual, *there is no way for us to protect you once you're inside.*

Both Chief Adcock and Chief Kent looked uncomfortable with Barlow's statement.

I considered his comment a moment. "I'll be on my own," I suggested, looking directly at him.

That's right. You and I will set up a code to indicate you need help, but there's no way to guarantee you'll be able to get to a phone to call me if you need me. Once you're inside you'll be completely on your own.

A shiver rattled my excitement. "Will I be expected to carry a weapon?" I had never fired a gun in my life. I had taken the requisite self-defense class for females wanting to protect themselves from attack back in college, but nothing more.

Barlow shook his head in answer to my question. *You'll be a maid. Maids don't carry deadly weapons. Going in you'll likely be considered suspect by everyone already on staff. Your acceptance will take time. Getting close enough to watch Hammond or his associates will require your total acceptance. The only way you're going to do any good is if Hammond lets down his guard in your presence. The only way you'll get out of there alive is if you don't blow your cover.*

Miss Walters… Kent flared his hands to draw my attention back to him. *We'll protect you as best we can any undercover operative. There are, of course, no guarantees. This assignment comes with undeniable hazards.*

Unless you blow your cover, Adcock spoke up, *there will be no reason for Hammond or his men to harm you. You'll be completely safe as long as you stay within the boundaries of what is expected of your position.*

We have a very small window of opportunity here, Kent urged. *Detective Barlow will provide the background information you need and the necessary training before you go in, but our time is sorely limited. You've given us hope, Miss Walters. Hope that we can finally hold Hammond accountable for his crimes. Without your help I'm not sure the feat is in any way feasible.*

How could I say no? My heart beat like a drum. This was exactly the break I'd been looking for. I wanted to do this. Wanted to put myself in a position to have some leverage. But first I needed some guarantees.

"If I agree to do this," I said bluntly, "what assurances do I have that I'll be allowed to pursue a career here at Metro as an investigator?"

Chief Kent smiled, his relief palpable. *Miss Walters, you help us bring down Hammond and you can pick the division of your choice. We'll see that you get the training you need and the future of your career will be yours to do with as you please.*

I bit my lips together to hold in a victorious *yes*. There was no question, I intended to take the assignment. Truth was, I wanted to run around the table and hug both chiefs for offering me this fantastic opportunity, but I didn't want to look like a pushover.

"All right, gentlemen," I said, my pulse skipping in anticipation. "When do I begin?"

Before either of the chiefs could respond, their attention swung to the end of the table. Barlow had shoved back his chair and stood. He didn't speak or even spare the rest of us a glance before he did the absolute last thing I had expected.

He walked out.

Detective Steven Barlow made it to his office on the fourth floor before he got the call ordering him to return to Chief Kent's office. He slammed the receiver into its cradle and stormed back to the stairwell. His rage grew with every step he took. By the time he'd reached the sixth floor his temper was out of control.

He hesitated at the door that would take him into the elegantly appointed corridor leading to the chief of police's office. He had to get his anger back under control. He was this close, he mentally pictured a two- or three-millimeter expanse between his thumb and forefinger, to blowing his career. He had to take a step back, regain some badly needed perspective.

The deal was done. Merri Walters had taken the bait, hook, line and sinker. It wasn't bad enough that she'd risked her life to set that trap for Sawyer. Steven shook his head slowly from side to side. How in the hell had she come up with that scheme? If he'd ever met a woman more determined to prove she could do anything he'd blocked the memory from his mind. This deaf lady was one ambitious woman. He'd looked into her professional and academic history. There was nothing in her background that indicated motivation for such a drastic change in character…except the loss of her hearing.

Steven could almost understand her need to prove her worth in spite of the devastating tragedy. But proving her worth was one thing, agreeing to a suicide mission entirely another. His fury peaked again. The very idea that Kent and Adcock would use the vulnerable woman made him want to rip off their heads and…

Enough. He shook off the fury. He had to pull it to-gether here. Had to think rationally. Going off the deep end with his superiors wouldn't help. As much as he hated what was about to go down here, he had to be a part of it. No one knew as much about Luther Hammond as he did. He had been the one to develop the contact with the cleaning service. It was up to him to make sure this went down as planned.

As arrogant as it sounded, he was Merri Walters's best bet at surviving this assignment, whether she real-ized it or not.

Steven opened the door and strode down the quiet corridor until he reached Chief Kent's office. His sec-retary, Sarah Walters, had already gone home for the evening. Just as well. Anything she might overhear could prove detrimental to the confidentiality of the case where the Walters family was concerned.

"Detective Barlow." Kent motioned to a chair in front of his desk.

Steven took the seat and waited for the hailstorm to start. This wouldn't be the first or the last time he would be dressed down by Kent or Adcock…or both.

"You, of all people," Kent began his monologue, "un-derstand the importance of this case."

Steven slammed the door shut on the memories that instantly tried to surface. Kent's comment didn't re-quire an answer. His chief was well aware of Steven's feelings about Hammond. He hated the bastard for more reasons than one, but he wasn't going there now. It had taken Steven a long time to learn to handle his hatred for the man…he had to hang on to that control now.

"We have one shot here, Barlow," the chief urged. "We might never have a chance like this again. We have to stop him."

Steven stared directly at the chief, allowed him to see exactly how he felt before he spoke. "You're right. This is our best shot at stopping him. But we have female investigators in Metro. Using a civilian isn't necessary."

The chief heaved a sigh and leaned back in his chair. "It's so easy for you, isn't it, Barlow?"

Since he wasn't sure what the chief meant by that remark, Steven kept his mouth shut.

"You see everything as black or white. Play by the rules. Never deviate."

Steven shrugged. "Isn't that what we're here to do?" What was so wrong about doing the right thing? Making the best choices? He knew that most of his peers took the other route, bending the rules and stepping on toes as necessary to get the job done. He supposed that was why he wasn't very well liked around the bullpen. He refused to bend the rules, rejected even the possibility of presenting himself in a way that disrespected the gold shield he carried.

Chief Kent's expression hardened. "I'm not going to play that holier-than-thou game with you. Yes, we have female detectives, but none of them can read lips. None of them has the power to put Hammond at ease in this way. Miss Walters wants this opportunity. Hasn't she made that quite clear? You can make this happen, Barlow. I know you. If there is anyone in Metro who can do it, you can." Kent smiled knowingly. "You'll make it happen and you'll keep her safe. I have complete faith in you."

For several moments Steven couldn't speak without fear of blasting the chief. Yeah, he would do everything within his power to keep the woman safe. That went without saying. The problem was, outside of a miracle straight from God, he doubted anything he or anyone else did would be enough.

Merri Walters had agreed to walk into her own death trap.

Chapter 6

I dropped my bags to the floor and looked around the large sanctuary.

"Is this a church?" I asked the question but I already knew the answer. I knew a church when I saw one.

Detective Steven Barlow paused alongside me and turned his face toward mine. *It used to be. Now it's a sanctuary of another sort.*

"A safe house?"

He shrugged. *Sometimes. Other times we use it for a special operations base or training facility.*

Taking a deep breath I looked around again. Stuffy. The air reeked of age and disuse. Whatever the Metro cops had used the place for, it still smelled like an old church.

The entry vestibule and main sanctuary led to one big open space, like a gym. No pews or pulpit. Lots of workout equipment, including a punching bag and a few pieces I didn't recognize.

Barlow tapped my arm. When my gaze reached his he jerked his head to the right. *This way.*

I picked up my bags and followed him across the expanse of hardwood floor. I wondered if our steps echoed in the cavernous space. My imagination conjured up the remembered sound. A soft thwack thwack. Like that. Yeah. Probably. My attention then settled on the broad shoulders of the man, Detective Barlow.

He'd picked me up at my house at the crack of dawn this morning. We'd driven around for almost an hour, to lose any possible tail he'd explained, before arriving here. Last night when Sarah called to quiz me about my meeting with the chiefs I'd given her the same story I'd given my parents. An opening at a school in Knoxville had come available and Chief Kent had thought of me. He understood my desire to work in investigations so he'd considered this three-week course in cold-case profiling the perfect answer.

The family had swallowed the bait.

My attention shifted back to the man who'd brought me here.

Not married, I decided. He didn't wear a wedding band, but that alone was not definitive proof. I had asked Helen the last day we worked together. She had laughed. Almost wet her pants before she managed to stop. According to Helen, who had worked at Metro for half a lifetime, Steven Barlow was married to the job. No mere woman would ever have a chance snagging the handsome detective. It would take a very special woman, she had insisted, to break the man's fierce focus on his work.

Since I wasn't in the snagging market or particularly special it really didn't matter to me. I was simply curious. Given that I would be working closely with him on this case I needed as much information as possible. My life, to some degree, depended upon him and his reliability. From all accounts I didn't have anything to worry about, reliability-wise. My research indicated Steven Barlow was one of the finest detectives employed in any Metro division.

Barlow led me into a short hall off the sanctuary. He indicated the four doors lining the hall. *The kitchen and two bedrooms.* He glanced at the fourth door. *Bathroom.*

The living area that once served as home sweet home to the priests assigned to this church, I concluded. I followed my new mentor through one of the doors into a sparsely furnished bedroom. Narrow wooden cot, a modest dresser and night table with lamp.

Barlow placed the bag he carried for me on the cot. *I'll take the room across the hall.* He moved back to the door. *When you're ready, join me in the gym.*

A spiritual sanctuary turned workout gym. I sure hoped this old church would give me an extra in with God. According to Barlow, this was a suicide mission and I needed all the support I could get. I stared at the door he had closed behind him. We had our work cut out for us. That's what he'd said on the way here.

He didn't have very much faith in me. I found it ironic as hell that he'd brought me to a church to train me. Then again, I don't know that the place was his choice. I surveyed the room again. Well, I liked it.

I didn't take the time to put anything away. I wouldn't actually be here long enough to bother with unpacking. And I definitely didn't want to keep Barlow waiting. I pulled my hair back into a ponytail. Checked the ties of my sneakers and headed for the sanctuary…gym. I'd worn sweatpants and a T-shirt since he'd suggested I come prepared for a workout.

Barlow waited at the front of the room, where the pulpit would have been, near a long metal table. The table and a couple of metal folding chairs were the only pieces of actual furniture in the large room.

He pointed to one of the chairs. *I'd like you to study these photographs and the name that goes with each.*

I nodded and took a seat. A dozen photos were spread across the tabletop, and each was labeled with a name and brief history. Barlow left the room. I didn't have to turn around, I felt his withdrawal. Unable to quell my curiosity, I turned around just to make sure I was right. Good. I was working hard to focus on the details in an effort to maintain a keen awareness of all my remaining senses. I needed my working senses as sharp as possible.

Turning my attention back to the business at hand, I

surveyed the photos, none of which meant anything to me until I reached the final one.

Luther Hammond.

He was younger than I had expected. Mid to late thirties, around the same age as my detective mentor. And he was quite good-looking for a mobster. Not that I'd ever met any mobsters, but he didn't look anything like the ones portrayed in the entertainment business. He looked like the typical, elegantly dressed businessman one would meet on the street with briefcase in hand.

Dark hair, gray eyes. Hardly any lines on his face. Tall. The photo wasn't just a headshot. It was of Hammond in a restaurant I didn't recognize. In the past couple of years I hadn't gotten out much. He faced the camera and was talking to another man, while a number of others stood around him. His posse? I looked through the other photos to see if any of the faces matched the ones in the photo with Hammond. Only two. Mason Conrad and Victor Vargas. His bodyguards? Both stood close, maybe one or two steps behind him. Now, these two men looked dangerous.

Barlow reached past my shoulder and tapped Conrad's photo. I just about jumped out of my chair. My hand went to my throat as I fought to catch my breath. So much for sharper senses. When my gaze finally latched on to his, Barlow said, *Hammond's second in command and personal bodyguard.*

So I had been right about Conrad. Almost as tall as his boss but younger, Conrad had dark hair and eyes. At least I'd done something right. I inhaled another deep breath and then nodded for the detective's benefit.

You seem a little jumpy this morning.

Barlow was right. I was jumpy. I'd had hardly any sleep. Who could sleep on the eve of a step this big? "Didn't sleep well," I offered in hopes of derailing the suspicion I saw in his eyes.

He was proving every bit as perceptive as I had suspected he would be. He studied me a moment longer before turning back to the photographs and pulling up the other chair.

Now we work. Again his gaze held mine for a beat too long after he'd made the statement, ultimately ratcheting up my tension another notch.

For the next hour we reviewed the photographs. I memorized each name and face while Barlow explained how each man and the one woman factored into Hammond's dirty life. The woman, Cecilia Woodruff, was an au pair. Somehow I had missed that part. Barlow explained that Hammond had an eight-year-old daughter named Tiffany. The mother, Heather Masters, a woman to whom Hammond had never been married, had died four years ago from a drug overdose. Barlow rummaged around in a folder and withdrew a photograph of a beautiful child. Long dark hair and the same gray eyes as her father. Looking at the child made me sad. She would be the one to suffer in all this. If this operation proved successful she would lose her father.

Don't do that.

I shifted my gaze from Barlow's lips to his eyes in an attempt to read the motivation behind the statement. The only thing he let me see was the intensity that occupied those analyzing eyes more often than not.

Hammond has to be stopped. Sympathy for his daughter can't get in the way.

"I know that," I admitted, though my heart ached for the child. "Is there a relative she can stay with once her father is out of the picture?"

Barlow shrugged, though I felt certain he knew the answer. He simply had no intention of sharing it with me. I let it go. We had a lot of ground to cover. Getting caught up on this one issue was a bad idea.

By noon I understood why few others in Metro liked Detective Barlow. He was relentless and unfeeling.

Mathers, who is he? The demand hadn't come out any nicer the second time than it had the first. The ability to hear wasn't necessary. I could see the lines of tension in his face, the tightening of his mouth.

I looked away from him and started to pace once more. I'd given up on keeping a seat an hour ago. I didn't know who Mathers was. I couldn't remember. He wasn't one of the men in the photographs. I had those down. He…I scrubbed at my forehead. I just didn't know.

A tap on my shoulder jerked my attention back to my taskmaster. *Hammond's West Coast contact. Mathers is his West Coast contact.*

"Why do I need to know who he is? It's not like I'll see him!"

Barlow stared at the floor a moment. Judging by the tension radiating through those broad shoulders I'd say he needed to get a firmer grip on his emotions the same as I did. I forced myself to take three slow, deep breaths. I had to calm down. Getting angry wasn't going to help.

That blue gaze collided with mine once more. *You're right,* he said. He'd calmed down considerably if his relaxed expression was any indication. *You most likely won't see this guy. But I need you to be aware of all that you read on the lips of Hammond and his associates. There are names and phrases that signify crucial elements related to this case. You need to be able to recognize the relevance of the intelligence you gather.*

"Mathers," I muttered, "his West Coast contact." I nodded and took a deep breath. "Who's next?"

Let's take a break, he said. *We'll resume our work after lunch.*

Unbelievable. I watched him walk away. The man was human after all. Required food for fuel. I chastised myself for being so unkind. I should give Barlow the benefit of the doubt. Just because I knew he didn't want me on this case and I'd heard all the rumors about how he didn't have any friends was no excuse to judge him harshly.

It was up to me here to get our relationship off on the right foot. The least I could do was try.

With a ham and cheese sandwich, complete with

pickle spear and chips, and a nice big glass of iced tea, I was ready to chow down. Barlow, showing his gentlemanly side, waited until I had seated myself at the small kitchen table to join me. He didn't, however, wait for me to begin eating.

I took a moment to consider that today was the first time I had seen him in anything other than a suit. Though he didn't wear sweats like me, he did have on faded jeans and a plain gray T-shirt. He'd traded in his Italian leather shoes for sneakers. Though he looked far from relaxed, he did look nice. I shouldn't have been surprised. A guy as handsome as Barlow would look good wearing most anything.

"Do you have family, Detective?"

He paused in the devouring of his sandwich. Barlow was just as intense about eating as he was everything else. I wondered for a time whether or not he intended to respond before cleaning his plate.

My family is in St. Louis.

A Missouri boy, huh? "You grew up there?" Who knew? All this time I'd thought Barlow was most likely a born-and-bred Tennessee boy.

Yes.

Well, that was certainly the short answer. "Any brothers or sisters?" I persisted.

Two sisters.

Okay, now there was something we had in common. I was the only girl in my family and he was the only boy. "Older or younger?" I intended to have all the details. He might as well admit defeat now.

Younger.

Aha. I would bet this week's powerball lottery offering that growing up with those two younger sisters had forged some of that brooding, overprotective persona. I barely managed to keep the smugness off my face.

"Where did you go to college?"

He pushed his empty plate aside and stared at me with something like tolerance. *Is all this going somewhere in particular?*

Touchy. "I…" I shrugged in an attempt to play off the ferocity in his eyes. "I was just curious."

I graduated from the University of Missouri. I've never been married, haven't even been close. I call my family a couple times a month but rarely get home for a visit. I date from time to time but I don't bother pretending I want a relationship. Sex is good but I'm not interested in strings or attachments. Any more questions?

I shook my head and redirected my attention to my lunch. My appetite had pretty much vanished, but I forced myself to eat just the same. No way was I going to let him see that his attitude bothered me. I realized that's exactly what he wanted. He figured if he humiliated or frustrated me I'd give up and let it go. Well, Detective Barlow didn't know me very well. I had no intention of giving up on anything. Not this case, not myself, not even him. I shivered as his words echoed inside me. He wanted the world to believe he felt nothing, needed no one, but I had a sneaking suspicion that his "back off" growl was more about self-preservation.

Someone had hurt him. Really badly. I wondered why Helen hadn't known about that. Of course I was only speculating, but the one thing I had always been good at was reading people.

A cold, hard reality settled onto my shoulders. If I'd been so good, why hadn't I realized the man I was supposed to marry wasn't all I thought him to be? As soon as the going got tough, he got going. Walked out on the plans we had shared…away from us.

I stood. Dumped the lunch I couldn't finish in the trash and placed my plate in the sink. I was over that. Yes, it still hurt a little when I let it sneak up on me like this, but I didn't dwell on it. If my turkey of an ex-fiancé walked in right now, I wouldn't want him back. I had a new life. Plans, finally, for a fulfilling future. If I got through this operation successfully, I could have a career with Metro that offered an opportunity to make a difference.

Nothing else mattered to me right now.

I tamped down the guilt I felt about lying to my family. If things went wrong and I ended up…dead, my family would feel betrayed. My heart dragged downward like a stone in my chest. I didn't want to hurt my family.

Forcing the notion away, I decided there was only one thing to do…I could not fail. Whatever else happened, I had to succeed. I would get the evidence Metro needed on Luther Hammond. I would not get myself killed in the process. And I would break through that icy exterior and make Detective Barlow respect me for what I was doing.

I'm going to approach you from behind. When you feel my arm around your neck do your best to free yourself.

I nodded, then turned my back to him.

Several years ago I had taken a routine self-defense class. The kind designed to help women guard against rapes and muggings. After half an hour on the mat with Steven Barlow, I realized just how pathetic the course I'd taken actually was.

His right arm came around my neck, pressed against my throat. Instinctively I stiffened. My fingers curled around his arm, but he was far too strong for me to hope to pull him loose. With his free hand he manacled my left arm and drew it back toward his midsection, indicating that I should elbow him hard there.

I nodded my understanding. He moved my arm again, showing me the same move. I nodded a second time. I got it. I'd learned a similar move in the original class.

He stepped away from me and I turned around to face him. Frustration lined his face. What had I done wrong? What did he want me to do?

I need you to show me what you can do, he said, the features of his face tight with irritation…or maybe it was just the frustration. *Do it for real.*

Now I was confused. "You want me to actually try to hurt you?" That didn't make sense.

I want you to protect yourself from me, he reiterated, the tension he'd radiated relaxing ever so slightly.

A test, I decided. Maybe he thought if I couldn't prove my ability to fend off an attacker he would have an excuse to call this whole thing off. He would cite my inability to defend myself. I would go back to filing closed and cold cases and he would find another way to do what had to be done. For the first time since Chief Kent had called me into his office and proposed this operation, I realized just how badly Barlow wanted me out of the scenario.

Well, he was not going to get his wish.

"All right." Without meeting his eyes first, I turned my back on him. I didn't want him to know that I was on to him now. Bring on the test.

His arm went around my neck, closed in on my throat. I smiled as I mentally finalized my plan. I reached for his arm with both hands, tried to pull him away. He yanked me against his hard body and held me tighter. I struggled with his arm a few seconds before sagging as if I'd surrendered. When his arm relaxed ever so slightly I slammed my left elbow into his gut. I broke away as his upper body jerked forward with the spasms the blow to his midsection had caused. I didn't stop there. I twisted to face him, hooked my leg behind his and shoved him hard. He went down like a fallen oak against the floor.

He was back on his feet in almost the same instant. He dusted himself off and presented me with a crooked grin. Well, there was a first. I definitely hadn't seen that before.

Good job.

Pride swelled in my chest. What do you know? I'd impressed the iceman.

From there we went through a number of scenarios, some I'd encountered before in my self-defense class, many more I hadn't. In the end, I felt fairly confident I'd impressed him.

Funny how that feat had become more and more important to me as the day had dragged on. I'd barely had any sleep and adrenaline was all that had kept me going.

I didn't realize how exhausted I was until after we'd shared spaghetti that Barlow had prepared himself. He didn't say much, mostly talked about how important it was that I remembered the names and faces. I agreed and didn't prompt any additional chitchat. Detective Barlow wasn't very good at it. And I was too tired to keep up the sparring. Eventually I'd excused myself and showered. My legs felt like leaden clubs. I just wanted to lie down and drop into blissful unconsciousness.

My eyes had just closed and my brain had started to shut down conscious processes when I felt the mattress shift. In that moment of denial before my brain and body got on the same sheet of music, I told myself I'd simply turned over and hadn't realized it.

Then I felt another shift. My eyes flew open but the

room was black as pitch. I opened my mouth to scream but a punishing hand came down over it before I could expel the sound. The full weight of a body settled on top of mine. My hands went to a hard chest and pushed.

The scream died in my throat. My heart threatened to burst…and then my olfactory sense kicked into high gear. I recognized his scent.

Detective Barlow.

Fury whipped through me. What the hell did he think he was doing? The fingers of his free hand closed around my throat. My eyes widened with new fear. What if I was wrong? What if it wasn't Barlow? Could I trust my senses?

My blood stung with the renewed rush of terror searing through my veins.

I had to do something. Had to fight back. My knee jabbed toward his groin. He moved quickly, deflecting the blow. But I took advantage of that momentary distraction and slammed the heel of my hand into what I hoped would be his nose. He thrashed atop me. I flung my fists at his face. Kicked hard and twisted to roll him off me.

We hit the floor in a tangled heap of flailing arms and legs. I scrambled loose. Managed to get to my feet and race to the door. I jerked it open and flew out into the hall. "Barlow! Barlow!" I wasn't taking any chances as to whether or not my attacker was someone besides him.

The overhead light came on. I blinked to adjust to the

sudden brightness. I whirled around and came face-to-face with a rumpled-looking Barlow.

My first instinct had been right…it was him. The mental pat on the back I owed myself was temporarily overridden by irritation. "What the hell was that about?" I demanded.

He swiped at his bruised nose. He wasn't bleeding, but obviously the sting from the blow was still there. I couldn't help getting a little joy from that.

Very good, Walters, he said as he combed his fingers through his hair, straightening it. *But you should have realized it was me. It's very important that you use your other senses. Since you can't hear the enemy coming, you have to attempt to feel him coming. Pay attention to your instincts.*

I moved in close, nose to nose. "What makes you think I didn't?"

That crooked grin that he rarely allowed to make a public appearance did so just then. My pulse reacted and I wanted to kick myself.

Good answer.

I rolled my eyes and headed back to my room. I couldn't decide if he was yanking my chain because he could or if he felt it necessary to measure my reactions in the most unexpected situation. At least the most unexpected for me. I certainly hadn't anticipated his climbing into bed with me.

I shivered in spite of myself at the remembered feel

of his weight. His chest had felt incredibly lean and hard. The man was definitely all muscle.

He stepped in front of me just as I reached my door. *Let's review.*

I didn't have to locate a clock and check the time to know it was nearly midnight. It had been well past ten o'clock when I dragged myself from the shower. Since I hadn't managed any sleep last night, I could definitely use some tonight.

"Can't we do this in the morning?"

I need to know that despite being tired you can still recall all that you need to.

A part of me wondered if he got some sort of cheap thrill out of being in control, but that didn't mesh with what I knew about his professional reputation. This guy was focused, relentless. He didn't let anything stand in his way.

"Let's do it, then."

He led the way to the sanctuary, and without hesitation I recited the name that went with each face spread out on the table. It wasn't that difficult. I'd spent four years as a schoolteacher. Part of my job had been learning new names and faces in a timely manner.

Just as I was feeling pretty damned proud of myself he tossed new pictures, ones I hadn't seen before, onto the table with the ease of a poker dealer laying down cards for a lone player. The faces and setting were different in each photograph. I frowned, wondering what each scene meant. Business meetings or social gatherings?

Quickly. Barlow tapped the first photograph. *Name the faces you recognize.*

Okay, okay. I popped off each name without hesitation. Then we moved on to the next one. It wasn't until photo seven that I stumbled.

Look again, he ordered.

I recognized Luther Hammond and his two personal bodyguards…the child and the au pair, Cecilia. Surely this one was a social function. I hoped Hammond didn't involve his daughter in his dirty business. Clearing the distraction from my head, I scanned the two faces I couldn't seem to recognize. I closed my eyes a second to search my short-term memory banks. Nothing.

"I don't know this man," I admitted. I tapped the second face. "That one, either." I resisted the urge to flinch. I wasn't sure which was worse, his disappointment or my own feeling of defeat. With more dread than I'd felt since this intensive-training session began, I lifted my gaze to his.

Good.

Surprise and irritation immediately replaced the dread and disappointment. His lips twitched, but to his credit he kept any hint of a smile off his face.

You don't know these two. Hammond had both of them killed about three months ago. He suspected this one—he pointed to the unfamiliar face standing closest to Hammond—*of flipping on him.*

"What about this one?" I indicated the other stranger. Barlow held my gaze for a moment before he answered. Something in his eyes forewarned me that what he was about to tell me would be less than palatable. *This one was his daughter's godfather.*

Something deep inside me shifted as the words filtered through my soul. "Why did he kill him?" Had Hammond suspected that the two men were involved in a scheme to bring him down? That seemed the most likely scenario since he'd killed them at the same time.

Hammond had him executed because he thought his daughter had grown too attached to him.

I stared at the little girl in the picture and then the man holding her hand. How could anyone do that to someone their child cared about? I shuddered. What was I saying? How could he kill anyone period? How could a mere human take such liberties with human life?

Barlow reached out and took my chin in his hand and turned my face toward his. My breath caught in surprise…or something…at his touch. My gaze settled on his lips in anticipation of his words.

Don't be fooled by his elegant manners or his exquisite taste in clothes. Luther Hammond is a killer. If you make a mistake, he'll kill you, too.

Chapter 7

"This is where I'll be staying?"

I shifted my attention from the three-dimensional model of the Hammond mansion to Barlow's face.

Yes. This—he waited until I took note of the suite of rooms on the model and then fixed my gaze back on his lips—*is the corridor that connects your rooms to the kitchen and rear staircase.*

His hand moved to the second story. My attention alternated between the model and his face as he identified each space in the enormous house. *Hammond's room. Tiffany's. The au pair's next door. Mason Conrad is the only member of Hammond's security who resides in the house. The others use the guest house. Conrad's room is here.*

Mason Conrad. This morning I'd studied the profile Barlow had provided on him. At thirty-three Conrad had risen from a homeless bum to Hammond's right-hand man. Conrad hadn't even graduated high school. But he did possess the all-important street smarts and the one vital characteristic a mob leader searched for within his ranks: absolute loyalty.

My mentor rested his hand on my shoulder to regain my attention. A little jolt of electricity accompanied his touch and startled me…just a smidge.

Most of Hammond's business is likely conducted in this room, he said, oblivious of my unexpected reaction since he simply gestured to the study off the entry hall and continued, *but you may find opportunities to learn pertinent information almost anywhere in the house.*

"If the study is his primary place of mob business, is there no way to get surveillance bugs in place?" Maybe it was a dumb question, but they had the complete layout of the house, from the cleaning service, I presumed. Why couldn't someone from that same service plant something? A high-tech listening device like the ones I'd seen in movies. I didn't know the official name of the devices or even how they actually worked, but I knew they existed. It seemed awfully elementary to me.

We tried that once. The man who planted the bug was executed. We never found his body.

My chest constricted. Why did I keep forgetting that…the whole idea of mobsters and planned executions were just too foreign to me…too surreal. "Oh," I choked out. He'd warned me last night that the slightest mistake could cost me my life, ensuring another sleepless night. Maybe on some level I still didn't get this whole Hammond gangster world. How could anyone be that utterly ruthless?

Walk me through the house again.

Strong-arming my full attention back to the nifty model, I dredged up the necessary information. I'd done this half a dozen times already. But since knowing the house would help me escape in a hurry if need be, I did as I was told. Upstairs, downstairs and the grounds, including the guest house, massive garage, terrace and pool. I didn't miss a beat. I had the layout nailed. This appeared to please him.

Excellent.

The strangest fizz of heat erupted beneath my belly button. I didn't get it. It wasn't like this was the first time I'd seen him smile at me much in the same way I'd smiled at my students when they succeeded in a task. I mean I fully understood how defenseless my inability to hear left me. However hard I attempted to focus my other senses, I recognized that frailty. I had to learn every seemingly insignificant bit of information he had to teach me. But this other reaction…this feeling of…I don't know…attraction, maybe…was just too weird.

Let's discuss the profiles on each significant player once more.

I picked up the first folder, read the name and then began to recite what I had learned about the player described within. Each time I stole a glimpse of Barlow from the corner of my eye, he seemed to be analyzing my profile. Or, even more unsettling, watching my lips move. I moistened them, tried not to be unnerved by him or his assessment. Watching his lips was necessary for me to know what he was saying, but he didn't have that excuse.

Maybe lack of sleep was playing tricks on my ability to reason. The forced proximity didn't help. It had been almost two years since I'd spent this much time alone with a man who wasn't related to me by blood.

Then an epiphany sneaked up and grabbed me by the throat. That was the whole problem. I was feeling off-kilter because he's a man and I'm a woman. His undivided attention in this one-on-one environment made me restless. That's all it could be. Kind of like an ex-smoker getting a whiff of a freshly lit cigarette after months on the tobacco wagon.

I hadn't dated or even gone out with a male friend since losing the ability to hear. Why now? I needed my hormones to wake up and start making a fuss right now about as badly as I needed another hole in the head.

Nah. That couldn't be happening. I'd just about decided becoming a nun might be my next profession. Maybe I only needed sleep. A nap after lunch before we moved on to my self-defense classes would probably do the trick. Remembered heat rushed through me without warning. Okay. Maybe the nun business was out after all. I suddenly felt reasonably certain that any unnecessary touching would not help matters either way.

Wait. I paused mentally. Maybe this wasn't about hormones or sleep deprivation at all. I'd just had my first professional success, in solving that murder case, since walking away from my teaching career. Didn't a coup of any sort, professional or personal, induce a certain level of excitement? Of course it did. I was just so out of practice that I had somehow mistaken one kind of anticipation for another.

Whew. That was a relief. I definitely did not want Detective Barlow thinking the handicapped woman had a crush on him. I didn't need any pity attention, especially not the sexual kind. The next relationship of that nature that I ventured into would not have a damned thing to do with pity or my disability.

Barlow's hand collided with mine just then as we both reached for the same folder. As if prompted by a domino effect, our gazes bumped into each other next. For a fraction of a second they held, then he looked away. But not before I recognized the glint of desire…of heat…simmering there.

Impossible. I barely kept my mouth from gaping in disbelief. I had to be mistaken.

Mistake or no, there was no way to deny what had twisted through me during that fleeting space in time. I read the next name and forged ahead with what I knew Barlow wanted to hear. I evicted any other thought from my mind. This mission was far too important to risk getting involved in any shape, form or fashion with my teacher.

Before we move into our self-defense session, Barlow said when we'd resumed our work after lunch, *I'd like to go over some special gadgets I picked up for you.*

I nodded and moved toward the table where a new box sat waiting. The nap I'd hoped for hadn't panned out. Barlow had even questioned me about names and faces and locations as we ate lunch. Time was short, he'd said, we need to take advantage of every moment.

At the table he reached inside the box and withdrew what looked like a PDA, a small handheld personal computer similar to the ones people used to electronically store their daily calendars, addresses, et cetera. This one came with its own neat little shoulder strap. Compact, sleek-looking. I was impressed, but I had no idea what he wanted me to do with it.

Since Hammond can't know about your lip-reading ability, and sign language would make you a liability as far as he's concerned, you'll use this instead.

He turned on the device and a screen appeared. *Whenever anyone needs to convey information to you, they'll do this.* He took a moment to tap a few keys, then passed the PDA to me and the message read: *Do you remember the final move I taught you yesterday?*

I looked up at him and nodded.

The crooked smile that rearranged his too-serious

expression into one of breath-stealing quality made me quiver inside. He reached into the box once more and produced a cellular phone. The flip-top style.

This one works a little like a walkie-talkie, he explained. *You don't have to hold it up to your mouth to speak. Use it like this.* He demonstrated by holding the unit about seven or eight inches from his mouth and saying hello. *You can read what the caller has to say on the screen. It's fully equipped for the hearing-impaired.*

I didn't want to burst his bubble, but the one I owned worked very much like that. Unfortunately he'd wasted his or Metro's money on that one.

I know what you're thinking, he said when my gaze moved back to his face. But this one has something yours doesn't. *Because we want to be extremely careful to whom you pass along information, which you might not be able to keep to yourself until a face-to-face meeting is feasible, you need to be certain to whom you're speaking when you make a call.*

Now I was impressed. "How does it work?"

I must have looked a little bewildered or a lot awed. That lopsided smile broadened. *You place your call.* He entered a number and handed the phone to me. Then he reached into his pocket and pulled out his cell phone and answered it. When he said Barlow, his name appeared on my screen and a statement beneath it confirmed his identity. My phone would ID the name of the person connected to the number from which the call came. But this one was way cooler. It actually ID'd the *voice* of the caller.

"Wow."

He closed his phone and put it away. *The voice identification only works for those who have been added to its database. Me, Chief Kent and Chief Adcock. Always attempt to contact me first. Kent or Adcock should be last resorts.*

I saw the line of his jaw harden ever so slightly when he mentioned Chief Adcock's name. It wasn't the first time I'd noticed it.

"What is it you don't like about Chief Adcock?" The question was out of my mouth before I could swallow it back. I had no business asking such a thing. Judging by the way his face blanked, he felt the same way.

Chief Adcock is my boss. Whether I like him or not is inconsequential.

Judging by the cold, hard look in his eyes, he didn't merely dislike his boss, he despised him.

"I had a principal like that once," I offered. He'd been a real turkey. None of the teachers had liked him.

Barlow shook his head slowly from side to side. *Trust me, you didn't have one like this.*

Though I couldn't hear his voice and analyze the way he said the words, I could pick up nuances from his face and eyes…if he allowed me to. He did not. Whatever the beef between Adcock and Barlow, he had no intention of sharing the gritty details.

From there we moved on to self-defense. By the time

I had my taskmaster's permission to hit the shower I was exhausted but somehow wired at the same time. Considering the way his every touch had me ready to scream in unexpected frustration, I might just have to resort to a cold one.

I double-checked the lock on the door—I'd learned from experience that Barlow liked showing up at the most unexpected times. In the name of making sure I was fully prepared, of course. Not that I actually doubted his motivation. If I had come to understand one thing, it was that Barlow was definitely all work and no play. I might get a glimpse of male approval in those piercing blue eyes once in a great while, but he quickly vanquished the weakness whenever it occurred. Maybe, I mused, the good detective simply needed to get laid about as badly as I did. But I would never admit that to him or anyone else in a million years.

I stripped off my sweaty T-shirt, rolled down my jeans and kicked them aside. My hands hesitated at the latch of my bra. I stared at my reflection in the mirror over the sink and wondered what Barlow saw when he looked at me.

The bra fell away and I stared at my unrestrained breasts. Not bad. A C cup and still perky enough. My gaze traveled downward. I didn't exactly have what you'd call six-pack abs, but I was certainly slim enough. Ab crunches never had been my favorite exercise. My hips flared slightly and my legs were toned from my aerobic workouts.

I stripped off my panties and considered how long it had been since a man had seen me naked. Two years, three months and one week. I dismissed the thought before dragging it out to the days and hours.

I'd let my auburn hair grow longer, but I rarely bothered with anything but a ponytail or a braid. Just now, with it falling around my shoulders, I wondered if I should wear it down more often.

I scrutinized my face, still pretty much unlined despite that year of pure hell after facing the fact that my hearing would not return.

Now that I thought about it, not much else about me had changed…except the way I viewed myself. I was no longer a viable commodity on the dating market. But then, my ex-fiancé's decision to walk away from our two-year relationship could have something to do with that.

Turning away from the mirror I shoved the shower curtain aside and climbed in. My brain immediately evicted my ex-fiancé and resumed its obsession with my mentor. Why in the world was I torturing myself this way? No one, not Barlow or anyone else, would want a deaf wife. It was one thing to marry someone who for whatever reasons became deaf in the course of the marriage, but choosing a hearing-impaired mate from the get-go couldn't be expected of any man. Being deaf complicated life. I couldn't imagine anyone purposely wanting to complicate their lives.

I closed my eyes and allowed the hot water to sluice over my body. If I really looked at the situation with an objective eye, I would be the first to admit that I wasn't sure I would knowingly choose a mate with a physical impairment. Scrubbing the water from my face, I thought about that some more. I didn't personally know anyone else who fell into that category, but I felt reasonably certain of my conclusion. It was easy to say a person's frailties didn't count or that you didn't notice, but the truth was most people did, whether consciously or unconsciously. We're mere humans, after all.

As I smoothed the soap over my skin I amended that assessment a bit. If I met someone with an impairment, I certainly wouldn't hold it against them. *If* deeper feelings developed, I couldn't imagine not allowing them to evolve fully. But that's just it. The likelihood of a man who knew my circumstances looking to me for a permanent relationship was about nil.

Too depressing to dwell upon.

Admittedly, I couldn't keep hiding from life. My need to fulfill my professional expectations had forced me to take drastic measures in that department. Was this time with Barlow the trigger for pushing me to take steps in my personal life as well?

Here I went, overanalyzing things again. I had to remember that nothing but the operation mattered just now. I couldn't worry about anything else.

Guilt assaulted me with that last thought. I'd called my mom last night and lied to her for the first time since I was fourteen years old. Telling her I'd reached my destination and settled in still hung in the back of mind, nudging me with guilt every now and then.

I'd warned her that I might not be able to call again for a few days. She'd accepted the story without hesitation, only adding to my guilt fest.

Too late to worry about that now. Tomorrow morning I reported to the Hammond residence. I felt extremely confident in my knowledge of the situation, but I worried about meeting the man face-to-face. With Sawyer I'd managed to accomplish my goal without a face-to-face encounter. Barlow's warning that the slightest mistake could cost me my life didn't help. But that was his job. He had to ensure I was fully prepared.

I toweled my skin dry and wrapped my wet hair turban style. My terry-cloth robe felt warm and inviting against my skin. I cinched the belt tightly and took a deep breath before moving out into the dimly lit hall.

Barlow waited outside my room. The little hitch in my breathing was the only outward indication of my surprise. But inside, my heart pounded. He'd said we were through for the day.

I'd like to go over a few final items.

I couldn't read his face or eyes. I decided then and there he'd make a great poker partner. "Sure." My turban had already started to fall so I pulled it loose and shook out my hair as I waited for him to say whatever was on his mind. I assumed since he made no move to relocate to the gym that he planned to have his say right here.

You know the faces, the names. He folded his arms over his chest. *You understand his business dealings well enough to know what comments might carry weight. I'm even impressed with your ability to take care of yourself in the event of a physical attack.*

There was a "but" coming. I could sense it in his posture and the way he kept his face and eyes carefully devoid of expression.

That's all well and good, but since I can't talk Chief Kent out of moving forward with this operation, I need to make sure you understand exactly how I feel.

Like there was any question on that one.

"I believe you've made your feelings quite clear." No need to hear him say it all again.

He straightened away from the wall and set his hands on his hips. Irritation had tightened his jaw, but otherwise he kept his face clean of emotion.

This won't be like the situation with Sawyer. You'll be inside. His gaze narrowed and he searched my eyes. *Do you understand the full implications of that? You'll be in the middle of what's happening. Not outside, hiding in your car or the bushes, watching and waiting to call in backup. Inside, directly in the line of fire, where your every move, your every word will be scrutinized for threat. And backup won't be anywhere around. I won't be able to get to you in a timely manner when and if you're able to call. And you have to remember that a phone call should be your last resort, since all calls will be monitored.*

I clenched my jaw hard and told myself his words weren't going to elicit the fear I felt certain he intended. I knew he wanted me to back out, even now after all our hard work. He thought the operation was too risky. Thought I wasn't tough enough or smart enough to get the job done, much less stay alive.

"I fully understand what I'm walking into," I said firmly. I held the towel tightly against me and ordered my knees not to weaken. He'd gotten at least part of his wish. A line of fear had traced a path between my shoulder blades. As courageous as I wanted to appear right now, part of it was bluster.

Hammond and his men will be armed, he said as if I hadn't spoken. *Every single one of his associates has killed before. Conrad, Vargas, Hammond himself. Not one of them would think twice about killing you if anything at all feels wrong or out of sync.*

I swallowed back the lump of emotion his words had wrenched into my throat. "I told you I understand what I'm walking into. Why can't you just accept that?" Now I was angry. I'd had it with people treating me as if I wasn't capable of doing what needed to be done or making my own decisions. Yes, this operation carried a great deal of risk. I got that. But this was what I wanted. Any worthwhile venture carried some sort of risk.

You're an untrained civilian. He braced one hand on the wall just past my shoulder. The move put him even closer. I tried my best to ignore that subtle scent of earthy aftershave he wore. *I like you, Miss Walters.*

I'd had more than ample opportunity to suggest he call me by my first name, but I'd stayed out of that territory. He'd done the same.

I don't want your death on my conscience.

In the few days since we'd officially met at that construction site where Sawyer had intended to hide the skeleton in his past, not once had I doubted Barlow's motivation or his fierce dedication to duty. I didn't doubt it now. I took a moment and regarded the chiseled features of his face before fixing my gaze on his. "You really don't think I can handle this, do you?"

He moved his head slowly from side to side. *You seem determined to get yourself killed and nothing I say appears to be getting through.* He leaned slightly closer, forcing me to tilt my head back to see his lips. *Sleep on it. If you change your mind, no one will hold it against you.*

The oxygen evaporated in my lungs, and before I could drag in another breath he'd walked away.

There was no way to make him understand. I couldn't change my mind. I couldn't go back.

Steven Barlow stared at his cellular phone for several moments before he made the call he knew would obstruct sleep without making.

A groggy voice rasped across the other end of the line. It was past midnight but Steven didn't care.

"I hate to disturb you," he lied. The bastard that served as his superior officer shouldn't be able to sleep, either. He should be worrying about this operation more than anyone else, but, of course, he wasn't.

"Is there a problem?" Adcock demanded, an unbalanced mixture of uncertainty and impatience in his tone. He hated being made to wait. Hated even worse that there might be a problem with getting his pet project off the ground.

That would be his first concern. Not whether or not Merrilee Walters was all right or if she needed anything. To him, the only thing that mattered was that he got a shot at bringing down Hammond once and for all.

"Only the same problem I've reiterated to you over and over since Kent came up with this crazy scheme to use a deaf woman for this op." He was skating on thin ice, but he didn't care. The drawn-out silence that followed punctuated that reality.

"You'll be lucky to survive this op with your shield intact, Barlow," he warned. "I would suggest you remember to whom you're speaking. I will not tolerate any further insubordination. I've put up with too much from you already. Are we clear on who is in charge here?"

Steven ground his teeth hard enough to crack the enamel before he found some semblance of control. "Quite clear. You're willing to risk the life of an untrained civilian to have your moment of glory." Even he recognized he'd crossed the line with that one, but he no longer cared. Merrilee Walters would walk into a suicide mission at 8:00 a.m. tomorrow morning. He had to make at least one last-ditch effort to stop this.

"You do anything to jeopardize this setup and you'll hang for it, Barlow," Adcock snarled. "I will utilize every means at my disposal to ensure that you spend the rest of your life regretting it if you screw this up."

"I take it that's your final word on the subject," Steven returned, pushing the envelope even further. "Nothing I say is going to change your mind?"

"Are you recording this?" his chief demanded, suddenly suspicious or maybe worried about his own ass. "You're trying to trap me in the event something does go wrong!"

Steven smiled, couldn't help himself. "No, sir, I'm not recording this conversation, but that would have been a good idea, considering my ass is the one on the line when you get down to the nitty-gritty."

The chief wouldn't go down if this op failed, if a civilian was caught in the crossfire. It would be Detective Steven Barlow who paid the price. But he didn't care about that. He owed this final effort to the woman sleeping in the other room, even if she didn't fully understand it just yet.

"This conversation is over," Adcock snapped. "Watch your step, Barlow. Like you say, it's your ass on the line."

A definitive click signaled the end of the conversation. Steven closed his phone and laughed softly, derisively. The conversation had actually been over before it started. Chief Adcock and Chief Kent had made their decision. The operation was a go. Merrilee Walters was willing to take the risk and so were the powers that be.

Steven knew exactly how this would play out. If, major if, the op was a success, the chiefs would be heroes. The two would ride it for all it was worth. If anything went wrong, then they would step back, leaving Steven to face the unwanted press. But none of that bothered him. It was the idea that this woman—his gaze drifted to the wall that separated their bedrooms—was sacrificing everything. She would be on her own when it came right down to it. There was no way Steven could monitor her activities. Hammond was too sharp to allow any kind of electronic surveillance, even the latest and greatest technology, get past him. The best they'd been able to do was flyover surveillance.

All Steven could do was watch her walk into a world she couldn't possibly understand and hope for the best. She thought because he'd reviewed names and faces and profiles with her that she somehow understood what she was up against, but she didn't.

Luther Hammond had built himself a mansion on a hill overlooking all that he considered his, this city and all it entailed. His reach was ever broadening and expanding to include even uglier possibilities. He had no conscience, no care for life. On the surface he looked like any other well-to-do businessman, but he was like no other. He just didn't allow anyone to see it until it was too late.

Steven knew firsthand how ugly and cruel Hammond

could be. No one wanted to see him fall more than Steven. In spite of that burning desire, he still possessed enough human compassion to step back and consider the consequences.

Merilee Walters would be lucky to survive the week, and there was nothing he could do to stop her charge toward certain death.

Chapter 8

I clenched the steering wheel as I rounded the final curve before reaching the mountain's peak. Though I had lived in Nashville my entire life I couldn't recall ever having driven this particular road. Steep and curvy, it led farther and farther into seemingly nowhere. Folks in places like Colorado would call this a hill, but around here it was a mountain.

As the upward ascent leveled on the mountaintop my breath left me in an unexpected rush.

"So this is how the other side lives. Wow."

I'd seen my share of swanky mansions. After all, they didn't call Nashville "Music City" for nothing. Lots of music moguls and other celebs called Nashville home. The west side showcased some of the finest homes in the whole state, if not the southeast U.S. But this was a whole other level of elegance.

Ledges, the exclusive community Luther Hammond called home, was gated. I stopped for the guard and showed my driver's license, which included a warning that I was deaf. He checked his clip pad and smiled, then waved me through the massive decorative iron gates.

I relaxed my foot from the brake and allowed my Jetta to roll forward. It was a good thing no one pulled up behind me because I continued at a speed of about five miles per hour for a good portion of the drive through the impressive neighborhood. The houses were huge, at least eight or ten thousand square feet. Each appeared to sit slap in the middle of about five meticulously landscaped acres. Gorgeous trees and manicured shrubbery defined each space. Wide, welcoming driveways of cobblestone curved through the lush green lawns. Brick-and-stone homes were adorned with grand columns and towering windows.

About the same time I'd convinced myself that nothing could compare with the property I'd just passed, I reached the final address in the Ledges development. I'd looked at aerial views of the residence, but nothing had prepared me for the immensity of it. Hammond had purchased two side-by-side estate lots, each consisting of five acres, right on the bluff where he could look down upon the city of Nashville.

I eased into the long drive, paused for the guard who

stepped from the small guardhouse. Hammond's entire property was surrounded by a ten-foot decorative iron fence, reinforced by massive stone pillars every fifteen or twenty feet. Cameras were mounted strategically. Not to mention he had a guest house full of personal soldiers. A gated property within a gated community.

The guard motioned for me to pass. He didn't speak to me, and I assumed he'd been briefed on my condition since he hadn't attempted to communicate even before he looked at my driver's license.

The Hammond mansion made the others I'd seen thus far look like low-rent row houses. I'd studied the layout, understood that it was huge, but looking at it now, I hadn't really understood. This wasn't a house, this was a castle, sans the turrets.

I parked in front of the massive steps and emerged from what I now considered my rinky-dink car. The limousine-size Mercedes, as well as the Jaguar and the Hummer parked nearby would do that.

The soaring double doors opened before I'd climbed the first of the polished granite steps. I recognized the man waiting in the doorway immediately. Mason Conrad. He didn't speak, simply stood stoically waiting until I'd mounted the final step.

He wore a charcoal suit with matching shirt and tie. The dark on dark pairing looked good on him, complimented his swarthy features.

I drew in a deep breath, produced a smile and thrust out my hand. "Hello, I'm Merrilee Walters."

He looked surprised when I spoke. I couldn't be sure whether he'd expected me to be mute as well or if he'd thought my voice would sound peculiar due to my hearing impairment. Since I hadn't lost my ability to hear until two years ago, my speech was not affected—at least, not so far. His surprise gave way to confusion and I immediately offered my PDA.

"I'm sure you know I don't do sign language." I nodded to the PDA. "I can read anything you'd like to tell me. It's a bit of a chore for you, but it's the best I can do."

Long fingers deftly lifted the small electronic device from my hand. His fingertips brushed my palm and I barely resisted a shiver. Fear, I told myself. I couldn't start out allowing myself to be intimidated by the mere presence of any of these men. Conrad was tall, broad-shouldered and quite good-looking, and he was a killer. But I couldn't be afraid. I had to pretend I knew nothing if I wanted to survive. Barlow had made that immensely clear last night and then again this morning.

Conrad passed the PDA back to me with a smile that startled me all over again. I blinked, managed an answering smile, then focused my attention on the words he'd entered on the small screen.

Your pictures don't do you justice.

My heart bumped against my sternum. I wasn't sure whether he was joking or trying to be kind. I wore a rather drab gray dress with a white apron. My auburn hair was arranged in a generic bun and I hadn't bothered with makeup. But the worst fashion infraction was the white nurse's style shoes. Maybe he only wanted to put me at ease.

I turned my attention to the man standing between me and the door and somehow, God only knew how, kept my smile in place. "Thank you."

He stepped aside and gestured for me to enter ahead of him. I directed my feet to move, one in front of the other, until I passed through the final barrier into enemy territory. My heart was pounding, my pulse tripping, but I was here. I'd done it.

There were times when I felt grateful for the absolute silence…this was one of those times. The infinite quiet fit very much with the palatial entry hall. The ceiling soared nearly three stories to a towering glass dome that showered light downward, only to be splintered into a million shards of glitter by the multitiered brass-and-crystal chandelier. Shiny marble floors reflected the splendor from above. Even that magnificence was all but overshadowed by the massive, intricately carved detailing of the wood trim. An equally embellished mahogany table stood center stage, topped with a fragrant bouquet of fresh flowers. The deep, rich wine of the walls shimmered like blood pulsing with life. The idea made me shudder inwardly. And all of it, every single detail, merely set the stage for the grand staircase that flowed up onto the second-floor landing.

A hand touched my elbow, giving me a start. I worked up a smile for Mr. Conrad. He motioned for me to follow him. I knew where we were likely headed, the study, but I resisted the urge to lead the way. I had never been here before. I wasn't supposed to know which way to go.

The luxurious decorating theme carried through into the study. There wasn't a doubt in my mind that the elegance encompassed the entire house. All bought and paid for with dirty money. I gritted my teeth and held in the emotion that tried to surface. I couldn't let any resentment or hostility show. Not even for a second…not even the slightest glimmer. Barlow had warned me about that.

Conrad waved a hand over one of the jacquard-upholstered wing chairs flanking the desk. I sat down without hesitation. He left the room, but not for a second did I believe I was alone. That's another thing Barlow had repeated over and over, Hammond didn't leave anything to chance. He would be watching me. His associates would be watching me. No place within his realm was safe. No one trustworthy.

A frown needled my brow as I mulled over those final moments with Barlow this morning. He'd asked one last time if I wanted to change my mind. I'd said no. The look of finality…of resignation in his eyes had unsettled me more than any of his warnings. He truly believed I would fail.

I looked around the elegant room with its tasteful decor and palpable decadence. Maybe I was in over my head. There was always the chance I would fail. But I had to try. I had to do this. Not because I had known the man for whom Chiefs Kent and Adcock wanted to have their vengeance, not even for all the dirty business Hammond allegedly conducted. I had to do this for the people who lived in this city and who deserved to go to sleep at night with the certainty that someone cared enough to risk their life to stop this kind of evil from growing. I had to do it for me.

I closed all thought from my mind and focused on the room and its full-bodied character. The masculinity of the décor and the subtle scents: leather and citrus odors from the tufted sofa and the polish used regularly on the furniture permeated every square inch from the rich tapestry of the drapes to the imported wool rug sprawled on the glistening hardwood. A stone fireplace held court in one corner, four additional stylish upholstered chairs flanking it. In winter, with the gas flames flickering, the ambience would be as melancholy as a Norman Rockwell rendering.

The whisper of footfalls on the floor was not necessary for me to know when Mr. Hammond had entered the room. I recognized his scent. Barlow had insisted I become familiar with the cologne Hammond wore in an effort to distinguish his presence without having to turn around if my back were to him as it was at the moment. My gratitude for Barlow's intensive forty-eight-hour training session bumped up a notch.

Luther Hammond walked to where I sat. I looked up as he reached my peripheral vision, ensuring that a surprised expression claimed my face. I didn't speak or move. I waited for him to do so.

I'm Luther Hammond. He thrust out his hand.

I looked at his hand, then at him, allowing my surprise to evolve into confusion, before reluctantly clasping his hand. His handshake was firm. When he released my hand I offered my PDA and shrugged. "I'm sorry. I didn't understand what you said."

He studied me a moment, then nodded. When he'd completed his message he passed the PDA back to me. The words on the screen read: *I'm Luther Hammond. I'd like to welcome you to my home.*

I smiled. "Thank you."

Another lengthy scrutiny played out before he again reached for the PDA. Don't be nervous, I chanted over and over in my head. I had to stay calm.

This time his message read: *Your credentials are impeccable. I expect nothing but the best from you. Mason will show you to your quarters.*

I nodded. "I'll do my very best, sir."

At least ten seconds of assessment followed before he simply walked out. A man like Luther Hammond wouldn't waste time with the hired help.

I let go an enormous sigh of relief, but I kept my expression carefully schooled in the event I was being watched or taped or both. Mason Conrad appeared and indicated that I should go with him.

Mr. Conrad had to stop a number of times and wait for me to catch up to him. The house was awesome. I couldn't think of any place I'd ever seen on television, much less in real life, that even came close. But I'd have to get over that. I couldn't walk around this distracted all the time. The look of bored amusement on Conrad's face told me I wasn't the first to react in this manner.

"It's lovely."

He nodded.

When we passed the rear staircase in the immense kitchen I knew we were getting close. A few steps down a connecting corridor and he opened the door to the maid's quarters. Bedroom, bathroom and small sitting area. The rooms weren't nearly so grand as the rest of the house, but they were a serious cut above anything I'd ever rented or owned. Cozy and very, very nice. My bags had already been brought inside. The keys to my Jetta lay on the table near the door. Now, that was service.

I smiled to show my approval and appreciation.

Mr. Conrad entered a message into my PDA: *Let me know if you need anything else. I believe you already have your schedule and list of duties.*

"Thank you and yes, I have everything I need to get started."

He quickly entered another message: *Mr. Hammond insists that you take the day to get settled and familiarize yourself with the house.*

That was a nice break. "I appreciate that." If I said thank you again he would probably think I was a robot.

Conrad left the room and I took my time getting to know the place. So far, the experience was way different than I had expected.

Hammond was different. I'd seen pictures of him, but I'd somehow expected to sense an evil about him. I hadn't picked up any vibes like that. Strange. Even watching Sawyer from a distance I'd felt that he was dirty somehow. Bad to the bone. But I didn't get the first negative feeling from Hammond. Very strange.

I shrugged off the nagging thought and decided to settle in. That's what was expected of me. I sure didn't want to make anyone suspicious.

A little over an hour later I had unpacked my clothes. Only a few outfits. Jeans and casual blouses mostly. One dress, just in case. A half-dozen uniforms in my size with accompanying aprons already hung in the closet. I checked out the bed. Nice. Good sheets. Comfy mattress. The clock radio was outfitted for the deaf, complete with a small vibrating pad that went under my pillow. Lights on the phone and in various other places about the quarters, including above my door, would let me know if anyone rang my bell or called on my phone line. The phone, too, was equipped for the hearing impaired, not that I would be using it. Barlow had warned me that it would be monitored.

I turned on the television and checked the channels. Closed captioning appeared on the screen for my convenience. Everything the local cable company had to offer was there.

With my room taken care of, I decided to explore the house. I snapped my PDA onto its shoulder strap, draped it around my neck and let it hang to one side, then headed out. I knew the layout of the house by heart but I couldn't wait to see it all for real. If the rest was anything like what I'd encountered so far, it would be a real treat.

Downstairs I roamed around the kitchen some more. I discovered the cook and his assistant in the huge pantry. I wiggled my fingers at them and hurried out of their territory. Neither of them looked very pleased that I'd intruded on what looked like an inventory. I'd say a more polite hello later.

The dining room seated twenty-four and reminded me of the White House dining room I'd seen on a Christmas special once. More glittering chandeliers and gleaming mahogany furnishings. The walls in the dining room were painted a deep emerald and were adorned with lovely paintings.

A grand parlor that ran the entire width of the house on one side left me breathless all over again. I couldn't imagine cleaning a house this size alone. It would take a whole week just to dust the stuff in this one room. I would have been remiss had I not peeked into the two powder rooms located downstairs. Both were sufficiently elegant with their gold embellishments and jeweled mirrors.

I felt almost regal, even in my gray maid's uniform, as I ascended the staircase. Talk about glitzy. Five or six people could stand side by side and walk up or down this thing. A lovely runner held in place by brass stops ran the length of the staircase.

Upstairs I admired five bedroom suites. Enormous rooms with bathrooms the size of my living room back home. But the last one, the sixth one at the very end of the upstairs corridor, was the most special of all. A beautiful white canopy bed with pink linens and mounds and mounds of pillows and stuffed animals. Dressing table and bureau of matching white wood. A small table and chairs, complete with bone china tea set, sat in the middle of the room. Along one wall bookcases and a window seat had been built in. A book lay open on the cushions there. I wandered over and picked it up. *The Secret Garden.* One of my all-time favorites.

A little girl was suddenly standing next to me and I jumped. Gasped loud enough to startle her. I didn't have to hear it for myself, I saw the reaction on her little face.

I didn't mean to scare you. Are you the new maid who can't hear?

I opened my mouth to answer her and barely caught myself. My heart flopped. Close one.

I smiled and offered her my PDA. I showed her how to enter what she wanted to say to me. She laughed and said something about her computer. She wasn't looking directly at me so I missed part of it.

Tiffany Hammond sat down on the window seat, the strap of my PDA dragging me down with her. When she showed the screen to me it read: *How does it feel to be deaf?*

Typical question from a child and some adults. I thought about the question a moment, though I had answered it before. I had to remember to think about all my answers now. I was undercover…*careful* had to be my middle name.

"It feels like when you're in the bathtub and you stick your head under the water. Know what I mean?"

She nodded enthusiastically.

"You can almost hear things," I went on, "but it's more a vibration than a sound and it has to be really loud. Otherwise I don't hear anything but silence." I shrugged. "Except maybe the blood roaring through my veins when I get scared." I actually wasn't sure I really heard either of those things. Memories, my doctor had said.

She pursed her lips for a bit and thought about what she wanted to say next, then she tapped the keys: *Does being deaf make you scared?*

It was my turn to do some real thinking. My first thought was to say an unequivocal no…but that wasn't entirely true. Instead, I admitted, "Sometimes." I remembered the first time I'd gone for one of my runs and I'd kept feeling as if someone was watching me. I would stop every so often and turn all the way around. I couldn't see anyone and I'd wished so badly that I could hear. But I couldn't…there was only silence and, of course, the rush of fear in my blood.

At her expectant look I added, "Sometimes at night I wake up. You know, the way you wake up when some sound interrupts the night?" She nodded, her eyes wide with understanding. "'Course I can't hear anything so I just lie there wondering if I should have."

She chewed on her lower lip and I wondered if I'd said too much and frightened her. I definitely didn't want to screw up this early. Nor did I want to frighten a child.

The next thing I knew she was reaching toward me. She touched my ear. I sat very still and let her. Then she touched the other one, taking her time, performing a fairly thorough exam. When she'd examined her own, she looked straight into my eyes and considered what she saw for a time.

You don't look different or feel different.

I refrained from responding since she hadn't entered the comment into my PDA.

You look pretty.

My lips twitched with a smile. I bit down to quell it and forced my gaze back to hers.

She frowned and terror sliced through me. Her frown morphed into confusion. *Can you read my lips?*

Working hard to keep my hand from shaking, I offered her the PDA.

She accepted it but didn't look convinced. She typed in her question and handed it back to me. I shook my head, forcing a smile.

But you look at my lips when I talk, she argued aloud.

She suddenly looked away and I knew someone had come into the room. I turned, praying that whoever had walked in hadn't heard her last statement.

The woman who'd entered the room gifted me with a smile. I recognized her from her pictures. Cecilia, the au pair. When she'd smiled sufficiently at me she scolded Tiffany, *Don't be a nuisance, Tiff. You know she can't hear you. How rude is that, Tiff?*

I stood awkwardly. Was the maid supposed to fraternize with the family? God, what if I'd already overstepped my bounds?

Cecilia reached for my PDA without waiting for an invitation and entered a message: *I'm Cecilia, Tiffany's au pair. Nice to meet you.*

I managed another smile. "Merri Walters." I held out my hand. "Nice to meet you, too."

She brushed her palm lightly against mine, not a real handshake but that was fine by me.

Cecilia entered another message: *Tiff loves to ask questions. You'll have to overlook her.*

I certainly understood that. Having been a teacher of children just her age, I knew it well. But I didn't bother saying any of that. Instead I smiled and nodded, like the poor deaf woman I was.

Come along, Tiff, we have piano lessons in the parlor. Cecilia flicked one last smile in my direction and started for the door.

Tiffany hesitated, forcing her au pair to slow before reaching the door. *See you later, Miss Merri.*

Don't be silly, Tiff. Cecilia tugged the child toward her. *She can't hear you.*

Tiffany just smiled, as if she knew some secret no one else did.

I hoped like hell she didn't voice that secret suspicion to her father or anyone else.

Chapter 9

I made it through day two without any glitch to speak of. Mason Conrad had gone over Mr. Hammond's expectations with me just to be sure I understood my responsibilities. I'd spent the rest of the time, until 6:00 p.m., fulfilling those obligations. Not so difficult. Then I'd retired to my room and taken some time to mull over the people I'd met and the reactions my presence had garnered. All in all, I felt comfortable with how things had gone. I'd watched television, soaked in the tub, then watched some more TV until 10:00 p.m. had rolled around.

Unable to sleep I flopped over onto my side, fluffed my pillow and pulled the cover up closer around my

neck. The room was completely black with the plantation shutters closed and the drapes shut tight. The dark
hadn't ever really bothered me, not even when I was a
small child. I had always understood, even before
choosing to go undercover to get the goods on bad guys,
that it was what was in the dark one had to be afraid of,
not the dark itself.

Thinking of that now gave new meaning to the idea. In
this house, this grand palace, resided not one but several
men known for evil deeds. I couldn't help feeling the irony
of it. Every person I had met, male or female, had
seemed…normal. Other than the ball of nerves in my
tummy based on what I had read in the profiles Barlow had
provided, I'd encountered no reason to feel uncomfortable.
Everyone had been polite, kind, very businesslike so far.
My only awkward moment had been with the child.

Since her au pair, Cecilia, had played off the little
girl's comment, I wasn't actually worried. Yet a part of
me recognized that it could happen again with one of
the adults. Somehow I hadn't thought of that. In order
to eavesdrop on conversations I would need to read the
lips of those speaking. I couldn't very well do that without actually looking at their mouths. I wondered vaguely
if Barlow had thought of it and had simply chosen not
to mention it considering I was determined to go
through with this assignment.

I damn sure wouldn't ask him. Giving him another
excuse to pull the plug on this operation would ruin
everything.

Rolling onto my back, I lay there and stared at the ceiling, not that I could see it but I knew it was there. After a quick inventory of my feelings I admitted that yes, I was afraid on some level. I'd be stupid not to be. But Hammond and his associates had no reason to suspect me. That was the beauty of the plan. Any background check they ran on me in addition to what the cleaning service offered in the way of my history would be clean, with the exception of the fact that I had two brothers in Metro. That didn't make me guilty of anything. Neither of my brothers was in Homicide or Narcotics. Simple beat cops, happy to do the grunt work required to keep the city clean and safe.

My work file at Metro had been taken care of. And even if, by some remote chance, one of Hammond's people discovered I'd worked there as a file clerk, the cleaning service had been instructed to plead sympathy. The owner would insist I'd been fired and he'd felt sorry for me. Some detective had taken advantage of me and I'd been fired and the incident banished from the files to protect Metro. If anything, Hammond should consider that a good thing since that would make me bitter toward Metro. Barlow had gone as far as to suggest that I might lay a little groundwork on the issue. If the opportunity arose to make some negative comment about cops in general and the like.

I could definitely do that. Between my macho, overprotective brothers and Barlow's penchant for arrogance, I had myself a cache of irritation to draw upon.

Barlow's image bloomed in my mind before I could stop it, and I allowed myself to ponder what he might be doing right now. For the first week I wasn't supposed to contact him unless I had something significant to pass along. After that I would make up an excuse to go into town every three days. I would call him once I was halfway down the mountain and he would provide a rendezvous point. I had to smile at that. Imagine, me, the deaf ex-school teacher working undercover. My heart picked up an extra beat. This was more like it. I just couldn't spend the rest of my life in that dungeon of a workspace filing and retrieving cases.

Not that there was anything wrong with that line of work. It was a great job for the right person, just not me. I wanted to do so much. Wanted to make a difference. Maybe it was a side effect of growing up with four brothers who all turned out to be the hero types. Maybe I suffered from hero envy. I'd accused my brothers of being adrenaline junkies. Could I be addicted myself?

Deciding the subject was far too deep and complicated to go into without a carb boost, I threw back the covers and climbed out of bed. I'd nibbled at my dinner, a little uneasy in the presence of the cook and his assistant. They were friendly enough, just a little nosy. I'd been so busy making sure I gave the right answers that I lost my appetite. Well, it was certainly back to full form now.

After turning on the bedside lamp I tugged on my robe. I padded over to the door and stood there a moment before opening it. I couldn't think of any way my going into the kitchen for a snack would be construed as aggressive or covert. It would seem normal, wouldn't it?

I drew in a deep breath and reached for the door, unlocked it and pulled it open in one quick action to ensure I didn't change my mind. The hall was empty but not quite so dark as my room had been. A lamp on a side table about midway down the corridor provided a soft glow sufficient for maneuvering. Once in the kitchen, muted under-counter and baseboard lighting gave the room a pleasant glow.

The room was massive with two refrigerators, one being a walk-in type, along with a walk-in freezer. I shivered at the thought of being locked in that freezer. I'd definitely watched too many movies.

Intricately detailed cherry cabinetry topped with gleaming natural stone counters filled the space, including an island that was about the size of my entire kitchen back home. The limestone floor felt cool beneath my feet. I liked all of it, though I never even hoped to live in a place like this. As ostentatious as the house was, it actually felt homey in a big-bucks sort of way. The scents of fresh fruits and lingering olive oil from the enormous Italian-style dinner the cook had prepared still permeated the room. I inhaled deeply, thinking of my favorite restaurant downtown.

I hoped Connie, the cook, had stored the leftovers. Connie was a guy and definitely didn't look like any Connie I'd met before. He stood about six-four and probably weighed a little more than a hefty side of beef, but he had the sweet sense of humor you'd expect in a guy a third his size who possessed absolutely no testosterone. His assistant, Marjorie, looked to be about fifty and did most of the unglamorous work like peeling potatoes and onions and cleaning up after Connie prepared his masterpieces. I'd seen the kitchen after he'd completed one of his creations. Thank God kitchen cleanup didn't fall within my sphere of responsibility.

I was in luck. Plenty of salad was stored in a clear plastic container in fridge number one. I'd learned that servable foods belonged in fridge number one, while food-prep items were kept in fridge number two, otherwise known as the walk-in. Made sense to me.

Along with the salad and vinaigrette, I decided on lasagna. I flipped on the light above the island and rounded up a plate and eating utensils. As quietly as possible I scooped out a portion of the lasagna and popped it into the microwave for a warm-up. I hoped the hum and final ding of the timer didn't wake anyone. Who was I kidding? In a house this size it would take a minor explosion in the kitchen to shatter the quiet of the luxurious suites tucked away upstairs.

With a heaping pile of salad in my bowl, I re-covered the container and turned back to the fridge. The breath evacuated my lungs in one sudden whoosh.

Mason Conrad stood in front of the fridge, about two feet from me. He still wore the elegant black trousers, but his crisp white shirt now lay unbuttoned and open, showcasing a sculpted and tanned chest.

For about ten seconds I couldn't move or speak. He stared at me for the same, then dropped his gaze to the container of salad in my hands. Finally, when I'd about decided if I didn't make a move no one would, he reached for the container and took it from me. He opened his mouth to speak, but then seemed to think better of it. Instead, he held the bowl in one hand and patted his flat stomach with the other. The smile on his lips told me he'd meant the gesture to be a message.

"I'm starved, too," I admitted.

He turned toward the microwave. I noted the line of zeroes on the digital readout and realized the timer had just gone off.

I went to the microwave and removed the plate loaded with steaming lasagna. I bit my lower lip to hold back an ouch when I scarcely made it to the counter without dropping it. The plate had gotten a lot hotter than I'd expected. After pouring myself a glass of iced tea, I scooted onto a stool and dug in. I was pretty sure there was leftover garlic bread around somewhere but I didn't bother with it. Deciding to pig out had been before I'd had male company. Now I felt embarrassed by the sheer size of the portion I'd spooned out. As if reading my mind, Conrad scrounged up the bread and placed his bounty on the island directly across from me, then straddled a stool as if he'd done the midnight-snack thing a million times.

We ate without the distraction of chitchat for a time. Every once in a while I caught him looking at me. Un-

An Important Message from the Editors

Dear Reader,

If you'd enjoy reading romance novels with larger print that's easier on your eyes, let us send you TWO FREE HARLEQUIN INTRIGUE® NOVELS in our NEW LARGER-PRINT EDITION. These books are complete and unabridged, but the type is set about 25% bigger to make it easier to read. Look inside for an actual-size sample.

By the way, you'll also get a surprise gift with your two free books!

Pam Powers

Peel off Seal and Place Inside...

LARGER-PRINT
FREE BOOKS
EDITION

84

THE RIGHT WOMAN

she'd thought she was fine. It took Daniel's words and Brooke's question to make her realize she was far from a full recovery.

She'd made a start with her sister's help and she intended to go forward now. Sarah felt as if she'd been living in a darkened room and someone had suddenly opened a door, letting in the fresh air and sunshine. She could feel its warmth slowly seeping into the coldest part of her. The feeling was liberating. She realized it was only a small step and she had a long way to go, but she was ready to face life again with Serena and her family behind her.

All too soon, they were saying goodbye and Sarah experienced a moment of sadness for all the years she and Serena had missed. But they had each other now, and that is what

She held

Like what you see?
Then send for TWO FREE
larger-print books!

The Harlequin Reader Service™ — Here's How It Works:

Accepting your 2 free Harlequin Intrigue® larger-print books and gift places you under no obligation to buy anything. You may keep the books and gift and return the shipping statement marked "cancel." If you do not cancel, about a month later we'll send you 6 additional Harlequin Intrigue larger-print books and bill you just $4.49 each in the U.S., or $5.24 each in Canada, plus 25¢ shipping & handling per book and applicable taxes if any.* That's the complete price and — compared to cover prices of $5.24 each in the U.S. and $6.24 each in Canada — it's quite a bargain! You may cancel at any time, but if you choose to continue, every month we'll send you 6 more books, which you may either purchase at the discount price or return to us and cancel your subscription.

*Terms and prices subject to change without notice. Sales tax applicable in N.Y. Canadian residents will be charged applicable provincial taxes and GST.

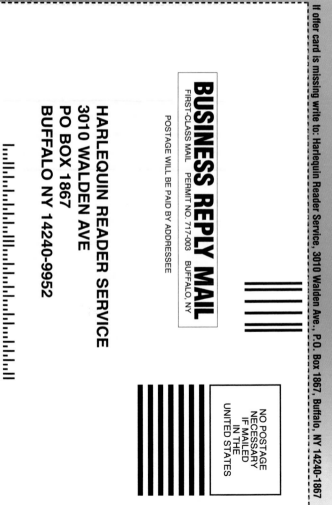

If offer card is missing write to: Harlequin Reader Service, 3010 Walden Ave., P.O. Box 1867, Buffalo, NY 14240-1867

BUSINESS REPLY MAIL
FIRST-CLASS MAIL   PERMIT NO. 717-003   BUFFALO, NY

POSTAGE WILL BE PAID BY ADDRESSEE

HARLEQUIN READER SERVICE
3010 WALDEN AVE
PO BOX 1867
BUFFALO NY 14240-9952

NO POSTAGE
NECESSARY
IF MAILED
IN THE
UNITED STATES

fortunately he caught me far more often. I hadn't eaten with a man like this in quite some time. Barlow didn't count since that had been work. My brothers and father didn't count, either, considering they were family. This was different. Though Conrad was actually work as well, he was a relative stranger. I knew facts about his background, but I didn't actually know him. I wondered if he was sitting there thinking the same thing. I had him at a serious disadvantage. He couldn't really talk to me, as far as he knew, without the PDA or a pad and pencil.

Taking advantage of the moment, I said, "Have you worked with Mr. Hammond long?" He had explained that he was Hammond's personal assistant. Yeah, right. Like I would believe that in this lifetime. Personal assistants didn't generally come in the muscle-bound, lethal-looking variety, at least not in any of the places I'd ever worked or visited.

He looked thoughtful for a moment, then held up both hands displaying all ten digits. Ten years. Of course I knew that, but I needed him to believe I had no idea.

"Wow. I guess you're really close after working together for that long."

He lifted one shoulder in a shrug. The move forced his shirt to gape open a little wider. Before I could stop myself, I'd checked out his pecs again. I blinked, then lifted my gaze back to his to find him watching me so intently that I had to look away, my cheeks burning with embarrassment. There was no telling what he thought.

I hoisted my attention back to my food, and as I did I saw in my peripheral vision that he'd started buttoning his shirt. Great. Now he thought I was a prude. I could appreciate a well-defined chest as well as any woman but I wasn't very good at communicating that sort of thing. I'd been out of the dating circuit too long.

Forcing down the last few bites, I hurriedly slid off the stool and stowed my dirty dishes in the dishwasher. He came up behind me, trapping me between the cabinet and his body and placed his utensils there as well.

I couldn't say for sure whether it was fear or some sort of wacky attraction, but with him this close my heart wouldn't stop pounding. A strange little tingle made my skin feel too tight.

Before I could escape, he'd taken me by the elbow and started escorting me back toward my room. Every step had my chest constricting tighter and tighter. Just because he seemed nice and looked handsome didn't mean he wouldn't take advantage of me. Why hadn't I thought of that? Why did I always wait until it was too late to consider all the repercussions of my actions?

At my door I turned to him, "Good night." I managed a tremulous smile and then went into my room.

He came in right behind me.

My throat quivered with the need to scream for help.

What in the world had I been thinking leaving my room in the middle of the night? This man was a killer and no telling what else. How had I let this happen? In just over twenty-four hours of arriving at the scene!

Seconds ticked by like hours with us standing there in the near darkness…my pulse throbbing erratically. Please, God, I prayed, don't let him hurt me.

As if I'd somehow telegraphed that message to him, the overhead fixture suddenly filled the room with light. Mason Conrad looked around my room, his gaze pausing briefly on the tousled linens, then he reached for my PDA on the bedside table. I licked my lips, ordered my heart to slow. Surely a man who intended to rape me wouldn't take the time to tell me about it.

He entered a message then handed the device to me. His note read: *I had a sister who was blind. If you need anything at all, feel free to come to me. Anytime.*

I blinked, felt my knees go weak with relief. I looked up at him and nodded. "Thank you."

His lips parted as if he wanted to speak, then he entered another message.

When I read the words I almost felt light-headed with some bizarre mixture of disbelief and fascination. It read: *You're very beautiful. Don't let anyone take advantage of that.*

I couldn't look at him right away but I knew he waited for me to do just that. I had to think. How could this be beneficial to my assignment here? And then I knew.

I lifted my gaze to his. "Thank you, Mr. Conrad. No one has said anything like that to me in a very long time." Part of me cheered my ingenuity. Another part, the needy female part, longed to hear more. How could that be? I knew who and what this man was. Apparently such a primal need knew no standards.

Another line was quickly entered: *Call me Mason.*

I nodded. "I appreciate your kindness," I finally managed to get out around the expanding lump in my throat.

That indecisive look marred his face again. I knew it well. He wanted to speak directly to me but saw the futility in it. People who didn't know I could read lips did that all the time. But this was way different from any other occasion I'd found myself in before.

He tapped out another message, then turned the screen toward me: *I didn't mean to make you uncomfortable, but I stand by what I said. All of it. Good night.*

I had two choices here. I could say good-night and usher him out the door or I could seal this moment of bonding with a more tangible move.

I took the PDA from him and placed it back on the table. Then I touched his arm. "You surprised me with your kindness, that's all." I smiled. "Good night."

That dark gaze held mine a moment more before he turned and walked out of my room, closing the door behind him.

I pressed my forehead against the cool wood and waited to the count of twenty before locking the door. I wanted to give him sufficient time to move away. With the door locked, I turned around and sagged against it.

Okay, what had I started here? Had that move been about this assignment or the unexpectedly resurrected need to feel like a woman? I hadn't wanted a man's touch or even longed for the company of the opposite sex in ages...not since my world fell apart two years ago.

Why the sudden burst of horniness? I shuddered inwardly at the word. I'd never considered myself on those terms. Calm, reserved, modest. Curious, yes. Ambitious even, but sexually aggressive? Not in a million years.

Maybe this new line of work brought out the tigress in me.

All this time I'd accused my brothers of being thrill-seekers, and look at me. Pressing the envelope at every turn. Seeing how far I could take the moment. Then again, Mason Conrad was Hammond's right-hand man. It didn't take a lifetime of detective work to recognize he was certainly the man to get to know.

A frown dug its way across my brow, nudging my conscience. Not now. I closed my eyes and scolded my stupidity. I would not feel guilty for using the guy. He was a murderer, no matter how handsome he looked or how nice he acted. There was no getting around the facts. I should consider myself lucky the guy'd had a handicapped sister and sympathized with my plight. That gave us something in common that I could work with. I had to remember that. I had to use every opportunity to gather intelligence.

Hammond couldn't be stopped until enough evidence had been gathered on him. Like Sawyer, he'd gotten away with too much for too long. I had to remember that.

I trudged into the bathroom and brushed my teeth

again. As I stared at my reflection I wondered how it was that I'd managed to contract that rare infection that had ultimately destroyed my hearing. I'd been raised to believe that God had a purpose for everyone. Somehow I couldn't see how his purpose for me had included losing one of my senses. But then, he worked in mysterious ways, right? Hadn't I heard that a thousand times in church? I had to trust something. I couldn't think of a better choice.

Climbing back into bed, I snuggled under the covers and my mind made the long, twisted journey from spirituality to sexuality. I began to count up the days since I'd last had sex. A long, long time. Did the lack of that kind of relationship in my life prompt this new living-on-the-edge mentality? I'd never felt precisely that way before. I mean, I hadn't been a prude or a homebody, but I certainly hadn't ever hobnobbed with mobsters.

Another frown tugged at my lips. How could Hammond and Conrad be such horrible people and appear so normal? I'd gone over that many times today, but no conclusive answer had welled from my gray matter. I should have tried to sleep, but somehow my mind wanted to tarry on the hows and whys of my life. Maybe it was just the lasagna. My mother always said don't eat right before bed, you'll have nightmares. Was this going to be a nightmare and I just hadn't realized it yet?

Detective Barlow had reiterated over and over how dangerous this assignment would be. But I hadn't let the concept sink past that first level of awareness. I didn't want to admit that this might be over my head. I wanted to do this…to bring down Hammond—the man no one else could touch. I shivered beneath my expensive sheets. Scary thought. Had the T factor penetrated that deeply? I hadn't ever thought of myself as the thrill type. Never bungee-jumped or rock-climbed or any of that other edgy stuff. I had always taken my risks in other ways. Like standing up to parents I suspected of child abuse or arguing with the administration when I felt the teachers would suffer over some new rule.

I lay there in the dark for a good half hour mulling over the inexplicable change. Was I having a midlife crisis early, prompted by the traumatic changes in my life?

I rolled onto my side and forced my eyes to close. I had to sleep. Tomorrow would be a long day. Though my duties were light, mostly ensuring that all was kept in order, at this point it still meant staying on my toes. If I expected to learn anything about Hammond and his illegal operations I'd have to be on my toes in more ways than one.

Heaving a sigh, I flopped over and curled my knees up to my chin. Mason Conrad's remark about my being beautiful just wouldn't stop intruding. I wasn't beautiful. I knew that. I looked in the mirror every day, for Christ's sake. I had nice hair and eyes and I suppose my face wasn't exactly homely, but I was certainly not beautiful by any stretch of the definition or the imagination.

It was entirely possible that Mr. Conrad had an ulterior motive just as I did. Perhaps he wanted more from me than tidying the rooms. I didn't get to be twenty-nine, almost thirty, overnight. I understood this kind of game, if that's what he was playing. I had no recourse but to play it out and see how it went. I intended to use him if the opportunity presented itself. That would make us even, if his motives weren't genuine.

Okay. Enough. I wasn't sleeping anytime soon. I kicked off the covers and climbed out of bed. I didn't bother with the light, just felt my way over to the immense window and drew back the drapes. I opened the plantation shutters and stepped closer to the window to stare out at the night sky. It was clear, filled with stars and a full moon glowing big and round. Gorgeous. The sky always looked prettier from high atop a mountain. The distraction of the city lights dimmed nature's glory.

No wonder those who could afford this kind of luxury were willing to deal with that steep, curving road. In the middle of June it wasn't a big deal, but in the dead of winter the only route leading to this exclusive neighborhood would no doubt be treacherous.

Piece of cake, I mused, with a Hummer. Hammond likely had his own helicopter at his beck and call, too, whenever he needed it. The man definitely had it all.

The gaslights placed strategically about the property lent an Old World quality to the shroud of darkness now blanketing the landscape. Come to think of it, the lights along the streets as well as the crooked private road linking this prestigious spot with civilization below had all been gas rather than the traditional electric lamps.

The gas lamps didn't give off nearly as much light; then again, that was likely the point.

Was I bored or what? I'd spent an entire ten minutes speculating on the illuminating power of various light fixtures. I could pace. The bedroom was every bit as large as my entire place back home. I wouldn't venture out into the hall again for anything. I'd already played it dicey enough on that score. I wasn't leaving this room again until 6:00 a.m. unless there was a fire or other disaster that rendered the premises unsafe.

Something moved on the other side of the lawn... near the fountain. I shook my head and peered even harder through the darkness. Nothing except the massive fountain complete with a lovely angel atop it that stood in the middle of a beautiful courtyard where the Hammond family no doubt held many a social function. I hesitated at the idea of calling anything held at a place like this a barbecue or cookout. The sparkling pool lay beyond the terrace and looked even more inviting by moonlight.

I folded my arms over my chest and blew out a breath of disgust. I needed sleep. I couldn't do my best work without enough sleep. Though I only had the one experience to draw upon, I felt certain sleeping most of the day while I followed Sawyer around at night had been the key to staying alert.

I squinted. Okay, now that time I really saw something move. I put my nose so close to the glass it was practically pressed there. More movement.

A face came into view via the dim glow from one of the gas lamps and I gasped, almost stepped back.

Victor Vargas. Hammond's other personal body-guard. Then Hammond himself passed through that same faint reach of illumination. What were they doing in the dark? I tried my best to see past where they'd stepped from the darkness but I saw nothing. My breath caught again when a third man appeared.

Mason Conrad. Still dressed in those black trousers, but the white shirt stood out like a beacon in the night. What the hell was going on out there at this time of night?

When I would have stepped away from the window, Mason Conrad's attention shifted in my direction. My heart shot into my throat, missing a beat before it slid back down and began to pound once more. Though I couldn't see his eyes through the darkness, despite the meager glow around him, I could have sworn he looked right at me.

He stood there for what felt like forever, staring, not moving a muscle. I felt like a deer caught in the head-lights, unable to move or even blink.

Just when I was certain he would point an accusing finger in my direction, he walked away, following the others to wherever they'd disappeared.

The instant oxygen filled my lungs once more as my brain jumped into overdrive. What were they doing out there? Did I need to know…?

Yes.

Before reason could poke itself into the mix I quickly

threw on my black stretch pants and matching long-sleeved T-shirt. Black socks and shoes. I shoved my hair into a black baseball cap. This was the only disguise I'd brought with me.

I imagined that Barlow would have croaked if he'd known I'd packed any such outfit.

Preparation was half the game, right?

Holding my breath once more, I did the one thing I'd sworn I wouldn't do again tonight…I stole out of my room.

By the time I reached the parlor my heart was beating so hard that arrest might very well be imminent. I had decided that the front and back entrances were out of the question.

Two sets of French doors led from the parlor out onto a side section of the terrace. Huge decorative pots filled with blossoming foliage offered some amount of cover.

Night had cooled the air, but still I felt sweat form on my skin. I was scared. As much as I wanted to do this—needed to do this—I was a little afraid of the consequences.

I grappled for my bearings and surveyed the yard. One of the garage doors had been raised and light spilled from the big hole it left. I figured that's where the trio had gone.

Keeping my respiration shallow, I eased away from the terrace, careful to stay in the shadows. When I reached the garage there was no way I could risk being seen at the open door, so I flattened against the closed one next to it. There were actually six bays, each with its own overhead door. Each door offered a small row of windows, which allowed me to peer into the enormous garage.

The three men were huddled around a fourth man. This new man was seated and...

My eyes widened in disbelief.

The fourth man—his back was to me so I couldn't determine who he was—was tied to the chair. Horror charged through me.

I resisted the urge to look away. Had to see if I could learn anything from whatever they were talking about. I struggled to block all other stimuli...forced myself to focus on the faces of the men speaking. First Conrad... then Hammond.

You know how this will end. Hammond said this to the man. I missed whatever Conrad had said. Couldn't make my brain work fast enough.

There was no way for me to guess the man's response.

Just tell us what you know and we'll make it quick.

I blinked, understood perfectly what that likely meant. Mason Conrad uttered this comment without so much as a flinch.

The man tied to the chair shook his head adamantly. Victor Vargas, Hammond's other right-hand man, threw back his head and laughed. Hammond and Conrad laughed, too, but without all the exaggerated body language.

They were going to kill this man.

I had to do something....

I looked around, but then realized that Hammond was speaking again.

...is up to you. I will get to the bottom of this.

Damn. I'd missed something.

Hammond looked at Vargas, who nodded once.

The need to act burned in my chest. I had to...

Terror obliterated the rest of my thought. Hammond and Conrad started toward the open door.

I had to hide.

Frantic, I glanced side to side.

Ran hard and fast.

Then flattened myself against the end of the garage a split second before the two men exited.

I held my breath for fear they would hear me panting. My heart all but stopped as they moved toward the same door I had exited from the parlor.

Conrad hesitated before going in...just long enough to glance at my bedroom window.

I had to get back into that room.

Now.

Ten seconds after the two had disappeared into the house, I shot one last look toward the open garage door, then hurried toward the terrace, careful to stay in the shadows.

I flattened myself against the wall of the house next to the French doors and watched for any sign of Vargas in the spotlight offered by that one open garage door.

When I'd screwed up my courage, I peered into the

parlor, which was still dark, and determined that Conrad and Hammond were no longer there.

Holding my breath, I slipped back inside. I stood very, very still for a long time. I couldn't be sure how long. When I felt relatively certain no one was close by, I moved from the parlor to the corridor that led to the kitchen and my quarters. I surveyed the dimly lit hall. Prayed no one would step into it about the time I did. Explaining away the outfit would be impossible.

My pulse pounding in my brain, I ventured into the hall and then rushed into my room and locked the door.

I didn't relax until I'd checked all three rooms, under the bed and in the closet to make sure no one was hidden thereabouts. I peeled off and hid my night camouflage. Then I stared out the window and wondered what had happened to that man.

The garage was dark now, the door closed.

I felt numb…terrified.

And there wasn't anything I could do.

Chapter 10

At 6:00 p.m. on Wednesday I retired to my rooms and shed the outfit that designated me as the hired help. I climbed into the shower and let the water glide over me without putting forth any effort to cleanse my skin.

Three days had passed and nothing. I had no idea what had happened to the man I'd seen in the garage. The doors had been closed ever since that night. Not a single opportunity had arisen for me to try to get inside.

But I knew he was dead. It didn't take a genius to figure that one out. Vargas had killed him.

A shudder quaked through me.

I closed my eyes and tried to block the troubling thought. How could I have ever imagined that I could do this? Temporary insanity, that's all it could have been.

Luther Hammond held his meetings behind closed doors. Not a single opportunity had arisen for me to oversee anything…other than what had happened in the garage, and I hadn't learned anything from that. Detective Barlow hadn't attempted to contact me and I, of course, hadn't reached out to him. My silence spoke loudly and clearly. I had nothing to report.

He was no doubt disappointed but not surprised. My failure would be seen as proof of his original conclusion. Sending me into this operation had been a mistake. He'd probably already gone to Chiefs Kent and Adcock to see if he could pull the plug on my participation.

I opened my eyes and clenched my jaw in determination. No way was I going to let that happen. The need to prove myself surged stronger than ever. If I failed now my family would never let me live my life the way I wanted. Sarah would eventually find out about this little undercover operation and she would, for my own good, tell my brothers. I shuddered at the idea. I could not let that happen.

Taking my time, I washed my hair and smoothed the soap over my skin. I let the hot water relax me. All involved in this operation had known it might take time. Weeks, even. No point in getting worked up just yet. I had to stay calm, stay focused.

After toweling my skin and drying my hair, I slipped on a pair of jeans and a pale yellow blouse. I could use a nice walk. The weather was perfect, not too hot. I'd stayed inside most of the time the past few days, familiarizing myself with the house and the people who lived there. Getting a better look around outside might prove beneficial later.

This time I planned to do it while it was still daylight. I shivered at the idea of how I hadn't been able to help that man. I'd told myself over and over that it might not have been what I thought. Maybe they'd sent him on his way with a message…yeah, right.

Taking a couple more deep breaths to relax myself, I strolled into the deserted parlor and out through the French doors. The terrace and backyard were deserted as well so I meandered across the cobblestone and headed for the very back of the property where the high iron fence hugged the edge of the cliff. The view was magnificent. To my right stood the detached six-car garage. I shuddered. On the left was the two-story guest house that the guards and anyone else who lived on the property called home.

Speaking of guards, I noted the two men roaming the boundary of the property. Both wore suits and ties and neither paid any attention to me.

I still couldn't help thinking that Conrad had somehow seen me in the darkness through my window before I'd ever gone outside. But that was impossible. My room had been completely dark. He couldn't have seen me. I hadn't mentioned the incident and didn't plan to.

The day after my little adventure I'd jumped every time anyone entered whatever room I worked in. I kept remembering what Barlow said about how I would be watched. What if someone had seen me leave my room all dressed in black? What if they knew I'd seen the man in the garage?

Finally I'd had to stop thinking about it. No one nabbed me and dragged me away. No one said a thing about that night.

The wind picked up a little, whipping my hair in front of my face. It would be dark soon. It was almost seven. I imagined that Hammond, his daughter, Cecilia, Vargas and Conrad were preparing to sit down in the massive dining room. The cook, his assistant and I dined in the kitchen around eight o'clock, which was fine by me. Despite how nice Luther Hammond and Mason Conrad had been to me, I didn't appear to have much in common with the others. A smile slid across my face. Tiffany was another story. We got along great. The last two days she'd tricked me into reading to her before her afternoon quiet time. I was aware that she could read quite well herself, but she liked my voice… or so she said.

Cecilia didn't seem to mind. She'd scolded Tiff the first time, but I had assured her that I was okay with it, which appeared to be the au pair's primary concern.

A frown nudged across my forehead. Mr. Vargas was the biggest mystery to me. I got the distinct impression that he didn't like me at all. He avoided me for the most part and had yet to type a message on my PDA. More often than not he merely glowered at me when faced with my presence. I didn't know what I'd done to get on his bad side, but I planned to stay out of his way as much as possible. He, apparently, did most of the dirty work.

I tucked my hands into my pockets and walked along the fence with no particular direction in mind. The guest house was built with the same classic red brick as the house. I wondered if the interior decorating was similar to that of my rooms. Since the guys who lived here were responsible for everyday cleaning up with the exception of laundry, I'd had no excuse to check it out, but I didn't see any harm in venturing inside.

Climbing the three steps, I convinced myself there was no reason to feel uncomfortable about it. No one had told me the guest house was off-limits.

Just inside the front door an entry hall sprawled into a long hallway that stretched to the rear of the house. The front entry of the main house was laid out in a similar manner, only with a lot more pomp and circumstance.

As I'd guessed, the guest house decorating was nice and neat, like my rooms, but not nearly so elegant and luxurious as the main house. A standard, rather unspectacular staircase led to the second level and the private rooms of those housed there.

I wandered to the end of the hall, passing a parlor, kitchen and a small bathroom. I was curious to see if there was a back porch or deck. There was. I pushed open the French-style door and stepped out onto the smooth wooden decking. Cushioned seating made for a perfect place to sit and enjoy the view of the valley below. Very nice. The breeze felt stronger here, or maybe it had just kicked up some more as dusk descended. I inhaled deeply, relishing the clean mountain air. Another perk of living high above the city and all the unpleasant by-products the perpetual growth of a metropolis entailed.

The windows and street lamps below glowed as if the whole city had been draped in Christmas lights. I mentally pinpointed the neighborhood where my parents and three of my older brothers lived in traditional ranch-style homes. A few blocks away was my own little home. Beyond that the downtown location where another of my brothers had purchased a modern city loft. A sigh heaved from my chest. As much as I hated to admit it, I missed them. The other night I could scarcely eat for thinking about how everyone would be gathered at my childhood home for dinner. Everyone but me.

I rolled my eyes and turned away from the gorgeous view. What was wrong with me? Feeling sorry for myself. How silly was that? My mind kept replaying what I'd seen in the garage. I had to get past that. I knew what these men were before I came here. That they seemed so normal by day had nothing to do with the truth.

Goose bumps skittered over my skin as another gust of cool evening wind blew over me. Might as well go back to the house. I stepped back into the hallway and blinked to focus in the darkness. No one had bothered to turn on any lights just yet. Halfway down the hall I stopped when the front door opened. A lamp on a table near the door came on and I immediately recognized

Cecilia and Vargas standing in the entry hall near the front door.

I couldn't say what it was that made me press against the wall and keep quiet, but I did. This far down the hall the shadows concealed my presence. I felt certain it was past seven, and I couldn't understand why these two weren't dining with the boss. But what intrigued me the most was the way the two looked at each other.

I will not give up.

Cecilia made the statement with an odd expression on her face. Fury, maybe. What was she angry about?

Vargas said something back to her, but I couldn't make it out since he stood at an angle to me. Cecilia faced him and I could see her clearly.

She braced her hands on her hips. *I know what I want and I will have it.* She smirked. *Do you think I'm doing all this for nothing?*

Whatever Vargas said to her then really made her mad. Her hand flew up to slap him, but he manacled her wrist before her palm contacted with his jaw.

My pulse tripped in the tense three or four seconds that passed before he jerked her menacingly close. Just when I thought they were going to resort to violence again, he kissed her hard. Shock jarred through me. Were Cecilia and Vargas having an affair?

That didn't seem likely. The two were total opposites from what I'd seen. Cecilia appeared far too proper and, well, snobbish for a plain old workingman like Vargas.

Not to mention she was outgoing and talkative and he was the silent, brooding type.

But when the highbrow au pair snaked her arms around the man's neck and dived headfirst into the kiss, I had to amend my assessment.

Now, this was truly sad. I was supposed to be eavesdropping on mob business and here I was playing Peeping Tom to Cecilia's love life. How sick was that?

Just when I felt certain the two would have sex right there against the door, Vargas scooped her into his arms and carried her up the stairs. My jaw dropped in something akin to jealousy. Okay, I'd definitely crossed the line with that one. Somehow I had to find my balance in my personal life. I couldn't keep pretending it didn't matter.

I sneaked cautiously to the front door and slipped out. Nearly stumbling down the steps, I caught myself then walked determinedly across the yard toward the terrace where I'd exited the main house. The sooner I got back to my own room, the better I'd feel. The sooner I could forget…that everyone else in the world had a sex life but me. Jesus, how had my own sex life, or lack thereof, entered the equation?

Something in my peripheral vision distracted me. I slowed to a stop. A side door at the end of the garage facing the guest house stood ajar.

I glanced at the house, then looked back at the door. Did I dare?

I'd never noticed that door before, then I remembered it on the model Barlow had shown me. It was almost dark. I could either keep standing here arguing with myself or I could go into the garage and check it out.

What would be my excuse for going in?

My tongue darted out and moistened my bottom lip. I could be looking for Conrad. Mason, I amended. He'd told me to call him Mason. I was bored. I thought he might want to watch a movie with me.

Okay, that was totally lame, but it could work.

I sauntered over to the open door, made sure my movements weren't hurried in any way. I glanced around the long garage thankful for the last of the day's light, noted the vehicles parked there. The Mercedes dominated the place where the man had been sitting. I walked all the way around it, coming back to my starting point.

The six-figure automobile occupied the last bay—or the first, depending upon which end you started. I surveyed the other vehicles, pretending to admire them.

Now or never.

I dropped down onto all fours, tucked my PDA into my waistband and peered under the Mercedes.

Relief, disappointment or maybe a little of both washed over me. There was no blood on the concrete floor beneath the car. I don't know what I'd expected. Maybe a big old puddle with murder written in the now-thickened fluid.

When I would have pushed back up, something caught my eye. Something crinkled and white. Small. I squinted, looked again. A few feet from the tire on the front driver's side. I crawled closer to the tire and reached beneath the car. I could almost get it. I strained…stretched my fingers.

Light suddenly blared down from the ceiling.

I froze. My face flattened against the cool concrete.

From my position on the floor I saw two feet move up next to one of the vehicles in bay three or four. The accompanying door had yawned open.

I held my breath…didn't move.

The feet disappeared. Got into the car. Then the car slowly rolled out of the garage. Moments later the door closed and eventually the overhead light went dark again.

During this entire time I didn't even breathe. Every ounce of blood in my body had surrendered to gravity and pooled against the floor, leaving the rest of me numb.

When my heart started to beat once more, I squeezed my body under the edge of the vehicle…got a hold on the object with the very tips of my fingers. I got it! Scrambling up onto my knees I saw that it was a crumpled business card. I didn't recognize the name. I shoved the card into my pocket, dusted myself off and stole out of the garage.

Once inside the house I peered back through the glass door to make sure no one had followed me. The guards were nowhere to be seen. Cecilia and Vargas were likely far too preoccupied to be following me around. Then again there was always the chance one of the other residents of the guest house had seen me.

My chest ached. I slowed my breathing and finger-combed my hair before moving forward. I'm okay, I told myself.

I don't know what I was thinking going into the garage like that. This card could have been in there for months. I doubted my trouble would yield anything significant to this operation. I'd likely only succeeded in almost giving myself a heart attack. I glanced at the towering grandfather clock that made itself at home on this end of the huge corridor, cutting the downstairs part of the house in half. It read 7:45.

With nothing else to do I moved through the house until I'd reached the kitchen. I peeked inside and frowned. Where was the cook? And the organized chaos of his having prepared dinner? The kitchen sparkled like a shiny new dime. No way a meal had been prepared here in the last few hours. I sniffed the air. Yet, somewhere I smelled food…pizza, maybe.

Puzzled, I headed to the dining room. Empty. The banquet-size mahogany table gleamed, the generous bouquet of fresh-cut flowers reflecting on the rich wood.

Where was everyone?

Had I missed something?

I turned back to the hall and bumped into a broad male chest. A moment of pure fear tightened in my throat before I recognized to whom the chest belonged.

Mason Conrad.

He couldn't have seen me fleeing the garage… could he?

"Sorry," I muttered. I tried to back up a step but I stumbled in my haste. I'd been doing a lot of that tonight. He steadied me.

Whoa there.

I blinked, forced my gaze to his and away from his lips.

Somehow, God only knew how, I dredged up a smile. "I'm sorry," I repeated. "I'm not usually so clumsy."

He reached for the PDA that forever hung on its strap around my neck. I'd gotten so used to it resting against my hip as I went about my daily routine that I scarcely noticed it anymore.

Are you looking for someone, Miss Walters?

Working hard to appear calm, I read the note he'd written. I shook my head in answer. "Just wondering if Connie had the night off."

An aha expression claimed his face. He quickly entered another message. *I guess no one told you that Wednesday is pizza night. Connie and Marjorie usually take the night off. Mr. Hammond and Tiffany are in the den. I'm sure you're more than welcome to join them.*

"Oh, that's all right." My nerves screwed into a thousand tight little jerky knots at the idea. I gestured to the kitchen. "I can fend for myself."

He lowered the PDA, his fingers brushing my hip as he released it. A little jolt of awareness went through me at his touch. I ordered it away. The very idea was crazy. But standing here looking into those dark eyes made me feel jittery, I had to admit. Just another indication of how badly my personal life had suffered the past two years. I, evidently, bordered on desperate, in more ways than one.

He wrapped his fingers around my hand and tugged me toward the den. No. No. I didn't want to intrude on Mr. Hammond's father-daughter pizza night. How did I get that through to him?

"Really, I shouldn't intrude," I urged, but Mr. Conrad paid me no mind.

"I could—"

Too late. He opened the door and moved inside, dragging me behind him. A popular kid's program played across the wide-screen television. Mr. Hammond and his daughter were red-faced from laughing at something one of the characters had said or done. This was the only time Tiffany looked really happy, I realized. When she was with her father. She sat very close to him on the sofa, a piece of pizza in her hands, her face bright with happiness. Her father looked much the same way, only his pizza was on a plate. No tie, no business suit, just a dad with his little girl enjoying a favorite program.

The one thing I had learned the past few days in snooping through the mail and pilfering through any papers I came across as I tidied the various rooms was that Luther Hammond supported numerous charities. The man donated a small fortune, especially to the ones that helped needy children.

Why would a man who loved children so much be involved with the selling of drugs or the promotion of prostitution? It just didn't make sense to me.

Of course, please, have her join us.

I jerked my attention back to the here and now just in time to catch Mr. Hammond's remark. Apparently Mr. Conrad had conveyed my lack of knowledge regarding pizza night.

Tiffany tossed her pizza back in the box and ran over to greet me. She grabbed my hand, the one I only just noticed that Mason Conrad still held on to. The little girl tugged me toward the sofa where her father still sat.

She looked up at me and smiled. *You can sit with me, Miss Merri.*

Fear banded around my chest as the little girl stared up at me and waited for a response.

I blinked, considered what I should do. I didn't have to look to know that all eyes were on me.

Tiffany slapped her forehead with her right hand. *Silly me!* She snatched up the PDA and entered her comment for me to see.

I read it and forced a smile. "I'd love to sit with you, Tiff." I glanced at her father. "If you're sure it's all right."

Luther Hammond made a dismissive gesture. His daughter urged me over to the sofa and we sat down together. Then she served me a slice of pizza on a napkin. Before I could stop her she'd rushed out of the room.

Her father watched me. A thousand butterflies had taken flight in my stomach. If I dared take a bite of pizza just now, I felt certain I would hurl it right back up.

"I'm sorry, Mr. Hammond," I said abruptly, unable to hold back the words. "I didn't mean to intrude."

He studied me several moments longer, then held out his hand. Understanding quickly cleared my confusion. I shuffled my pizza to one hand and pulled the PDA from around my neck with the other. I held it out to him.

My heart galloped as he typed the words he wanted to relay to me. From the corner of my eye I saw Mason Conrad pour himself a drink of something. With the liquor bottle in hand he walked around the sofa and freshened his employer's drink as well. Hammond thanked him, then returned his attention to the PDA before passing it back to me.

I moistened my lips and read the message. *No need to apologize. You are a part of my family now.*

"Thank you."

Tiffany returned with a can of cola for me. She retrieved her pizza and scooted onto the sofa. The little girl watched until I'd taken a bite of my pizza before she resumed the devouring of her own.

Before long I got caught up in the moment and found myself laughing at the antics on the television. Conrad had turned on the closed captioning for me. Occasionally I would look up to find him watching me. Each time I shivered in spite of my best intentions not to. I would need to talk to Barlow about this. No, I couldn't do that. He would know for sure just how pitiful my personal life had been these past two years then. Or, at least, he would suspect.

I told myself that Conrad watched me like this because he was suspicious of me. But I hadn't forgotten the things he'd said to me that first night. I couldn't forget now the way he'd touched me, then and a few moments ago. So carefully and delicately, as if he feared I might break. Very strange.

I had to remind myself that these men were evil. I couldn't prove they had killed that man I saw tied to a chair, but I would be stupid to believe otherwise.

When the program ended, Hammond clicked off the television. Tiffany fussed about it, but her father insisted it was time for bed. I was surprised to see that it was past ten already. I hadn't realized two hours had gone by.

I stood in preparation to go and Hammond held up a hand for me to stay. The unspoken request sent a new kind of trepidation skating through me.

Mason Conrad sent an unreadable look in my direction as he escorted Tiffany from the room. I wondered if he knew something I didn't or if that look had been one of concern. I remembered well his warning that I shouldn't allow anyone to take advantage of me. Is that what the next few minutes were going to be about?

I sure hoped not.

Or had Tiffany told her father that she thought I could read lips? Had that awkward moment tonight been all he'd needed to convince him that it was possible?

Or maybe someone had seen me leave the garage.

Mr. Hammond picked up the PDA, gestured for me to join him on the sofa and then entered a lengthy message. It was all I could do to keep my hand from shaking when I took the PDA from him and read what he'd entered.

I'm very pleased with your presence, Miss Walters. My daughter is thrilled. She loves it when you read to her. Are you happy here so far?

As hard as it was, I met his gaze and produced a smile. "I'm very happy here. Tiffany is a pleasure." I stood. "Thank you for sharing your pizza with me."

When I would have turned to go he stood and placed a hand on my arm. The way my heart banged against my rib cage you would have thought he'd grabbed me by the throat. Instead, his touch was light, unassuming.

He took the PDA once more, typed for a few moments, then handed it back to me. The message read: *Please indulge my curiosity. Do you miss the sounds of everyday life?*

Those gray eyes searched mine during the brief hesitation as I wrestled with the best way to answer his question. He suddenly closed his eyes and shook his head. *What a thing to ask,* he said, not really meaning the words for me, but I read them on his lips.

When his gaze met mine once more he looked genuinely sorry for having put the question to me.

"Yes," I said. I pulled in a deep breath and thought about my answer again. "I guess I miss the little things the most." I stared out the massive windows where trees, their tops barely lit by the moon, swayed in the breeze. "The sound of the wind in the trees. The water dripping from a leaky faucet." I shrugged. "That kind of stuff more than anything."

He reached out, squeezed my arm, then walked away. I watched as he left the room, uncertain if I'd said the wrong thing somehow. I remembered Barlow had said that Tiffany's mother, Heather, had died of a drug overdose four years ago. Did Hammond still grieve the loss? Had something I said triggered a memory?

I didn't know. After hanging the PDA strap back over my shoulder, I decided to clean up the pizza-party mess. It was my job after all. Why put it off until morning?

By the time I'd tidied the room and headed for the door with the dirty dishes, Mason Conrad had returned. I jumped when he walked into the room, but quickly managed a smile. He grabbed the now-empty pizza box and the rest of the items I couldn't carry and followed me to the kitchen.

While I loaded the dirty dishes into the dishwasher, he took care of the trash. He didn't offer to start a conversation. I followed his lead. Oddly, I found his presence reassuring. I wasn't certain I'd ever understand how that was possible, but it was.

Before I mentally beat myself up again for enjoying the company of a bad guy, I reminded myself that making friends with these people was part of the mission. This is what I was supposed to do. And, after all, it had been Vargas who'd stayed behind to do…whatever they did to that other man. I shivered.

With the last glass in the rack, I looked up at my helper and said, "I guess that's it. Thanks."

He nodded and I hurried past him. There was no need to drag out the moment.

I went straight to my room and locked the door. I leaned against it and took a moment to enjoy the idea that I'd surely passed another test. I was part of the family now. Accepted unconditionally.

Nothing I'd seen tonight actually amounted to anything as far as the case went, but I felt loads better about where things would go from here.

I was definitely on the right track.

I would give Barlow the business card I'd found in the garage and tell him what I'd seen. If it was nothing, then so be it. But there was always a chance it was something.

Chapter 11

Friday morning I actually worked up the nerve to take a much-needed run around the property. Keeping up with my usual workout hadn't been high on my priority list of things to get done since my arrival, but I couldn't forsake my physical training. I'd gotten up extra early and asked Connie what he thought about the possibility. He didn't see any problem, so I went for it.

A couple of the guards scowled at me, but other than that I didn't encounter any problems. A quick shower and change of clothes later and I started the day's chores. Making beds. At home I always made my bed before going off to work, but here I made nearly half a dozen beds, including Mason Conrad's and the one in which Luther Hammond slept.

This morning I lingered in Hammond's bedroom. This wouldn't be the first time I'd looked around a bit, but my confidence seemed to increase more each day. Especially since he'd made me feel like such a part of the family on pizza night. And since I hadn't gotten caught in the midst of any of my other exploits, I was feeling a little cocky.

I wasn't sure whether today's newly discovered bravado was good or not, but five days without learning even a snippet of useful information served as a strong motivator. I had the business card, but without a dead body or any other clues I doubted it would mean much.

I could not fail at this assignment.

I smoothed my hand over the down-filled comforter and straightened the pillows, my determination growing with each passing second. I glanced at the door. Closed. I was the only one upstairs. Cecilia and Tiffany were out by the pool that filled the space between the garage and the guest house. Vargas, Conrad and Hammond were in the private study in a meeting. A little extra snooping could be chanced.

Chewing my lower lip, I made up my mind. Failure was not an option.

In the process of putting away freshly laundered socks and designer briefs, I'd managed to pilfer through the drawers of the bureau and dresser. As far as the bedroom went, there wasn't anything to find. Except maybe in the closet. I hadn't been in the closet. His suits and shirts were professionally laundered. There was absolutely no reason for me to go into the closet.

I summoned some of that new courage and plunged ahead. I strode straight to the closet and opened the door. A gasp stole my breath.

The closet was larger than my whole bedroom back home. "Incredible," I murmured.

I wandered inside, my eyes wide with awe. Wow. There must be three dozen suits hanging in here. Maybe a hundred shirts. An endless row of casual-wear trousers. Racks of elegant ties and handmade Italian leather shoes. I inhaled deeply, enjoying the pleasant scent of his aftershave, or maybe it was cologne. Expensive, subtly seductive. The underlying aroma of polished leather and starched shirts didn't detract from the glamour or the appeal.

My fingers trailed over the fine silk and imported wool of the designer fabrics. So this was what *real* money felt like. The kind of material that caressed the skin like a lover's touch rather than merely covering it. This guy didn't have a closet, he had his own personal mall.

Something on the floor captured my attention. I frowned, tried to determine what it was. A ticket. I leaned down and picked it up. Children's Hospital Fund Raiser, $25,000. I shook my head. Hammond had purchased a very expensive dinner to support the children's hospital. How could this man, the one who went above and beyond the call to help children, be the monster Barlow had painted him out to be?

I rubbed my thumb over the ticket as if I could somehow uncover the truth…swipe away the words ultimately letting me see the lie. But that didn't happen. This side of Luther Hammond was real, genuine.

A tap on my shoulder sent me whirling around with a start, the PDA bouncing against my hip, to find Mason Conrad staring down at me. The ticket slipped from my fingers and fluttered to the floor.

"I'm sorry…I…" Okay, get a hold of yourself. I dragged in a ragged breath. "I…" Tell the truth, a little voice screamed in my head. "I just wanted to see." I surveyed the contents of the closet in emphasis of my admission before turning back to the man watching me so very closely. "I'm sorry."

Reading him was impossible. He reached for the PDA and didn't look at me again until he'd entered his message.

Mr. Hammond is an intriguing man. Your curiosity is normal.

I nodded as I balled my trembling fingers into fists.

He touched my chin with the tips of his fingers and lifted it so that I had no choice but to meet his gaze once more. He smiled and relief made my knees weak…or maybe it was his touch. I told myself to ignore the acrobatics act going on in my stomach, but it was impossible.

He was right. Luther Hammond did intrigue me…but it was this man that moved me in some way I couldn't explain…couldn't ignore.

Just when I thought I'd survived the encounter, the pad of his thumb slid over my cheek. My breath hitched, sending my pulse into overdrive.

His expression changed so suddenly I almost swayed with the abruptness of it. He withdrew his hand and indicated the door.

Stunned, more by my reaction to him than his actions, I moved past him as quickly as I dared with my legs feeling like limp noodles. Before I reached the bedroom door he was at my side once more. I hesitated. He reached for the PDA.

Almost forgot. Connie needs you in the kitchen. That's why I came looking for you.

I read the words and nodded my understanding. "Thank you."

His gaze lingered on me a moment or two longer and then he left. I moved more slowly, giving him ample time to descend the stairs before me. Rather than take the main staircase, I opted for the rear service stairs that would take me directly to the kitchen. I struggled the entire way to catch my breath and slow my heart rate. Part of me felt reasonably certain that Conrad harbored no additional suspicions about me, but another part of me worried that maybe I was wrong.

But there was no ignoring that he felt something besides friendliness or suspicion toward me. I could no longer deny that the man was attracted to me for some reason. Maybe his sympathy for my impairment was getting the better of his judgment. Whatever the case, I had to be more careful.

Connie had worked himself into a real tizzy by the time I entered the kitchen. He started talking to me a mile a minute and waving his arms frantically. I let my mind conjure from memory the sounds that matched his tirade. I did that a lot.

Though I understood quite clearly what he said, at least the parts he uttered while looking my way, I allowed confusion to show.

Apparently Marjorie, his assistant, had gone home sick and he had no one to serve lunch to Mr. Hammond and his guests in the study. I would be the first to confess that Connie, fantastic cook though he might be, was a large, awkward man. Serving his fabulous dishes on fine china and pouring coffee from a silver pot into delicate little cups could prove quite dangerous for the ones being served.

Connie stopped mid-rant. *Dear God, I forgot. You can't hear a damned thing I'm saying.* After taking a few seconds to calm himself, he reached for the PDA and entered the relevant parts of his rampage onto the screen for me to read. I nodded my agreement.

The big cook scrutinized my appearance. *You'll do as you are.*

I frowned so he'd think I didn't understand. He waved it off and ushered me toward a lovely, albeit laden, silver tray. Four delicate china plates, the necessary silverware and cups with saucers.

Connie quickly entered his instructions on the PDA. *Set the conference table. Then you'll serve.*

I nodded and took the tray to do as he told me.

In the study I found Hammond and three male guests

seated around the fireplace. It was apparent the four had been in deep discussion before I entered the room. A cursory glance was all my appearance garnered. I set the table the way Marjorie set the one in the dining room. Good thing I'd watched her once or twice, since I'd never been that good at keeping up with how it was supposed to be done. Which fork went where…which side for the water glass, et cetera.

When I returned with my newly filled tray, the men had already taken their seats around the table. I hoped I wasn't supposed to have said anything, because I didn't. With water goblets in place, I filled each, then proceeded to do the same with the coffee. The sandwiches, prepared on croissants, came next, and then the scoops of potato salad nestled in crisp green lettuce leaves. Connie's careful planning had made the job relatively simple. I was thankful.

Hammond smiled at me as I left the room the last time. I managed an answering smile. Didn't miss the comment made by one of his guests. *She's a looker. Have you had her yet?* The harsh look Hammond shot in his direction pleased me a great deal. Just something else to shake my confidence in the accuracy of Barlow's assessments of the man. Okay, enough with that. Looks were often deceiving. I knew that better than most.

Thirty minutes later I started the cleanup work. I watched Hammond and his guests as much as possible. From what I had gleaned, the discussion revolved around a new development of some sort in Nashville.

More high-end housing to meet the increasing needs of the more affluent flocking to Music City.

I decided then and there that I had to start keeping up with the news and current events. It amazed me how little I knew about the changes taking place in my own city. Amazed and disheartened me. It was my civic duty to be informed. How could I vote with any competence? I used to be so much better at living my life. When had I become so self-absorbed? So full of self-pity and withdrawn from the real world?

One of the men came over to the table to nab his still half-full coffee cup before I could load it onto my tray. *I'm not finished with this, sugar.* He winked at me.

I managed a tight smile.

He patted my bottom and I gasped. *You're a pretty thing,* he said as he performed a quick visual sweep of my body.

His attention suddenly jerked back to the others seated around the fireplace once. His gaze swung back to me with an expression akin to mortification. I'd missed whatever Hammond said to him, but judging by my employer's lethal stare it hadn't been nice.

I left the room with my tray. By the time I returned, two of the men, including Mr. Roaming Hands, had left. I wondered if the abrupt departure had anything to do with me. Hammond and the other gentleman were at his desk now going over something that looked like blueprints.

I slowed my movements, taking my time so that I

could delay my departure as long as possible. Covertly I watched the two men. I could see Mr. Hammond's face quite well. His side of the conversation appeared to be in response to various questions. *Yes, that's the plan. No, a date has not been set just yet. Things are proceeding as scheduled.*

As I set the last glass on the tray the atmosphere in the room suddenly shifted. I looked down just in time for Hammond to glance in my direction. My heart jerked at the close call. When I'd regained my nerve I shifted my gaze in that direction again.

Everything had changed in those few moments. Hammond's face had hardened to a mask of unpleasantness I had not seen before. The other man's profile looked every bit as flinty. *If he gets in the way, you know what to do,* Hammond stated with what looked like malice.

Another of those sudden jolts kicked behind my sternum. I didn't get the visitor's response, but it was not nice. Even from a side view his scowl was clearly visible.

I don't like doing business this way, Hammond told him. *But I won't let him or anyone else stop me. I've come too far to turn back now. I put him where he is, I can remove him just as easily.*

The governor? The mayor? All the political possibilities ran through my mind. Had his money put some important figure in office? That's certainly how it sounded. But then he could be talking about the CEO position of some corporation or even one of his main contacts. He was talking again so I forced myself to focus on his lips.

You tell Mathers if this deal goes south he's a dead man.

I dropped the cup in my hand.

I scrambled to clean up the mess. I glanced up to find both men staring at me. "I'm sorry, Mr. Hammond," I offered softly. I don't know how I kept my face devoid of emotion, but somehow I did. At least I hoped I did.

He smiled and nodded.

I gathered the last of the dishes and started from the room, but not before I saw Hammond say, *Don't worry, she's deaf.*

Thank God.

I barely managed to get the heavy tray back to the kitchen with my legs going all rubbery and shaky on me. Mason Conrad glanced at me as I shoved the tray onto the counter. I finagled a smile for him. He returned the gesture, then shifted his attention back to the paper in his hand.

I don't know how I did it but somehow I completed my chores for the day. The next few hours dragged by like a mini-eternity. Hammond's words kept playing over and over in my head. *You tell Mathers if this deal goes south he's a dead man.* Mathers, the West Coast connection.

I had to find a way to get to Barlow. To tell him that something was definitely going down, or, at the very least, on the table. I just had to find out what. But Barlow needed to know that a higher state of alert was needed.

At least now I knew the truth…Barlow had been

right about Hammond. He wasn't the kind, generous man he pretended to be. He was ruthless and a killer.

That evening I waited at the specified location, my nerves jangling. The smell of overdone hot dogs wafted from behind the counter of the hole-in-the-wall fast-food spot. At first I'd been bothered by Barlow's choice of a café for the meeting. Then, when I arrived, I realized why he chose it. No one who operated in Hammond's circle would be caught dead in this place.

I didn't even know anyone who would patronize such a sleazebag joint. I stared at the cola on the grimy table in front of me and wondered whether I should risk a sip.

Half a dozen other patrons, most less-than-friendly-looking and definitely the type one would find on skid row, loitered around the small dining area. The tiled floor hadn't seen a mop in so long that it was hard to tell if the color was red or brown.

I swallowed. Told myself I wasn't hungry, though I hadn't eaten since breakfast.

Barlow walked in, and all thought of grime and the various food poisonings one might get from dining here flew out of my mind. He didn't spare me a glance, simply strolled up to the counter and ordered a hot dog and cola.

My throat constricted and I hoped the order was part of his cover. But when he slathered the hot dog with mustard and ketchup and took a bite I knew it wasn't. My stomach twisted at the mere thought.

He sat down at my table, looked at my untouched drink and then at me. *You aren't hungry?*

I peered at the hot dog in his hand and tried my best not to let my distaste show. "I'm fine," I lied.

Barlow jerked his head toward the counter. "Frank here makes the best hot dogs in town."

I looked around the small, ah…quaint café, and nodded. "That's good to know."

Barlow leaned forward as if he didn't want anyone to hear his next comment. *Don't let the appearance fool you.* He shoved the hot dog toward me. *Try it.*

I stared at it, then shook my head. "I don't think so." I would be the first to admit the concoction smelled good, but there was no way I was taking a bite out of it.

Come on, Walters, be a sport.

I licked my lips and told myself he'd thrown down a gauntlet. I couldn't refuse.

Praying I wouldn't regret it, I took a bite. The taste exploded in my mouth. Not the ketchup or mustard but the spicy meat. "Wow," I confessed. "It *is* good."

Barlow smiled, one of those lopsided ones that only he could pull off. *Truth is, everything behind that counter is more spotless than the highest-rated joint in the city.*

Two hot dogs later, I got down to business and told Barlow all I'd learned during Hammond's meeting and about the man in the garage. I'd given him the crumpled business card. He made no comments about the name embossed there. I could only assume it wasn't familiar to him. He'd have to check it out, I supposed.

You didn't recognize any of his guests? He'd asked that one already. He seemed much more concerned about the meeting today than the poor man in the garage the other night.

I mustered my patience. "No."

Anything else to report?

I thought about that one for a moment. I wasn't sure I needed to tell him this part, but then again...

"Mason Conrad," I began. "I think I can get close to him." The memory of him touching my cheek made me shiver. "I think he...likes me."

The reaction I got was far from what I had expected. I blinked, resisted the urge to lean as far from Barlow as possible. His glower was lethal.

I want to be absolutely certain we're clear on this, Barlow said, his face as hard as granite. *Under no circumstances are you to get involved with any of these men. Mason Conrad is a killer. He could be using you. Just because you believe they've all accepted you over the course of the past week doesn't mean it's true. Conrad may be attempting to get under your defenses.*

I shook my head. He didn't know all the details. "You don't understand. He—"

No. A muscle flexed in his tense jaw when he snapped out the word. His entire demeanor loudly telegraphed his fury. *You don't understand, do not get involved with Conrad. Stay clear or I will pull the plug on this operation.*

"I should get back."

I'd stormed out of the café and reached my car before he slowed me down. He took me by the shoulder and turned me around to face him.

I know this is difficult. Your eyes tell you one thing, while your brain warns of another. Hammond and his people put on a great show. But Conrad is a killer. He won't hesitate to kill you if he suspects for a single second that you're up to something. Don't doubt my word. You can bet that guy you saw in the garage the other night is a goner.

I looked away. Didn't want to hear his words. I wanted to argue that Vargas was that man's killer. Maybe I had been naive about the thing with Mason Conrad, but I wasn't completely stupid. I didn't appreciate Barlow treating me as if I were a total idiot.

He took my face in his hands. My breath stalled somewhere in my throat. *Listen to me,* he said when he'd forced my gaze back to his lips. *You want to believe the best in people and that can be a mistake. Trust me on this, Merri. Stay away from Mason Conrad.*

I opened my mouth to argue with him. To tell him I wasn't a complete fool, but something in his eyes stopped me. He was no longer looking at my eyes…his gaze had dropped to my lips. When he at last looked at me again I saw the longing there. Heat detonated inside me, warring with the feelings of frustration his reprimand had elicited.

As if he'd realized his mistake he released me, backed away a step. *Be careful.* With that final warning he walked away. I watched in astonished silence.

It had to be my imagination. I knew my limitations. It wasn't possible that two men would be attracted to me. I was handicapped, for Christ's sake. What did I have to offer anyone? I was the one suffering from the attraction malady, not the men in my life. Apparently I was also suffering from delusions.

Maybe Barlow was right. Conrad was likely trying to determine if I was on the up-and-up. Barlow, well, he probably just felt sorry for me. I had to get a grip here. No man would really want me.

My ego stinging, I got into my car and backed out of the parking lot. I drove, my thoughts preoccupied with Barlow's warning. How could I have been so stupid? Of course Conrad wasn't really attracted to me.

It was a ploy to distract me. To get close to me. The same ploy I'd hoped to utilize. Only I lacked the experience to get one step ahead of my enemy. No matter how I tried to kid myself, it was becoming more and more clear that I was not cut out for this kind of work.

Several blocks later I stopped for a light. I heaved a sigh and told myself I had to get over it. I had managed to bring Barlow some information. Something was going down with Hammond and his people. Some sort of deal. A man connected to Hammond's organization was likely dead. That was something, wasn't it?

In my peripheral vision a couple on the sidewalk snagged my attention.

Sarah and my *brother.*

Oh, my God!

I slid down in the seat, praying they wouldn't look this way. If Michael saw me I would be done for. Between him and his wife they would put two and two together and come up with five…my scam would be uncovered. Although it was already dark, the street and shop lights made me plenty visible to pedestrians on the sidewalks. I should have insisted on meeting Barlow somewhere out of town.

Sarah and Michael stopped and peered through the windows of a small shop. My curiosity getting the better of me, I squinted to see what they were looking at. My eyes went wide with recognition. A baby boutique. Sarah turned to Michael and smiled. He kissed her, then rubbed her tummy.

She was pregnant! A big, goofy grin stretched across my face. I was finally going to be an aunt!

The light changed and I let off the brake. I couldn't resist one last look at my brother and my best friend. They looked so happy. They still stood in front of the shop, arms wrapped around each other.

At least something was going right.

My favorite sister-in-law was pregnant. My parents would be thrilled. A frown elbowed its way onto my face. Wait. Had she known before I left? Why hadn't she told me?

Maybe she'd only just found out.

The urge to call her was very nearly overwhelming. But I couldn't do it. Lying was something I found particularly hard to do. Especially when it came to my family. I couldn't take the risk that she would recognize the lie in my voice if she asked how things were going at my school.

I floated up the mountain, then smiled for the guard at each gate. I parked near the garage, didn't encounter anyone else as I made my way inside and to my room. I'd dropped by a store I seldom shopped at and picked up a blouse before my meeting with Barlow. That way I wouldn't return to the house empty-handed. I tossed my purchase onto the couch in my room and headed to the kitchen. I could use a bottle of water or a glass of iced tea. Anything to dampen my parched throat.

What I really needed, I realized as I opened the bottle of Evian, was a long workout to burn off this adrenaline. Another run at this time of night wouldn't be too smart. Between the meeting with Barlow and the close encounter with Sarah and Michael I was pretty worked up.

I decided on a stroll around the house to see what everyone was up to. I had to keep my eyes open for any additional info or any new faces.

No one in the study or dining room. I glanced at my watch, almost nine. Maybe Hammond had gone out. Cecilia was likely upstairs tucking Tiffany in for the night.

I hesitated at the door of the den and took a second look. Tiffany was huddled on the sofa watching TV Land, her favorite channel. Surprised that she was still up I walked into the room and pinned a smile into place. It wasn't difficult, I loved the kid.

When she looked up, my smile faltered.

Her eyes were red and swollen from crying.

I immediately sat down next to her and took her into my arms. She sobbed even harder then. I rocked her like a baby and murmured kind words. She cried for a long time before she looked up at me and said, *I hate Cecilia.*

I shrugged and tried to look confused, but she ignored my signals.

She's mean to me all the time. I hate her. Tiff's bottom lip poked out. *I think she only keeps this job because she wants my dad to like her.*

I made no comment, just held her tightly and smoothed a hand over her silky hair. How could I have misjudged Cecilia so profoundly? I'd thought she seemed nice. Well, there had been a moment yesterday when I was reading to Tiffany that I'd thought she didn't look too pleased, but nothing really specific.

I closed my eyes and held on to the sobbing child. What if I was in too deep here? Hell, I couldn't even spot the bad guys when I'd had advance knowledge of their identity.

Tiffany pulled out of my arms and stared up at me, her cheeks wet with tears. *I wish you were my au pair.*

I tugged my PDA around to where she could see it. Somehow it had ended up behind me. I offered it to the child. "I'm sorry, I don't understand."

Tiffany just stared at me as if to say, sure you do.

I'm going to bed. She climbed out of my lap and headed toward the door. I wasn't sure what to say. Any words I'd thought might be useful deserted me when my gaze landed on Cecilia standing in the doorway.

When our gazes collided she managed a stiff smile. She turned as Tiffany passed her and followed her charge. Despite her smile I hadn't missed the sheer hatred in her eyes. Apparently my blossoming friendship with Tiffany bothered Cecilia more than I had suspected.

Way more.

Chapter 12

I wasn't quite so chipper the next morning as I went about my duties. I hadn't slept well the night before. I kept thinking of the look on Cecilia's face when she discovered Tiffany and me in the den. I couldn't be sure how much she'd overheard of what the little girl had to say. The best I could hope for was that she would assume I hadn't understood any of the conversation, thereby preventing her from being even more angry than she no doubt would be considering the child's assertions.

The idea of her taking out her fury on Tiffany worried me. Had actually kept me distracted all morning. I looked for the child first thing. Smiled at her while she devoured her cereal in the dining room with her father.

He'd noticed and gifted me with one of those looks that said he appreciated my affection for his daughter.

I just couldn't reconcile the two sides of the man. The man I had come to know over the past week was gentle and generous. He loved children and went to extraordinary means to help those less fortunate—which was most of the civilized world. Yet, I'd seen with my own eyes that he would order the execution of another human being if things didn't go as planned or if he wasn't happy with the outcome of a particular venture.

I smoothed the fresh pillowcase on the fluffy pillow and set it into place. I had to remember, God knows Barlow had told me often enough, that I wasn't here to understand these people. I was here to gather information and pass it along, nothing more.

With a heavy sigh I bent down and picked up the pillowcases and sheets I'd removed from the bed. This was the last room. Mason Conrad's room.

His name popped into my head at the same instant the scent permeating the sheets, an aroma that was uniquely his, filtered past my preoccupation. I felt overly warm instantly, as if he'd walked into the room and touched me the way he had before.

I closed my eyes and forced away the ridiculous thoughts. I just couldn't keep dwelling on the way he looked at me or how kind he was to me. Barlow was right on that score. There was every reason to believe that Conrad might be using me, making sure I was who and what I'd claimed to be.

Funny thing was, after a two-year drought, I was suddenly inundated with male attention, and quite frankly, I felt a little off balance.

Before I'd trudged halfway across the room the door burst open and Tiffany bolted in.

Hi, Miss Merri!

I smiled, couldn't help myself.

"Good morning, Miss Tiffany," I teased.

She grabbed my left hand, causing me to have to shift my load to one arm. *Come on, you gotta visit with me!*

I manufactured a look of confusion. "What?"

Oops! She pressed her hand to her mouth. *Guess I forgot.* Then she gestured for me to follow her.

Feigning uncertainty, I allowed the child to tow me to her room. She picked up the book we'd started yesterday and showed it to me. She pointed to the book and then to herself. *I want you to read some more to me.* She tapped the book again, then her chest.

The sweet little girl looked so hopeful. How could I say no? But I had work to do. The beds were all taken care of and the laundry, save for the bundle in my arms, had been tossed down the chute, but there were a dozen more little things to do downstairs.

"Let me finish up with my work downstairs and I'll read to you when I take my lunch break. That okay?" I infused as much excitement as I possessed just then into the words. Not for a second did I want her to think I didn't want to read to her. But I had to remember why I was here…that had to take precedence.

Tiffany looked past me. I turned around to find Luther Hammond waiting in the open doorway. My face heated with embarrassment. What would he think with me standing in the middle of his daughter's room with a bundle of laundry in my arms? Getting fired was very close to the top of my don't-want-to-happen list, right under don't get caught.

Hammond spoke to his daughter as she loped over to him, the love for her evident on his face as well as in his posture. How could he love his daughter so much and have such little regard for the life of others? I barely resisted the urge to shake my head at the paradox he represented.

When he looked up again he moved in my direction. My heart bumped out a faster rhythm but, incredibly, I kept my composure in place when every instinct screamed at me to make my excuses and get out of there.

Hammond lifted the PDA from beneath my load of laundry and entered a message that read: *Your kindness toward my daughter means a great deal to me. Never concern yourself with your duties if she requests your attention. You have my permission to use your own judgment in how you utilize your time.*

"Yes, sir." I hoped my voice didn't squeak, but my throat felt tight with trepidation.

He laid the PDA back against my hip, then patted my arm once, reassuringly, before leaving the room. I worked hard to control my breathing so that Tiffany wouldn't see how anxious the scene had made me. She yanked at my arm and I looked down at her.

Grinning widely, she said, *You don't need to be afraid of my father. He likes you.* She glanced back at the door. *More than Cecilia, I think.*

As hard as I tried not to react to Tiffany's words, I couldn't resist a glance at the door. Having Cecilia overhear a comment like that was not a good idea.

Tiffany pulled at my arm again. *We have a secret.* She pressed her finger to her lips, then added, *I'll never tell.*

By the grace of God I kept my own smile in place. Lying to myself any longer was out of the question. This child knew my secret. I could only pray that she would keep it.

I skipped lunch to make up for the time I'd spent with Tiffany. Technically I understood that it wasn't necessary, but I didn't want Connie or Marjorie to start looking at me with the same suspicion that I now saw in Cecilia's eyes. When she'd discovered me reading to Tiffany in the middle of the morning her expression had turned blatantly accusing, as if she fully suspected that I was out to get her job.

Trying to influence her otherwise would be pointless, so I didn't. I just went about my chores and ignored her. Probably made bad matters worse, but I didn't care. I had a job to do and it didn't include appeasing her.

I mentally stopped myself for a moment. Okay, that was catty. Was I jealous of Cecilia? Maybe. She was beautiful and had all her senses. Sure I was envious. She was an au pair and I was a mere maid. A smile tickled the corners of my mouth. But I was also an undercover agent and she was just…a bitch with a fancy job title.

A tap on the shoulder brought me around and face-to-face with Marjorie. She was several inches shorter than me and a couple of decades older, fifty maybe. Her hair had gone gray and she, apparently, didn't care. But she had nice brown eyes. I would wager there wasn't a jealous or vain bone in her body. I liked her more every day.

She entered whatever she had to say into the PDA: *Thanks for covering for me yesterday.* She made a yucky face. *Twenty-four-hour bug or something.*

"No problem. I was glad to do it," I assured the kind woman.

She nodded appreciatively, then entered another message: *Do you mind picking up the dry cleaning at the guest house and putting it into my car? The cleaning team failed to do that this morning. I've got my hands full cleaning up after Connie right now, but I'll take it into town when I go home this evening. I'm just afraid I'll forget it if it's not in my car.*

"I'll be glad to."

Marjorie entered directions on where to look and I was off. Any excuse to get out of the house was fine by me. The sun was still high in the sky and the weather was perfect. The cleaning team had come in and started the vacuuming while I read to Tiffany. Two men and one woman, the team worked efficiently. In just a few hours they'd finished their tasks, leaving gleaming surfaces all through the house. If I'd had time to follow along and watch, I'm certain I would have found them quite amazing and picked up invaluable tips.

Locating what looked like a large walk-in closet off the kitchen on the first floor of the guest house wasn't difficult. The main chute brought laundry down from all the upstairs bedrooms. A commercial-size washer and dryer took up space on one wall, while shelves of fresh linens, sheets, blankets, towels and the like lined another. The open plantation shutters on the one window allowed for looking out onto the deck and the magnificent view behind the guest house. The bag marked with one of the city's dry-cleaning business logos sat next to the washing machine.

Just as I reached for the bag, movement on the deck stole my attention.

Vargas had walked to the banister and lit up a cigarette. A plume of blue smoke rose above his head and was then carried away by the ever-present breeze that mountaintop living afforded. This man was a complete enigma. He never spoke to me. Had only said hello that first time we were introduced and nothing since. When in the main house he paid no attention whatsoever to Cecilia, but I hadn't forgotten their secret rendezvous the other night. I wondered about that.

A frown worried my brow as I thought about what Tiffany had said. She believed Cecilia was interested in her father. If that were the case, then why the affair with Vargas? Maybe Tiffany was wrong. Then again, maybe Cecilia was more calculating than I knew. She certainly had no use for me anymore. Not that there was any real love lost, but I didn't need or want her causing me trouble.

I hoisted the laundry bag into my arms and started to head back to the main house when Cecilia joined Vargas on the deck. Okay, I had to see what these two were up to now. Hammond and Conrad were in a meeting. Tiff and the rest of the staff were back at the main house. These two could be up to most anything. Mainly I just wanted to see what they would do next, given the opportunity.

Letting the bundle fall back to the floor, I eased closer to the window and pressed against the wall right next to it so I wouldn't be easily seen if either of them looked in this direction.

Cecilia started off on a rampage. Since her back was to me I had no choice but to watch for Vargas's responses to get some gist of the conversation.

She's just a maid. A deaf one at that. She's no threat to you, doll.

I'd been right. Cecilia was threatened by my relationship with Tiffany. And maybe the child was correct as well in her assumption that her au pair was after her father. I could see that.

Cecilia flung her arms high and went on another tirade. The move jerked her blouse loose from the waistband of her skirt. Vargas noticed.

All you have to do, he said, grabbing her by the arms and pulling her close, *is keep your cool until this is over. Mathers will take care of the rest. Hammond won't even know what hit him.*

I went ice cold. I tried to assess what those last two statements meant, but my mind could wrap around only one possibility. Vargas and Cecilia were plotting with Mathers to overthrow Hammond or maybe kill him. My heart pounded so fast I could hardly breathe, but I had to pay attention…had to see if Vargas said more that would help shed additional light on their plans.

If you lose your cool, you'll blow the whole plan. We have to keep the status quo until the time is right. Any wrong move right now could ruin everything. All eyes are on Hammond. We have to do this right.

Vargas pulled her closer still and she pounded on his chest with her fists. He only laughed, then said, *I know how to take the fight out of you.*

He ripped off her blouse. I gasped. Almost backed away, but some morbid fascination held me in place. He pulled her bra down and sucked violently on the bared breast. Her fingers fisted in the fabric of his jacket and her back arched, giving him better access to the flesh he plundered so ruthlessly.

My trembling fingers went to my lips. I told myself to turn away, but somehow I couldn't. I needed to…see. I rationalized my actions with the idea that I might learn more information. But it was a lie. I simply couldn't look away. The cold hard fear that had filled my veins gave way to a forbidden heat…a lust that burned red hot. Truth was, I missed the feel of a man's hands on my body. I needed to be wanted. A wounded moan welled in my throat.

As I watched, Vargas pushed up the hem of Cecilia's skirt and ripped off her skimpy panties. My hand trapped a gasp as he hefted her legs up around his waist. Her fingers were in his hair and she kissed him frantically…as if she couldn't get enough of how he tasted.

As he braced her against his torso with one hand he used the other to wrench open his trousers and pull himself free. I stumbled back a step at the sight of his hard, upright sex. He brought her down onto him in one brutal plunge. Her entire body reacted, tensing, bucking. Her mouth had opened in a cry of ecstasy that stirred memories of my own cries of need…sounds I'd almost forgotten.

I backed up another step. I couldn't watch any more. Watching them brought to the surface just how badly I ached to know that kind of fulfillment once more. How had I let my personal life fall apart? I grabbed for the bundle and turned to go, but bumped into an immovable wall.

Mason Conrad.

For several seconds I couldn't breathe much less speak. Need still throbbed deep inside me…angst still tightened my throat. Finally I managed to say, "I'm sorry. I…I came for the laundry." I wanted to be afraid… to be embarrassed. Instead every part of me that made me female was either stinging with anticipation or drenched with want.

His gaze dropped to my breasts and I felt certain he could see the rock-hard peaks of my nipples through my clothing. Heat rushed to my cheeks. I didn't have to look behind me to know that beyond the window the sexual activity had likely increased in ferocity.

He reached down and took the heavy bundle from me. The move prompted another harsh intake of breath. He noticed.

The bundle fell to the floor. He moved in closer to me, his eyes searching mine for resistance, I presumed. I could muster none. His hands came up to cup my face and I shuddered with the shivery sensations cascading over me.

I shouldn't do this, he murmured just before his lips descended to meet mine. His kiss was gentle, not at all like the one I'd witnessed beyond the window. He tasted hot and sweet, like cinnamon gum. His lips felt firm and velvety. At first I couldn't move…just stood there enjoying the taste and smell of him. The feel of those firm lips moving on mine. I reached up and placed my hands against his chest, felt the contours beneath the fabric. He felt warm and hard, like I'd detected before. Muscular and male.

He drew back from the kiss and stared into my eyes. The smile that tilted the corners of his mouth made my heart flutter even more than his noninvasive kiss had. How was that possible?

He took one step back from me and reached for the PDA. I watched his big, strong hands as he entered his message as deftly as if those powerful hands had been made for such delicate work rather than what I knew for a certainty he was entirely capable of.

I accepted the PDA and read his message. *I shouldn't have done that. Forgive me for being unable to actually regret it.*

I laughed softly, glanced quickly over my shoulder and was thankful the coupling had concluded. When I met Mason Conrad's eyes again, I said, "I wouldn't want you to regret the sweetest kiss I've ever had."

Sweet. He shrugged. *I can live with that.*

I bit down on my lower lip to stem the laughter that bubbled up in my throat at his typical male reaction. No guy wanted his kiss to be called sweet, but he couldn't know I'd understood.

I read his new message on my PDA: *I'll try to do better next time. That is, if you're interested in a next time.*

I couldn't say for sure what possessed me just then, but I let the PDA drop back to my side and I reached up and grabbed him by the ears. "What's wrong with now?" I pulled him down to me and kissed him with all the crazy, mixed-up feelings churning inside me.

I'd never cared for porn movies or the whole voyeurism thing, but I had to admit that watching two people have savage sex combined with the fact I had deprived myself for more than two years had me wanting more *now.*

I thrust my tongue into his mouth and explored to my heart's content. His hands rested on my hips, but he made no move to push the moment to the next level. I leaned into him, felt my body mold to his. He was so warm and as hard as a rock. He felt big and strong and I wanted him.

With my heart slamming mercilessly in my chest, I'm certain the roar of blood had affected my ability to think clearly. I couldn't let this…

He took the decision out of my hands and pulled back, breaking the intense connection.

I fought to catch my breath. "I'm sorry." I shook my head and struggled to clear it. "It's just been so long since anyone touched me." I looked directly at him then and said exactly what I felt. "Too long. I didn't mean to let this…" I shrugged. "To let it get out of control."

For several seconds he just stood there staring at me. I could see in his eyes that he had enjoyed the kiss, that he wanted me, but I couldn't read what he was thinking. Yet, I sensed the war going on inside him.

That's a real shame, he murmured, with no intention of my knowing his words.

He pulled the strap of the PDA over my head and set the handy device aside on the nearest shelf. I lost my breath when he reached for me again. His movements slow, fluid, he turned me around and untied the apron, allowed it to fall to the floor.

For the first time fear entered the scenario. I knew without doubt where this was headed. Could I really do this? Should I?

My hand went to my mouth and I held back a tiny cry of anticipation when he lowered the zipper of my dress. His fingers trailed over my skin, then he pushed the fabric down my shoulders and I held it there, turned to him with a question in my eyes.

I wish I could make you see that you don't need to be afraid. That you don't need to simply wish for something...

The words touched me so but I couldn't let him sense I'd understood. It was so difficult not to respond.

He tugged the dress from my arms where I'd trapped it over my breasts. It puddled around my ankles. He lowered his face to my breast and suckled me through the fabric of my bra. I couldn't push him away. I just wasn't strong enough. I needed this more than I had realized.

The fabric that separated his hungry mouth from my breast was suddenly gone. He ushered me down to the floor. The idea that I should stop this flitted through my mind, but I couldn't resist. I needed this so desperately.

I arched my back in anticipation as his mouth moved down my belly. My fingers got lost in his hair and I wondered how it could possibly get any better than this. When he dragged my panties down my legs and then kissed his way back up my inner thigh, I knew it was only going to get better.

His attention reached my sex and my bottom came off the floor. I whispered his name. Fought to control the barrage of fiery sensations tugging at me. I felt myself coming already. It had been so very long.

His tongue was inside me, in and out, circling my opening in slow, teasing strokes. His lips moving over the flesh on fire for him. His fingers kneaded my bottom. I couldn't hold it back any longer. I pressed my hand over my mouth and stifled the cry that accompanied my release...my first in more than two years.

When my body fell slack against the floor, he kissed his way up my rib cage, then settled against me as if my climax had cost him as much energy as it had me. He looked into my eyes a moment, then kissed my cheek.

I reached for him but he pushed up to his knees, then stood. Startled and mortified, I scrambled to find my clothes. By the time I'd pulled on my panties and bra he was gone. I slipped back into my dress and tied my apron into place. I'd need a mirror to check my face and hair.

I pressed my hands to my face, humiliation sinking fully. Now I comprehended the term *pity fuck*. Only he hadn't actually taken it all the way, just gave me what I had been needing. How thoughtful of him.

I grabbed my PDA only then, noticing that he'd left the poor deaf maid a message.

Whenever you're ready to do this right, let me know. I definitely want to touch you. Again and again.

I set the PDA aside and ran a trembling hand over my face. Okay, maybe it hadn't been about pity. I wanted him like that, no question there. But was it the right thing to do? Was getting close to him going to help me learn more? Or was my desire to pursue this avenue purely physical, purely selfish? Barlow had warned me to avoid this dicey territory. He would blow a fuse if he found out…

Jesus, I had to find a way to get the information I'd just learned to him. Vargas and Cecilia were up to something and Mathers was involved.

Going back into town this soon might be a risk, but I had to take it. This couldn't wait.

I pressed my hand to my chest. But first, I had to gather my wits…had to compose myself after my own forbidden encounter. Barlow could never know that part.

Chief Ike Adcock was an ugly son of a bitch by anyone's standards, but as far as Steven was concerned, he was a hardhearted bastard to boot.

"I think you're going soft on me," Adcock offered. He leaned back in his leather executive chair and pumped up the whole I've-got-you-right-where-I-want-you look of triumph.

"I'm telling you she's getting personally involved with the players and that increases the risk." Barlow wanted more than anything in this world to climb over that desk and beat the hell out of the arrogant bastard.

Adcock straightened the lapels of his suit, the one that likely cost a month's salary and no mere chief should be able to afford. "You said the whole operation was a risk, now you're complaining when it actually starts to pay off. What's going on here, Barlow?" He eyed Steven skeptically. "You letting this get personal yourself?"

The whole conversation was pointless. Steven threw up his hands. "Fine. You let her get herself killed." He braced his hands on his superior's desk and allowed him to see just how pissed off he was. "I'll make sure everyone knows you let this happen."

Adcock sat up straight, the whole good-old-boy demeanor disappearing in the blink of an eye. "Don't you threaten me, you piece of shit. You wouldn't even have a shield at this point if it wasn't for that idiot Kent. You do whatever you have to do to keep her alive. If she ends up dead it won't be anyone's fault but yours. Now, get the hell out of my office. I don't want to see your face again until you have something we can use to take Hammond down."

Steven walked out of Adcock's office without making a response. What was the use? Adcock wasn't going to change his mind any more than Steven was.

One way or another, the next time he got Merrilee Walters away from Hammond, he had to make sure he kept her away. As badly as he wanted to win this, he didn't want her to end up dead.

Maybe Adcock was right. Maybe he was going soft. There had to be a way to do this without getting an innocent, untrained civilian killed.

Chapter 13

Going out last evening had proved impossible.

The rest of the day frustration had played havoc with my ability to think clearly. When six o'clock finally arrived, Hammond had asked me to watch Tiffany for the evening so that Cecilia could join him for dinner in town.

Talk about infuriating. I'd wanted to tell him not to trust her, that she and Vargas were up to something, but, thankfully, my brain had somehow managed to fend off the stupidity long enough for me to do the right thing.

Too bad it had been a little slow on the uptake. I still couldn't believe that I'd practically had sex with Mason Conrad.

My shuffling of magazines on the table in the parlor

abruptly ceased as the images frolicked through my mind, leaving me helpless to do anything but get warm and tingly all over again.

What had I been thinking?

This assignment *did not* include having almost-sex with one of the players involved. If I'd had any question on that score, Barlow had made it more than clear in our meeting at the hot dog joint.

Why hadn't I listened?

I puffed out a lungful of frustration and plopped the stack of magazines into a reasonably neat pile. I forced myself to move about the room, tidying as I encountered anything out of place.

My mother would say I'd lost my mind. I stilled. My mother could never, ever know about the incident. The family, those who were supposed to love me the most, would skip counseling altogether and go straight for having me committed as quickly as possible.

I glanced at the clock for the hundredth time. It read 5:58. I might as well put my few cleaning utensils away and get ready to go. Since no one had approached me to do otherwise, I planned to go into town. I swallowed back another lump of apprehension. Staying here all day, knowing what I knew, was one of the hardest things I'd ever done.

Connie and Marjorie were eyeball-deep in dinner preparations when I passed through the kitchen. I hurried and put my things away in the laundry room and checked to see that the coast was clear before I went to my room. The fewer people I ran into the less likely I would get waylaid. I had to check in with Barlow, had to pass along this information.

As I quickly changed, I considered how much simpler it would be to just call him and tell him what I knew. But he and the chiefs had feared that calling from anywhere on the property, even using my nifty secure cellular phone he'd provided, wouldn't be safe. Though I'd certainly had my moment of stupidity, I hadn't crossed into complete idiocy just yet.

I tugged on a T-shirt, fastened my jeans and slid my feet into comfortable mules. I didn't bother taking my hair out of the French twist I'd fashioned it into for work. I grabbed my purse, tossed the PDA into it and took a slow, deep breath before sneaking out into the corridor.

The coast was clear when I checked first left then right. Good. I slipped into the hall and headed for the front door. If Connie or Marjorie saw me out of uniform with my purse in tow, they would know I was planning to escape for a while and I would be forced to answer the inevitable questions. Where are you going, Miss Merri? Didn't you just go out the other night? Got yourself a boyfriend in town?

I hated lying unless it was absolutely essential to my continued good health under present circumstances.

The entry hall was deserted as well. Thank goodness. I'd almost made it to the door when I felt a firm hand land on my shoulder.

To my supreme relief I didn't jump out of my skin. I'd almost grown accustomed to having one or more of a dozen people walking up behind me when I least expected it.

My relief was short-lived when I turned and found myself toe to toe with Cecilia. From the expression on her face she was ready to launch an interrogation of her own into my activities.

It wasn't like I hadn't been expecting this. I'd just hoped to delay it for a little while longer.

I manufactured a smile. "I thought I'd go into town. Do you need anything while I'm out?"

For a second that turned to ten she stared at me without making a response, then as if she'd only just remembered, she held out her hand.

Keeping my cheery mask of innocence in place, I reached into my bag, retrieved the PDA and placed it in her palm.

Her movements as she entered the message were stilted as if she barely contained her anger. I braced myself for whatever she had to say. It wouldn't be good. Her overpowering perfume offended my nostrils as it usually did. Not the cheap stuff sold at budget retail outlets. It was the hundred-dollar-an-ounce designer stuff and still I didn't like it. Or maybe it was just her that I didn't like. Somehow she intended to hurt Luther Hammond. Though he was no innocent by any stretch of the imagination, I despised disloyalty and this woman was as disloyal as they came. She was indifferent to Tiffany, a child, and she played the part of attentive and smitten employee in Hammond's presence, all the while having an agenda of her own. She made me sick.

The idea that I was doing something similar sat like a stone in my stomach. That *was* different, wasn't it?

With a glare of victory she passed the PDA to me. When I'd taken it, she crossed her arms over her chest and waited for my reaction.

I know what you're doing. It won't work. Cut your losses or you'll lose more than you bargained for.

For a single instant the remote possibility that she knew what I was really up to sent a twinge of panic through me, then I realized the real import of the message.

I looked her dead in the eye and said my piece, "I don't know what you're talking about. But—" I said pointedly when she would have reached for the PDA once more "—if you're talking about Tiffany, I would suggest that you watch your own step."

The look on her face at that moment could only be called murderous. She snatched the PDA out of my hand and entered another message before shoving it back at me. *I'm talking about Luther, you stupid little bitch. Stay away from him or you'll regret it.*

With that potent message glaring at me from the small screen she stormed off toward the parlor. I dropped the PDA back into my purse and walked out the door.

As I climbed into my car I thought of all the things I should have said to her like, I know what you're up to as well. I saw you and Vargas together. But I couldn't. That would only give her more reason to want me out of the way. I had to be careful around her. I stared up at the house as I circled the drive. She had been here long before me. Her opinion likely carried far more weight. I didn't need her going to the boss about me.

Not to mention that the boss's daughter already knew my deepest, darkest secret. If she said anything, perhaps thinking she was defending me somehow, I would be in deep trouble. The kind Barlow had warned would get me killed. I shuddered and shifted my attention back to my escape.

Once I'd made it through the gate, leaving the cozy community of Ledges behind, I fished out my cell phone and entered his number. The screen identified his voice after the first ring.

"We have to talk" was all I had to say.

He provided the destination and assured me he would be waiting for me there. Now, if I could just get through the meeting without telling him more than he needed to know.

Our rendezvous was the safe house. The former church where we'd worked together what felt like months ago but was, in reality, just over one week ago. He made a pot of coffee and we sat at the table in the small kitchen as I related the events of the previous evening and my most recent encounter with Cecilia.

Barlow didn't speak for a long time after I'd finished. He got up, poured himself another cup of coffee and stared out the window over the sink for a time. It would be dark soon. I felt restless. A part of me wanted to get back on that mountain. Maybe it was nothing, but it felt like something big loomed on the horizon. Some instinct nagged at me that things were about to take a turn for the worst.

Finally he turned back to me and started talking without preamble or comment on what I'd told him.

I've known for several months now that Hammond's West Coast associates weren't happy with him.

Well, that was news to me. We certainly hadn't gone over that in the brief training session.

I felt certain there would be a move to usurp his power. I went to Adcock with my concerns and he told me to forget Hammond and get on with my life. I ignored him and monitored the situation for further developments. Barlow sipped his coffee for a bit. I couldn't tell whether he just needed the caffeine or dreaded saying the rest.

Nothing happened, he went on. *Then this opportunity presented itself and you know the rest.*

He was leaving something out. I could feel it. I pushed up from the table and walked straight over to him. "What is it you're not telling me?"

For a full minute I felt certain he wasn't going to answer and then he did. *Adcock didn't want me digging around in this. But when I went over his head, he had no choice but to go along. He pretended the whole setup was his idea from the get-go. He's been taking credit for it ever since.*

Now, there was something I hadn't expected. "Why wouldn't he want to bring down Hammond?" It didn't make sense. My gut feeling when I met Adcock was that he wanted this as much as Kent did. The fact was, Barlow was the only one who'd bucked the operation. I kept that to myself.

Barlow shook his head. *I can't answer that for certain. I believe it has more to do with me than with Hammond. If he'd had his way, I would have lost my shield four years ago.*

I'd read enough of Barlow's case files to know he was one of the best detectives in Metro. The idea that Adcock would want to be rid of him was ludicrous. "What happened four years ago?"

No sooner than the words were out of my mouth I remembered one particular incident that had happened four years ago. The mother of Hammond's daughter had died from an overdose of drugs.

The enigmatic detective's lips tightened into a thin line, and he turned his back on me to stare out the window once more.

I'd obviously hit a nerve. I got up from the table and walked over to stand next to him. He placed his cup in the sink and braced his hands on the counter.

"I need to hear the rest," I urged, in hopes of drawing him back into the conversation. I had a bad feeling about what he would tell me, but I recognized that I had to know what he was leaving out. My life might depend upon it.

He turned to me with nothing short of reluctance. *It's my fault she's dead.*

A frown tugged at my lips. "Who?" I knew the answer but I needed him to spell it out.

Heather Masters. He looked away a moment. When his gaze collided with mine once more I could hardly bear to look at the pain there. *She was my one mistake,* he confessed.

I watched his lips as he told me about his plan four years ago. Even back then Metro recognized what Hammond was up to. The difference was Barlow had decided to do something about it way before the bureau had gotten involved. He'd made it his mission in life to get acquainted with Hammond's most precious plaything. A woman who'd borne him a child four years prior. Though he hadn't married her, Hammond kept her close for the child's sake. Barlow knew that he had other women as well. I found that odd, since I hadn't seen him with any women, other than Cecilia.

She trusted me, Barlow said. *We became friends first, then lovers. Hammond ignored her needs, wanted her to focus solely on the child. Treated her like a high-paid baby-sitter.*

I could imagine what that must have felt like. I didn't know the woman he spoke of, but I understood how awful the situation must have been for her.

The plan was for me to use her. Barlow closed his

eyes and shook his head. *I did get some useful information,* he admitted when he opened his eyes and continued once more. *But I got too close, took too many chances and she ended up dead.*

He'd fallen in love with her. Oh, my God. He didn't have to say it…I could see the hurt he'd suffered even now. "I'm sorry." I put my hand on his arm and he flinched as if my touch had pained him somehow. "You think Hammond killed her?"

His gaze landed on mine again and this time it was filled with fury and hostility. *I know he did. He called me, told me where I could find the body. Warned me to stay out of his business. And there wasn't a damned thing I could do about it because I didn't have any evidence.*

His words were like a sucker punch, knocked the wind out of me. How could the man I had come to know have done such a heinous thing? Then I remembered the way he'd looked when he gave his guest those orders the day I served in his private study. Yes, he was capable of murder. Definitely. He'd killed Tiffany's mother as well as her godfather. My God…he was pure evil.

"That's why you didn't want me for this assignment," I said, the epiphany striking with the impact of a load of bricks falling right on top of me. No wonder he'd fought this operation so fiercely. He'd already been down this road.

He took me by the shoulders, shook me gently. *Don't go back, Merri. I believe the coming hailstorm between Hammond and Mathers will take him down. I'm even*

*more convinced after what you've just told me. That man
you saw in the garage, he was one of Mathers's men.
His body probably won't ever be found. Let them kill
each other. I don't care anymore.*

His words left me speechless. Was this his way of trying to protect me? Was he willing to dash this opportunity to keep me safe?

All the reasons I'd had for coming into this suddenly
sprang to mind. This wasn't just about getting Hammond. This was about me. I had to do this. Had to prove
I could. But no one else understood that primal need.

I moved my head solemnly from side to side. "I can't
do that. I have to finish this."

He pushed away from me. Stormed around the room,
muttering what appeared to be curses. I couldn't be sure
since he wouldn't look directly at me. Outrage or frustration, maybe both, lined his face. Finally, hands on
hips, he stalked back over to where I still waited. His
nostrils flared with the anger twisting inside him. I knew
I should be scared, just a little, or maybe nervous, but I
wasn't. Of all the people involved in this case, I knew
without a doubt that Barlow would not harm me.

You're making the biggest mistake of your life, he
said, the difficulty of maintaining his composure apparent with every word he uttered.

I looked him square in the eye and said what had to
be said. "We all make mistakes, Detective. This has to
be done. *I* have to do it."

He reached for me again but hesitated, then dropped

his hands back to his side. *Merri, I need you to think about why you're doing this.*

That he kept calling me Merri and pressed me so urgently with that piercing gaze confused me. Was this some kind of trick to sway my decision? Nothing he could say or do would change my mind. He needed to understand that.

"You're not going to change my mind. I will see this through."

To prove you can do it even without your hearing?

Fury scorched the softer emotions churning inside me. "Don't pretend to know how I feel, *Detective.*" I refused to use his name. It suddenly felt too intimate.

But I do know how you feel, he argued. *You want to prove you can be whatever you choose to be and that's great.* He managed a halfhearted smile. *That's one of the things I admire most about you. But this is a mistake. This is too dangerous.*

I blinked, startled by his words or my own reaction to them. I wanted to rant at him for his preposterous presumptuousness, but another part of me wanted to bask in the idea that he admired anything about me.

Don't go back. This can be handled a different way.

Any lingering softer feelings his words had garnered vanished on the heels of his last statement. In other words, *I* couldn't handle it.

I retreated a step, putting some distance between us. "I have to get back."

Just listen to me, he appealed. *Bowing out of this operation won't mean you failed—*

"I don't want to talk about this anymore," I interrupted. "Just back off."

He scrubbed a hand over his face. I didn't give him a chance to regroup. I gathered my purse and draped it over my shoulder and prepared to go. He was my support system. Our meetings weren't supposed to go down like this.

When I reached the front door of the sanctuary-turned-gym, he stopped me with a hand on my arm. Reluctantly I faced him.

If I can't change your mind, at least promise me you'll be extra careful. Anything can happen at this point.

There was something about the absolute sincerity in his eyes that made me realize that he meant those words, all else aside. I didn't know for sure what was going down between him and Adcock or even between him and Hammond; clearly all three men had a shared history that had left scars. But the one thing I could be unconditionally certain about was the fact that he didn't want anything bad to happen to me.

For the second time since I'd met him, I so wished I could hear his voice. I tiptoed and placed a kiss on his cheek. He was the one looking startled now. "Thanks, Detective, I'll be extra careful."

He didn't let me go. He held me still with those eyes as he moved in even closer, the subtle remnants of the aftershave he'd used more than twelve hours ago making me quiver inside. I liked the way he smelled. I blocked the images of Mason Conrad that tried to intrude. That had been different, purely physical. He made me feel alive…made me think of sex. But this man, he made me feel something different…something far more intense and intimate.

For a long time Barlow simply looked into my eyes, then he reached up and touched my lips. I drew in a shaky breath at the feel of his fingers on my mouth. After each touch he kissed me softly in that same spot. My lips, my cheek, my nose, each closed lid. Then he drew back. My eyes opened and I saw the desire in his. The heat that slid through me was like the man, mysterious and intense. He kissed me more thoroughly on the mouth, but stopped short of letting the moment go too far. This time when he pulled away, he smiled, something he rarely did.

Be very, very careful. We have unfinished business.

I left Detective Steven Barlow with one certainty in my mind: he and I would definitely continue that kiss at a later date.

I smiled and slid behind the wheel of my Jetta. At last, something to look forward to on a personal level.

By the time I got back to the house, Connie and Marjorie had already cleaned up the kitchen. I scrounged up leftovers and sat at the island while I ate. I was still floating a little from all that Barlow had said and…his kiss. It was really strange. I shivered. I couldn't deny having enjoyed the sexual encounter with Mason, but the kiss Barlow—okay, Steven—and I had shared had been so much more real and powerful.

I sighed. Maybe there was something wrong with me besides the fact that I couldn't hear.

Mason Conrad suddenly appeared on the opposite side of the island. He smiled at me and I blushed at the memories of what he'd done to me on the floor of the guest house's laundry room. The idea that his memories were no doubt just as vivid made looking him in the eyes particularly difficult. My heart started to beat too fast and I told myself to calm down, but it was no use.

"Hi," I murmured self-consciously.

He nodded, the smile widening. He pulled an envelope from the interior pocket of his jacket and laid it on the counter. He pushed it toward me, then walked around the island to where I sat.

My breath evaporated in my lungs and I told myself to stay calm. The thing that had happened between us in the guest house couldn't happen again.

He leaned down and kissed me on the cheek, as if doing so were as everyday an affair as taking a breath, then he left the room without further ado.

When I'd pulled myself together I opened the envelope he'd left behind. I unfolded the single sheet of paper it contained and read the handwritten note. *Merri, come to my room tonight if you feel comfortable moving so fast.*

My fingers trembling, I quickly stuffed the letter

back into the envelope. I looked around the big kitchen just to make sure no one had seen me or the note.

"Oh, God." What in the world did I do now?

Okay, he'd said if I felt comfortable. That gave me an out. I had to keep that in mind. I stuffed the envelope into the pocket of my jeans and quickly cleaned up my dishes. The best thing I could do at this point was go to my room and lock the door. Mr. Hammond was nowhere to be seen, nor was Cecilia or Vargas. It wasn't like I was going to learn anything tonight.

I'd almost gotten to my room, almost made it to safe territory, when I ran smack into Luther Hammond in the corridor between the kitchen and my destination.

He smiled, gestured to my room and waited while I went inside. I pulled the PDA from my purse and offered it to him since he apparently had something to say. My heart thundered so hard I feared he would hear it. I refused to consider that he wanted anything less than hard work from me. Having two men display a certain desire for me was more than adequate, considering I hadn't gotten a second look in two years.

When I read the message my employer had entered I was flabbergasted. *It seems my dear friend Conrad is quite taken with you. Shall I tell him to back off or is the feeling mutual?*

What the hell did I say to that?

"It's fine, Mr. Hammond," I said, choosing what I hoped would be the safest course of action for my cover. "The feeling is…mutual." The words rang hollowly inside me, but what else could I do? My boss, a mobster, was standing in my room. I was alone. He wanted to know if his right-hand man was acceptable to me. If I intended to stay in this operation, I had to keep the players happy. I thought about Mason's note. At least, I had to keep them happy to a degree. "I just need to go slow."

Mr. Hammond nodded, then entered another message. *Excellent. Good night.*

When he'd left I took a deep, calming breath and counted to twenty before racing to the door and locking it. I leaned against it and pulled the note from my pocket. What in the world had I gotten myself into?

I didn't sleep that night. How could I? I worried that when I didn't go to Conrad's room he would come to mine. I tossed and turned. It wasn't like I would hear him breaking down the door if he chose to, though I doubted that scenario. Even so, I'd lain there watching the door, expecting the knob to turn any minute, until exhaustion had gotten the better of me.

Not taking any chances on running into him, I'd steered clear of the study this morning. He had evidently been tied up in meetings there. I performed all my chores throughout the whole house before finally going to that last room. It was lunchtime and I'd already seen that Hammond and the usual group, including Conrad, were gathered around the dining table. Now was my best shot at getting my work done in the study without bumping into the man who'd given me my first orgasm in more than two years. I almost laughed at that. He was good…would be good at what came next. I was single. What woman in her right mind wouldn't want him?

He's a killer, a little voice reminded.

Enough said.

I straightened the books on the shelves, then moved to Mr. Hammond's desk. I did the same thing every day. I surveyed every visible paper or note as I dusted. The desk always took me longer than the entire rest of the room combined. Today would be no exception.

As I lifted one set of documents, a note beneath the stack snagged my attention. "Mathers, 8:00 p.m., Tuesday night."

Was Mathers coming here? Jeez, Barlow was right. This was all about to come to a head. My heart knocked hard against my chest. Tomorrow was Tuesday.

I set the papers back down exactly where they had been and moved on to the next object on his desk, the calendar. I flipped to Tuesday and studied it while I pretended to tidy the desktop.

If I had been able to hear or if I had been paying proper attention to the changes in the atmosphere around me, I would have known when the door opened and someone walked across the room. But I was deaf and distracted so I didn't recognize Hammond's presence until he stood right beside me.

I gasped, jerked back from the desk as guiltily as if he'd caught me with my hand in his personal safe.

But his smile and the it's-okay gesture kept me from

going into an all-out cardiac episode. He pointed to the phone. I saw the light blinking there.

I nodded and moved out of his way. This was my chance to eavesdrop on a call. I couldn't leave the room. Summoning my bravado, I moved over to the conference table and started to polish the gleaming mahogany I'd already polished once. Since he made no move to usher me out, I continued.

I told you not to call me like this.

I started to tremble with excitement. This could be important. I couldn't take my eyes off him even if it meant risking that he might catch me watching him.

I'm going to take care of him tomorrow night. He's a dead man. Do you understand me?

His face had darkened with fury. I was damned glad that kind of anger wasn't focused at me. I forced myself to look away long enough to spray more polish so he would hear the hiss and feel comfortable that I paid him no heed.

Push me and you'll suffer the same fate as your friend Mathers. This conversation is over.

He slammed the receiver back into its cradle. I shifted my gaze back to the conference table. When I looked up again, nearly a half a minute later, he was gone from the room.

It took another two or three minutes for me to gather up my courage. When I had, I moved back to the desk and pretended to tidy it some more. As I did I checked the calendar again, noting the location of tomorrow night's eight o'clock meeting with Mathers.

All I had to do now was get back into town so I could inform Barlow.

After last night, I wasn't sure that was feasible. Would anyone be suspicious of my frequent trips down the mountain? Whether it drew unwanted attention or not, I had to try to get to Barlow.

The door to the study suddenly swung open once more. Cecilia, all fake smiles and looking as regal as ever, strode into the room.

She stuck out her hand for the PDA, which I, without hesitation, passed to her. I ignored her as she typed a lengthy message. I didn't even spare her a glance until she passed it back to me.

Today is reading day at the library. Tiffany would like to go. Mr. Hammond requested that you take her. Would you please change into more appropriate attire and prepare to do so?

There was no question that I loved Tiffany and was more than happy to take her anywhere. The part that got me was why in the world was Cecilia smiling? She couldn't possibly be happy about this.

"Sure," I told her. "I'd love to."

She gave me a cool nod and left the room, clearly assuming I would do as I was told.

By the time I had changed into slacks and a blouse, Tiffany waited for me by the front door. The excitement on her face almost allayed my misgivings about Cecilia's behavior.

I offered her my hand and she accepted it. I opened

the front door and started out. I couldn't say for sure what made me look back, maybe the prickling sensation on the back of my neck. For whatever reason, I did look back. Cecilia stood farther down the hall, in the shadows, staring after us. The smile she flashed me as our eyes met was pure evil. I didn't return the gesture. I closed the door behind me and hurried to my car. Someone had pulled it around to the front steps in anticipation of our departure.

Tiffany climbed into the back seat and I fastened her seat belt before going around to the driver's side and sliding behind the wheel. She had several books in her arms, probably ones that needed returning.

I waved to the guard at the gate of the Hammond property and did the same when I reached the final gate that allowed us to leave Ledges behind.

The eerie smile on Cecilia's lips kept haunting me. I just couldn't figure out what she was up to. I fished around for my cell phone. I didn't see any reason why I couldn't call Barlow and have him meet us at the library.

I frowned. My phone wasn't where I usually kept it in my purse. I dug frantically. Nothing. An alarm wailed in my brain. This was not good. Alternating my attention between the road and my purse I hunted some more. It simply wasn't there. I took a curve a little too fast and even Tiffany's head came up. I smiled at her in the rear-view mirror and focused my full attention on the road. I could call him from the library. It wouldn't matter. No one would have that phone bugged.

I took a deep, steadying breath and tapped the brakes to slow down a bit, but the pedal went all the way to the floor. Outright fear surged into my chest. I pumped the brake, but still there was no response.

I glanced at the rearview mirror to see that Tiff was okay and tried to appear calm when she looked up at me.

Oh, God, I prayed, please don't let this be what I think it is. I pressed down on the brake again…nothing.

No way could I take the next curve at this speed. Goose bumps spilled across my skin.

I had to try.

Chapter 14

For long minutes after the car crashed to a stop I wondered if I was dead. I couldn't feel my heart beating…or the blood roaring through my ears. I felt numb…I stared at the huge white pillow deflating in front of me. What happened?

My lungs abruptly seized and air filled them once more. With the oxygen came excruciating pain. A cry squeezed out of my throat. I balled my fingers into fists and gasped for more air…fought the pain.

The air bag, I realized, had knocked the breath out of me. I stared down at myself. No blood. I moved my head side to side. Wiggled my arms and legs. Okay, I was okay.

Tiffany!

Fear screamed through my veins, blasting against my impotent eardrums. Agony welled inside me as I jerked at my seat belt and cried out her name.

Please, God, don't let her be hurt.

I struggled against the damned belt. Tried to get loose. The rearview mirror was missing…only then did I realize that a limb had protruded through the windshield. Fragments of safety glass lay scattered around me…on the dashboard…on the seat.

Small hands suddenly tugged at my arm. I looked up into frightened gray eyes.

Miss Merri! Miss Merri, are you okay?

I hugged Tiffany hard against me and prayed I wasn't dreaming. Please let this be real.

She wriggled free of my fierce hold and wiped the tears from my face with her tiny hands. *Are you hurt?*

I had to laugh. Here I was shaking like a leaf, bawling my eyes out, and an eight-year-old child escapes her seat belt and climbs over the seat to see about me.

I hugged her again and kissed her once more. "I'm okay." This time I managed to get the seat belt loose.

Tiffany shook her head somberly. *The car's not okay.*

She was right about that.

After checking out the situation a little more closely, we scrambled out of the vehicle. I lifted Tiffany into my arms and visually inspected her for injury. We were both shaken and would likely sport various bruises tomorrow, but otherwise neither of us appeared to be injured. I stared back up at the highway where we'd gone off the road. It was a miracle we'd survived.

I'd managed to make that first dangerous curve, primarily because I hadn't met another vehicle coming toward me, which allowed me to swing into the other lane. Beyond that curve a section of guardrail protected a stretch of highway from a particularly precarious drop. With another prayer that what I'd seen in movies could work, I'd cut my wheels far enough so that I ended up sideswiping that guardrail. To my surprise the move worked, as it had definitely slowed down the forward momentum of the car a bit. The problem was when the guardrail ran out I couldn't swerve back to the left quickly enough and I ended up going all the way over the shoulder and down.

Way…way down.

I studied the path, noting the saplings I'd killed. I didn't know how in the world I'd managed to avoid the larger trees until we'd finally come to rest against these pines. I turned back to where my Jetta sat parked in the thicket, an evergreen scent angrily filling the air. Fortunately, between the guardrail, the saplings and the underbrush, the speed of my car had been slowed enough to prevent a lethal crash.

Thank God.

I felt faint all over again and my knees went weak.

Gathering my wits and my fortitude, I found a relatively clear spot and settled Tiffany down onto the ground. "Stay right here," I told her. "I'm going to try to find my phone." It had to be in the car. Had probably been in my purse all along, but I just hadn't been able to locate it while driving.

After an exhaustive search I realized I was wrong. The phone was not there. I remembered clearly unplugging it from its charger and putting it into my purse this morning. My purse had remained in my locked room until I'd grabbed it to make this trip.

I could no longer deny the only reasonable explanation. Someone had gone into my room and stolen it.

I stepped back and stared at my damaged car. The memory of the brake pedal going all the way to the floor without slowing the vehicle seared into my brain all over again.

"Oh, God."

Surely my brakes hadn't been tampered with. Failures did occur spontaneously from time to time. It wasn't completely impossible that it had happened now and my phone had gone missing at the same time. Terror snaked around my chest and tightened. The look on Cecilia's face when Tiff and I walked out of the house this morning loomed large in my mind. Her threat flashed next. *Cut your losses or you'll lose more than you bargained for.*

A tug on my arm brought my attention to the child, who had moved up beside me. *I'm scared. I want to go home.*

I lifted her back into my arms and hugged her reassuringly. "I know. It's okay. We'll get home."

If we climbed back up to the road, we could hitch a

ride with the next car that came along. There weren't any houses for several more miles.

Tiffany drew back, her face scrunched with worry. *I have to go to the bathroom, really bad.*

I nodded. There were tissues in my bag. All we needed was a private spot. I grabbed my purse, surveyed the thick woods around us and felt reasonably certain that wouldn't be a problem.

We made our way through the underbrush until we found a spot that looked safe enough for baring her bottom. I settled Tiff and my suddenly too-heavy bag onto the ground. While she took care of business, I kept watch in the direction of my crashed car.

I rubbed at my forehead, only then noting the ache there. I wondered if I'd hit my head somehow in the crash. I didn't remember doing so. Maybe it was just the jolt or some odd way my neck got twisted during impact causing the discomfort just now.

Branches moving in the distance snagged my attention, sent renewed fear rushing through my still-wobbly limbs. I grabbed Tiff, who had just pulled her underpants back into place and held her tight against me. "Shh," I urged against her ear. I could feel her little heart pounding just as mine was.

I held my breath, waited for a bear or other wild animal to emerge from nature's screen.

Vargas.

I almost stumbled back a step. Caught myself just in time.

My first instinct was to call out to him, but some deeper, more primitive feeling kept my lips firmly sealed. I kept my hand over Tiff's eyes so she wouldn't see, whispered softly for her to be very, very quiet. If she saw him she would want to call out to him, probably would before I could stop her. I couldn't let that happen until I determined his intent. He and Cecilia were in this together—whatever *this* was. If Cecilia didn't want me around, it made sense Vargas wouldn't, either. My heart skipped a beat. He was likely the one she'd talked into tampering with my brakes—assuming that's what had just happened.

I had to be sure.

Vargas made his way to the car and stuck his head in through the open driver's side door.

I watched and waited to see what he would do. My instincts continued to war inside me. What was I doing hiding like this? He was Cecilia's lover, that was true, but the bottom line was that he worked for Hammond. I held Hammond's daughter in my arms. There was no reason to believe Vargas wouldn't take us back to the house. Was there?

Still, I couldn't get past the idea that he represented some kind of threat. The images of him and Cecilia having savage sex flitted one after the other through my mind. This man was working against Hammond behind his back. I felt certain of it after having seen the things he said to Cecilia in the throes of passion.

There it was. That's why I couldn't trust him…

couldn't call out to him. The final look Cecilia had given me slammed into my brain next, along with the memory of my foot pressing hard on the brake pedal.

They had caused this. I knew it…felt it in every cell in my body. Not only would Cecilia be rid of me, but Hammond would be devastated…leaving him vulnerable.

Vargas pulled his cell phone from his pocket. I froze, focused on his lips. Maybe he would call for help. I didn't mind being wrong…especially not right now.

They're not here.

The fingers of his free hand fisted and slammed down on top of the car.

I jerked at the ferocity behind the blow, held Tiffany tighter to my chest when she did the same.

The car crashed, he said, his face a harsh mask of anger. *But they got out.* He listened for a moment. *How the hell do I know? I'm telling you they're not in the car.* His mouth twisted brutally with fury in the seconds that followed. *Don't worry, I'll find them. I'll take care of it personally this time.*

We had to get out of there.

Adrenaline pumped through my veins, prodding me to move. To hurry.

I crouched down and turned Tiff's face to mine while still holding her as tightly as I dared. I pressed my finger to my lips to indicate that she should be quiet, then I whispered, "We're in danger. We have to try to get to help."

I heard someone talking…was it—?

I touched my fingers to her lips to shush her. "Do you

trust me to take good care of you?" I asked softly. I didn't worry that she now had proof-positive that I could indeed read lips. Saving our lives was far more important just now than worrying about her knowing my lip-reading secret.

She nodded, her eyes wide with uncertainty.

"Then you have to do as I say. Be very, very quiet no matter what."

She nodded again.

I wrapped her arms and legs around me. "Hold on tight." She obeyed. I glanced back toward the car one last time and saw that Vargas was searching the area around it, likely looking for blood or some indication of a trail. It wouldn't take him long to find the latter. I had to hurry, but more important, I had to be very, very quiet.

Should be easy enough for a deaf woman, right? Yeah, right.

I pressed my lips to Tiff's ear and murmured, "If you hear me making noise, tug on my hair." The child nodded her understanding.

All I had to do was get away from Vargas and find a phone. Detective Barlow would take care of the rest.

I started forward, choosing the path that appeared to offer the least resistance. The underbrush rubbed against my clothes. I moved as quickly as I dared, praying Tiff would warn me if I made too much noise.

Deciding a straight path was not a good idea, I moved in a zigzag pattern.

I tried to recall my days as a Girl Scout, but I couldn't remember anything relevant to my current situation. I did recall vividly selling boxes and boxes of cookies. How hilarious was that?

The farther I moved into the woods, away from the scene of the crash, the more confident I felt about my ability to do this. I moved faster and faster. I was a little winded from carrying Tiff, but I'd be okay.

What if he was close behind me and I didn't know it?

I stopped dead in my tracks and turned around. The breath rammed in and out of my lungs as I visually searched the woods behind me.

Tiffany drew back, a frown marring her pretty face. *What's wrong?*

I moistened my lips and steeled my nerves. I had to keep going, couldn't let fear slow me down.

"I have another job for you, Tiff."

She stared at me expectantly.

"If you hear me making noise pull my hair like I said. Keep your eyes open, and if you see someone or something moving in the bushes behind us or running toward us, you yank extra hard, okay?"

Her eyes rounded with terror. *Is something after us?*

I summoned a smile for her benefit. "I don't think so, but I just want to be sure." I tapped my ear. "You know I can't hear a thing, so I need your help."

She nodded.

I pulled her close once more and started moving again, as fast as I dared. I lost all sense of time and direction, just kept going until my arms and legs felt rubbery with exhaustion.

Tiff yanked on my hair.

I ducked behind the closest tree. "What?" I whispered between ragged gasps for air.

She looked uncertain how to tell me what she had to say. *I hear something.* She lifted her slim shoulders in a shrug. *It sounds like a fountain…or water.*

For the second time recently I wished like hell I could hear again. Admittedly, hearing the sound of danger was a lot more important than hearing Barlow's voice. I remembered wishing I could hear how he sounded.

She pointed to my right. *That way, I think.*

I don't know why I considered it a good idea, but for some reason I wanted to find the water she thought she heard. Tiff had to give me a couple more directions but we finally found it. Nothing more than a wide, shallow stream. The water was crystal clear and upon seeing it my mind immediately conjured from memory the sound of flowing water.

Tiff turned my face to hers. *What do we do now?*

Maybe it was something I'd learned as a Girl Scout or maybe it was just another scene in a movie I'd once watched or a book I'd read, but some instinct made me want to follow the stream.

I stepped into the cool water and started walking in the direction of the flow. Without the underbrush to slow me down I could walk much faster. The water wasn't deep enough to work against me. All I had to do was keep going. Tiff would let me know if I started to splash too much.

The sun had dropped below the treetops when I realized I couldn't walk another step. I waded out of the water and dropped on the ground.

Tiff raised her head from my shoulder and looked at me with a question in her eyes.

"Sorry, sweetie, I have to rest. You listen and watch, okay?"

She nodded, then laid her head back on my shoulder. I didn't know how much watching she'd done for the last hour or so, but I felt fairly comfortable at this point. If Vargas had been going to find us I believe he would have by now. More likely he'd gone back for help.

Another reality suddenly hit me. Tiffany and I couldn't be allowed to survive. If we did, then Vargas and Cecilia's attempt on our lives would be revealed. I sat up straight and looked around. No way would he give up until he found us. And he couldn't go back for help. He couldn't, not without signing his own death warrant.

I stumbled back to my feet and started moving again. No way could I slow down considering what I now understood. We weren't meant to survive the accident. One way or the other, I couldn't be permitted to see Hammond again...to tell him what I knew.

And all this time I'd worried that working undercover for the police would get me killed. Who would have thought that getting too close to a kid would present the most danger?

* * *

It was almost dark and Tiffany was getting more frightened by the moment before we found our way to any sort of civilization.

The road was a small, curving one that likely connected at some point to the road coming down the mountain that led from the prestigious Ledges. We'd reached the valley, and judging by the power lines overhead there would be houses somewhere on this road. All I had to do was find one with a telephone.

Tiffany was restless in my arms. I reassured her over and over, but even I had grown anxious about my ability to get us through this.

After another half hour or so I saw rectangular blocks of light in the distance. Windows. A house. My pace picked up, despite the exhaustion clawing at me.

As I neared I could see an old model Ford truck in the driveway. It was too dark to make out the color. The house was more like a cabin, wooden siding, small and all alone on the road for as far as I could see. But lots of light poured from the unobscured windows.

I hesitated a moment before climbing the porch steps to consider what I would say. Tiff shivered in my arms. I hugged her closer, hoping to warm her with my own body heat. The night was unseasonably cool.

Finally, I gathered my courage and knocked on the door. I had to knock again before the porch light came on, making me blink. The door swung inward and an older man, maybe seventy-five or eighty, peered out at me.

If you're selling something I'm not interested.

Like I'd be selling anything at this time of night. I pushed a smile into place. "I'm sorry to bother you, sir." I shifted Tiffany to a different position to call his attention to her. "My car broke down. Do you mind if I use your phone?" God, please let him have a phone. "My little girl's tired and scared, and to be honest, so am I."

He looked from me to the child and back. *Come on in.*

Following him inside, I felt fragile with the overwhelming relief. I'd give most anything right now for a drink of water. Tiffany was likely thirsty as well. I didn't know how far we'd walked.

Phone's over there. The man gestured to a table near the sofa, then he swung a suspicious stare back at me. *It's not long distance, is it?*

I didn't think it was, but I couldn't be sure until I tried it. Hell, I didn't even know where we were.

"I'll be happy to pay you if it is."

He glanced at my arms, probably noting I didn't have a purse since I'd left it on the ground where Tiff had taken her comfort break, but he nodded his okay.

I lowered Tiffany to the floor but kept her hand firmly tucked into mine. She tugged on it when I would have headed for the phone. I looked down at her.

I'm thirsty.

I glanced at the man who waited nearby, dividing his attention between us and the television. Considering the program I'd interrupted, I estimated the time at around eight-thirty.

"Is it all right if she has some water?"

He nodded and trudged out of the room. To get the water, I presumed. I looked around and found a clock that confirmed my estimation of the time. Hammond would know something was wrong by now.

I sat down on the sofa and picked up the receiver. Another reality broadsided me. I bit back a curse. I couldn't use this phone.

The old man returned with the water, a glass for Tiff and one for me. I thanked him and covertly took a sip from each glass. Tasted fine. Not that I imagined this old man would have any reason to want to drug either of us, but frankly I was past the point of trusting anyone. I drank until it was gone. When he'd taken the glasses back to the kitchen, I pulled Tiffany into my lap.

"I need you to make this call for me." I touched my ear. "I can't hear, you know, and this phone doesn't have a screen for me to read from."

Okay. She picked up the receiver and held it to her ear. *You dial the number.*

"When the man answers," I told her before entering the final digit of the number, "ask if it's Detective Barlow. That's who I want to talk to."

Tiff nodded.

I entered the final number and waited, my pulse racing. I couldn't help wondering if Vargas was still out there trying to pick up our trail.

Tiffany's eyes told me she'd heard a voice on the other end. *Detective Barlow?* she asked. Her face clouded with confusion and her gaze shot up to mine, but the single word she uttered was what stole my complete attention. *Daddy?*

My heart jolted. I knew I'd dialed the number correctly. It should have been Steven Barlow on the other end of the line.

Yes, Miss Merri is here with me.

I wanted to grab the phone from her and demand to know how he'd gotten Barlow's cell phone...but it would do no good. I couldn't hear his response.

Tiffany's eyes widened with fear. *Yes, Daddy, I'll tell her.* She turned the phone to her shoulder and looked up at me. She swallowed hard, her small throat working anxiously. *Daddy said you're to bring me to the warehouse on Eighth Avenue right now or your friend Detective Barlow will have to pay your bill.*

A new kind of terror exploded inside me. He had Barlow. I couldn't imagine how...maybe he'd found his private number in my cell phone's log. Oh, God. Wait, my mind rationalized. Steven Barlow was too smart to fall for any of Hammond's tricks. And then I knew how he'd gotten trapped...they'd used me as bait, just as they were using him now.

But how could I be certain?

How could I confirm that they even had Barlow with them?

"Tiff, tell your father that I need confirmation."

She frowned. *What's confirmation?* She rubbed at her eyes. She was exhausted and confused. *If you owe my dad money I'll help you pay it back. I have a bunch of money in my piggy bank.*

My heart squeezed at her sweet offer. From the corner of my eye I saw the old man watching me. Unlike Tiffany he would know something was amiss, but I couldn't worry about that right now.

"Thank you, sweetie," I said gently. "Now, tell your daddy I need confirmation."

Tiffany did as I instructed. In a few moments another odd look crossed her face. She peered up at me. *I don't know this voice. It's a man.*

"Ask him if he's Detective Barlow."

Tiff asked the question. *He says yes.*

But it could be anyone. Tiff wouldn't know the difference. "Ask him what's the last thing he said to me." My heart had climbed into my throat. If they had him... he was as good as dead.

He said that... She asked him to say it again, then she looked at me. *The two of you have unfinished business.*

I went ice cold.

It was him.

Tiffany seemed to be listening again. Confusion had cluttered her face once more when she turned back to me. *He says he has faith in you and that he knows you won't let him down. You know what to do.*

Tears blurred my ability to see, and for the first time since this had begun I wanted to give up. To lie down and cry and admit that I couldn't do it.

I'd failed.

It's my daddy again, Tiff told me.

I braced myself for whatever he had to say next.

He said you have two hours. What does that mean, Miss Merri?

I patted her and managed a shaky smile. "It's just adult stuff. You tell your daddy I'll be there but that he should remember I have what he wants."

Looking uncertain she did as I asked.

A tremulous smile pulled at her lips. *Love you, too. Bye, Daddy.*

Tiff handed the phone back to me. *He told me not to tell you this part, but he said he knows where we are and that he'll send a car for us. My daddy'll help us.*

Oh, God. He'd traced the call. Barlow had told me that Hammond's people stayed on the cutting edge of technology.

I managed a smile to allay her worries. Telling her now that her father had no intention of saving me would be unconscionable. I patted the sofa. "Sit right here for me a minute, okay?"

She scooted onto the sofa and I moved across the room to where the old man waited, his expression stern and growing more suspicious by the second.

"Sir, I need your help."

Sounds like you need the police, he countered.

"We don't have time," I said with as much urgency as I could infuse into my voice and still keep it low enough so Tiff wouldn't hear. "There are very bad men on their way here right now. I'm sorry I've brought this trouble to your door, but they traced the call." I lowered my voice some more. "They want to hurt us. I need to borrow your truck."

His gaze narrowed. *I don't let anyone else drive my truck.*

"Then would you drive us to a safe place?"

He looked past me at the child sitting quietly on his sofa. *What kinda trouble you two in?*

"Please, sir, I don't have time to explain."

For three beats I felt certain he would refuse, but he surprised me. "All right. You take the girl on out there and get in the truck. I'll get my shotgun."

I didn't argue. We could use all the help we could get.

With Tiff's hand in mine we hurried out to the truck. I loaded her into the middle and dug beneath the cracked vinyl bench seat for the safety belt. Thank God it was a recent-enough model to have a middle seat belt. When I had her buckled in, I climbed in and se-cured my own belt.

Our cranky old savior opened the driver's side door and climbed in, as promised, his shotgun in hand. I pulled Tiff against me and patted her shoulder reassur-ingly.

Before he closed the door, and thankfully while the interior light was still on so I could see, he asked, *Where we going?*

I thought of my family, but I needed objectivity right now and I wouldn't get that from my overprotective

brothers or parents. There was only one person I could
trust completely and who I could count on for complete
objectivity.

Chapter 15

Helen Golden stared at me as if I'd lost my ever-loving mind.

You're kidding, right? She glanced across the room where Tiffany slept on her sofa. *She is Luther Hammond's child? You're supposed to be taking training... not cavorting with criminals!*

I shushed her. "Don't wake her up." Then I ushered my good friend into her cluttered kitchen. She worked and studied far too hard to bother with cleaning. Helen would be the first to admit it. If I lived through this I would owe her big time. Maybe I'd give her a month's free house cleaning. And I hated housework. "I don't have time to convince you, Helen. I need your help.

Now—" I sucked in a steadying breath "—are you going to help me or not?"

Helen studied my face for precious seconds—time I didn't have to waste—before committing. *You know I'd do anything for you, Merri. But this.* She shook her head. *This is like the whole Sawyer-Carlyle thing. This is dangerous.*

With a resolute nod I confirmed her conclusion. "Very dangerous. But Detective Barlow is a dead man if I'm not at that warehouse in less than one hour. Will you help me or not?"

All right. She clasped her face with trembling hands for a moment before she relented completely. *Tell me again what you need me to say.*

"You call Chief Kent or Adcock, whichever one you can reach. I'll go to the warehouse," I began.

In my car, she interjected.

I gave her a confirming nod. "While I distract Hammond and his henchmen, Chiefs Kent and Adcock can get backup into place."

Helen shook her head, her expression somber. *This isn't a good plan, Merri. You can't go in there alone.*

I looked at the digital clock on her microwave. "I have to go." There was no point in arguing the issue further. I wasn't going to change her mind. As long as she did what I asked, that's all that mattered. "Give me fifteen minutes head start, then make that call. Don't let Tiffany out of your sight."

Though my friend and co-worker didn't protest fur-

ther, I knew she didn't really want to let me do this. I
went back into the living room and left a kiss on the
sleeping child's forehead. I couldn't risk waking her. I
wasn't sure I could leave her if she cried.

And I had to go.

Steven Barlow's life depended upon me.

At the door Helen put her hand on my arm. When I
met her gaze once more I saw the fear there. *Please be
careful, Merri.*

"I'll do my best." I started to go, to leave it at that,
but I couldn't. "Listen, Helen, do me a favor. If this turns
out badly, be sure to let my family know how much I
love them and that I've always known deep down how
proud they are of me."

I left before she could respond. I hurried out to her
car, working hard to see past the tears blurring my vision. There was no turning back now.

The next move was mine.

The downtown section of Nashville's Eighth Avenue
was mostly fashionable offices and antique malls. But
at this time of night it was pretty much Deadsville. Most
of the nightlife was played out a few blocks away on
Second Avenue, where Tootsie's and the Wildhorse
Saloon, among numerous others, kept Music City rock-
ing until the wee hours of the morning on most any
given night.

I parked Helen's car in a public garage just off Second Avenue and walked the rest of the way. If I didn't

make it through this I didn't want Hammond to be able to track down Tiffany by locating the owner of the vehicle I'd arrived in. Jed Moffet, the man who'd driven Tiff and I into town, had offered to give me his shotgun, but I'd never fired a weapon in my life and I doubted it would prove useful for me.

After he'd dropped us at a convenience store, I'd called Helen to come and pick us up. If any of Hammond's friends tracked down Jed, I didn't want him to be able to give away our location. He would only know where he'd left us. I'd suggested he not go back home tonight, but the old man seemed pretty set in his ways so I couldn't be sure what he would do. I was scrambling here to make contingencies to cover all the bases. I'd learned that the hard way while tracking Sawyer.

Now, as I stood on the sidewalk opposite the building, which actually wasn't a warehouse per se—it was a posh antiques store of about ten thousand square feet called the Warehouse. Evidently Hammond owned it.

I sent one final prayer heavenward and did the only thing left I could do. I crossed the street and walked straight up to the front door. It was locked.

Startled and frustrated, I turned to go around back but someone grabbed my arm before I took my first step.

I whirled around and came face-to-face with Mason Conrad.

He glanced at my waist, probably looking for the PDA.

"I can read your lips," I told him. No need to keep up the pretense.

He looked at my lips a moment, then into my eyes. The cold, unfeeling stare I'd expected, to my surprise, was filled with disappointment.

Where is Tiffany?

I tried to pull free of his hold, but his grip only tightened. "She's safe."

His jaw tightened, and the cold, emotionless mask I'd initially expected fell into place. *You know he's going to kill you, don't you?*

A new wave of fear washed over me, but I stood firm. I knew what I had to do. I couldn't back down now. "Yes."

His expression as unyielding as granite, he unlocked the door and hauled me inside, then quickly locked the glass entry doors behind us. Beyond the front of the ritzy shop, the interior looked dark and deserted, but Hammond would be here somewhere. Conrad escorted me deeper into the consuming gloom, away from the plate-glass windows that allowed some amount of light from street lamps to filter inside. I scarcely noticed the venues of ancient collectibles on either side of the path he cut.

I blinked and squinted in an attempt to force my eyes to adjust to the lack of light as we moved deeper into the building, but I still couldn't see well enough to have any clue what lay more than two or three feet before me. He paused, fidgeted with something…I felt his arms moving, then he slid a large warehouse-type door open.

He dragged me beyond it and then ushered the massive door back into place.

Turning me to the left, he propelled me forward, toward a pool of light where Hammond waited.

My heart jolted as I recognized Barlow lashed to a chair. His face was bloody and bruised, one eye looked badly swollen. He managed a smile in spite of his split lip, and I had to fight back the tears crowding into my eyes. They were going to kill him.

Conrad grabbed my chin and forced my gaze toward Luther Hammond's furious face.

Where is my daughter? he demanded. The ability to hear was not necessary. The harshness of his demand was etched into every line and angle of his face.

I steeled myself and refused to allow him to see just how frightened I was. "She's safe."

Vargas stood behind Hammond, but I didn't see any sign of Cecilia. There were other guards about, loitering in the shadows beyond the pool of light where we faced off.

The slightest twitch of Hammond's hand and one of the guards stepped in front of the chair where Barlow had been secured. The first blow that landed against the detective's already-damaged jaw had my knees giving way beneath me. Conrad made sure I stayed on my feet.

"Stop!" I cried. I felt the hot burn of tears streaming down my cheeks, felt the churn of terror twisting in my throat. "Please," I begged. I couldn't let them do this. I had to do something…however futile it would be in the end.

Another of those insignificant twitches from Hammond and the guard backed off.

Tell me two things, Hammond said, *and I will make both your deaths as quick and painless as possible.*

I stood there for one infinitesimal moment and tried to reason what he'd said with what I knew about him. This was a man who went to extraordinary means to help children. One who gave generously of his great wealth. A man who loved his daughter unconditionally. One who'd been kind to me. How could he be this evil?

Where is my daughter? he repeated. *And what did you learn while in my employ?*

Hammond's head jerked toward Barlow. I looked just in time to catch his final words...*didn't learn anything.* He was trying to protect me, but I knew, as well as he did, that it wouldn't do any good.

At precisely that moment I realized what a mistake I'd made believing I could do this. It took a special breed of human being to do undercover cop work, a person who wasn't missing anything so vital as one of the five senses. My out-of-control curiosity and determination was about to cost Steven Barlow his life. Oddly, I didn't exactly feel defeated. I felt, for the first time in two years, like I finally knew who I was. I could stand up and be counted with or without the ability to hear. I might never get a chance to tell my family they were right, but I could do my very best to save Barlow from the danger I'd put him in with my overenthusiastic need to prove myself.

"He's lying to protect me," I said.

Hammond's gaze swung back to me. He smiled. *Really? In that case, tell me what you learned?*

"Let him go and I'll tell you everything, even the parts he doesn't know just yet."

Hammond laughed. *Don't be naive, Merri. Your detective friend isn't going to walk out of here alive any more than you are. You should know that. Metro needs to learn that I don't appreciate their futile attempts to get to me. You'd think they would have learned their lesson by now.*

I wondered if his reference was to the others who'd died trying to get info on him, maybe even Tiff's mother for becoming involved with a cop. Or his own daughter's godfather for getting too close to the very child he'd vowed to love and protect. I glanced at Barlow. The way he looked at me, as if the idea that I was about to be hurt was nearly more than he could bear. To his way of thinking I would be the second woman who'd died by Hammond's hand for being involved with him. So not true. My destiny had, I suddenly realized, always been my own choice.

Conrad snatched my chin and jerked my face forward.

Make this easy on yourself, Hammond suggested. *Answer my questions and we'll dispense with this unpleasantness here and now.*

"Don't you know," I challenged, "that letting him live will be far more damaging than killing him?"

Hammond laughed, his features falling into the kind smile I'd witnessed so many times. *My, my, Miss Merri, but you truly are a hero, aren't you?* His expression abruptly morphed into one of hate-filled savagery. *Now answer my questions!*

As if the Good Lord had suddenly sent me a message of salvation, I knew exactly what to say. "I learned that your West Coast contact, Mathers, is coming for a little visit."

Hammond's gaze narrowed.

"And you plan to kill him, take him out of the scenario. Tomorrow night at eight o'clock. I even know the location. So does Metro. So you'll have to reschedule unless you want to be caught."

His penetrating stare was nothing short of lethal. *Anything else?*

"Just one thing," I confessed. I turned to Mason Conrad and said this part in his ear so no one else could hear. "Vargas and Cecilia are working with Mathers. Your boss is supposed to die tonight in Mathers's stead. I swear this is the truth."

I drew away from him just in time to catch Hammond's demand to know what I'd said.

My gaze cut to Conrad to see if he responded. He did.

She said her only regret was that she hadn't taken me up on my offer. Conrad shrugged. *She must be nuts, too.*

Why was he lying?

Vargas came up beside his boss. *She doesn't know anything. Let's just get this over with. We'll find your daughter. She can't have left her that far away. If she's got family or friends, we'll find the kid with them.*

Fear for my family joined the mix of emotions churning inside me.

"Actually, I do know more," I cut in, hoping I sounded

hateful and not terrified. My words jerked Hammond's as well as Vargas's attention back to me. I felt Conrad's fingers tighten on my elbow but I ignored him, couldn't figure out why he didn't want me to spill this part. I smiled at Vargas, whose face clearly gave away his discomfort. Somehow he suspected I was about to tell on him. "Why don't you come clean with the boss yourself, Mr. Vargas? Save him from hearing it from me. You can blame the whole thing on Cecilia. I'm certain she can be rather persuasive. It wasn't your fault you got caught up in her web of deceit."

Confusion claimed Hammond's face. "What the hell is she talking about?"

Everything happened at once then.

Vargas swung his weapon in my direction. Hammond ranted at him.

Barlow's chair toppled over at the same instant that a brief burst of fire flickered from the business end of Vargas's gun.

Mason Conrad shoved me to the floor.

Some remote part of my brain wondered why help hadn't arrived. I tried to assimilate what had just happened but the bloom of crimson on the white shirt Mason Conrad wore stole my full attention.

I struggled onto my hands and knees and hurried to see how badly he was hurt. I was vaguely aware of the scuffle going on beyond me. Felt more than saw the fierce movements. Barlow was shouting at me. In my peripheral vision I saw his mouth moving, his eyes wide with fear or worry, but I couldn't deal with that right now.

Mason Conrad had been shot…had taken a bullet intended for me.

Mason stared up at me. He blinked once, swore.

Instinct kicked in. I tore open his shirt and attempted to stanch the flow of blood. The wound was low on the abdomen. Lots of blood.

Damn.

I needed to call for help.

Suddenly I was on the floor again. My face pressed against the oiled hardwood.

I felt the weight of Mason Conrad's body on mine.

"You're bleeding," I cried.

He didn't move or respond, just kept me pinned to the floor.

I was suddenly aware of booted feet moving around me. I strained to see Barlow. His chair still lay on its side. His gaze was focused intently on me. He kept repeating the same thing over and over, but the meaning wouldn't penetrate the haze fogging my brain. *Stay down! Don't move!*

Everything fell into place just then.

The booted feet belonged to what appeared to be SWAT. Vargas lay on the floor a few feet away, his eyes unblinking, blood flowing from a wound at his throat.

Backup had arrived.

I was suddenly free of the weight pressing down on me.

Chief Adcock helped me to my feet. *Are you okay, Merri?*

He looked me up and down, noting the blood. *Are you hit?*

I grappled for calm. "I'm not hurt…I…" My gaze dropped back down to Conrad. "He needs help." The blood…so much blood. The lower portion of his shirt was completely soaked. I crouched down next to him. Had to stop the bleeding. He tried to speak to me but his mouth wouldn't form the words properly or maybe I was too confused to follow. Fear ripped through me.

Strong hands dragged me away from him. I tried to jerk free. I had to help! "Let me go!"

Chief Adcock jerked me around to face him. *Merri, you take care of Barlow. I'll help Conrad,* he urged. *Please, I have the training…I know what to do.* He ushered me toward Barlow, his eyes reassuring. *There's no time to waste. Paramedics are on the way but I have to get this bleeding under control.*

He was right. He knew what to do. I was too hysterical to do anything right. I hurried over to where one of the guys decked out in combat gear was helping Barlow to his feet.

"Are you all right?" I shuddered, felt stupid for even asking the question. We were both alive…breathing was definitely all right. I surveyed his damaged face, then the rest of him. I didn't see any new signs of blood. Thank God.

Barlow nodded. *You?*

I forced my head up and down in an affirmative response. My entire body felt fragile, somehow…like I needed to lie down. Or throw up…maybe both.

As Adcock had promised, paramedics were suddenly swarming.

Luther Hammond didn't respond to attempts to revive him. I wanted to look away but couldn't. My brain just couldn't seem to pass along the proper commands to my limbs.

Hammond was injured badly…maybe dying.

He'd been hit center chest.

Tiffany…she would be alone now.

Somehow I managed to look away. Found myself staring back at where Mason Conrad lay, waging his own battle to survive. He had to make it. Adcock abruptly started waving his arms…demanding one of the paramedics to stop this guy from crashing.

Crashing?

I moved toward the evolving scene. Peered down at Conrad. His eyes were open. He didn't blink. Didn't move. So much blood. He looked dead, too.

An ache welled in my throat.

"Help him!"

The words roared out of me as I dropped to my knees. He couldn't die, too. He'd saved my life. Someone had to help him. It wasn't supposed to end this way.

I stared at his bloodstained shirt as the paramedic ripped it from his chest. Saw the leaking holes…one at his abdomen…one higher up.

My gaze moved back to Conrad's…he didn't look at me…still didn't move.

I closed my eyes and pushed the images away.
This was wrong.
Not the way it was supposed to end.

Chapter 16

I sat in the special waiting room assigned to the family and friends of patients undergoing emergency surgery. But Mason Conrad had no family or friends— well, at least no friends who had survived the shoot-out at the Warehouse.

Luther Hammond was dead. So was Vargas and all but one or two of Hammond's personal army. Mason Conrad was in surgery, his exact condition unknown at this point.

Barlow and I had been debriefed and now waited, alone, to learn the fate of Luther Hammond's closest remaining ally.

I couldn't meet Barlow's gaze. Partly because I was

sick to death with worry that Mason wouldn't live, but mainly because I knew he'd figured out that the man, a criminal, who'd put his own life on the line to save mine, had strong feelings for me. Feelings I'd helped to cultivate by succumbing to his kiss…to the feel of his hands on my body. Feelings I couldn't deny on my end.

I closed my eyes and forced the images away. I'd told myself that I was only doing what I had to in order to win his trust…to get more deeply into Luther Hammond's world. But that wasn't entirely true. I'd wanted Mason to touch me that way…had wanted him, but fear had kept me from rushing heart first into that forbidden territory. I'd skated the very fringes. Maybe it was that intense moment with Barlow, those chaste kisses, that had made me pull it back together in the nick of time. I opened my eyes and stared at my clasped hands. Speaking of the man waiting in this room with me, I felt something for him as well.

How was that possible? For two years I hadn't felt even the vaguest desire for anyone, and suddenly I'm hard-pressed to keep my needs under control. Admittedly, my feelings for each man had been unique. Like the men themselves. What I'd felt for Mason Conrad had been more about the excitement, the danger of getting close to him—the extreme heat. The idea that he'd wanted me had held its own kind of allure. No man had wanted me, or so it seemed, for two long years.

I stole a glance at Barlow. He stood by the single window in the room now, staring out at the starlit sky, his back turned to me. He did a lot of that when we were together. We hadn't talked about any of this, but the tension in the room was as thick as chilled Jell-O and every bit as cold.

I inhaled sharply, hating the too-familiar medicinal smell. I'd been in the hospital more times than I cared to remember. Had walked out of this very one without the ability to hear after days spent with a raging infection and accompanying fever that had almost gotten the better of me. My life had been pretty much upside down ever since. I'd been searching all this time for some way to fit in again. To play a significant role.

Oddly, that memory surfaced without its usual companion, bitterness. Strange that I should finally, after coming so close to death, after putting others in that same predicament, realize that I still counted in this life.

My entire family had shown up in the lobby. I'd gone down to see them about an hour ago. My parents had been so relieved they'd cried. It wasn't until that precise moment that I realized fully what I'd put them through.

Chief Kent had called Sarah once he was certain I was okay. Minutes later the whole clan had descended upon the hospital. My brothers were furious with me but not one of the big, macho guys could stay ticked off once we'd embraced. I would eventually get around to telling them they'd been right, just not right now. Michael had actually had tears in his eyes when he'd told me that Sarah was pregnant. Imagine, my big, tough brother crying.

After the intensely emotional reunion, I'd come back to this room to wait. Barlow hadn't asked how my meeting with my family had gone and I hadn't mentioned it. It was difficult to tell if he was angry at me or simply disappointed that I'd allowed myself to get involved with Conrad, with the enemy. It wasn't like I could have hidden it. The idea that he might be disappointed bothered me more than the possibility that he was angry.

Images and sensations from the one time that Barlow had kissed me bombarded my senses before I could batten down my defenses. *We have unfinished business.*

I shivered as the words filtered through my mind, influenced the rhythm of my heart. He'd begged me not to go back to Hammond's house. He'd wanted to protect me, just as Mason Conrad had during that final showdown.

Sadly, I hadn't done so well protecting Detective Barlow. He'd confirmed that the call log on my cell phone was the way Cecilia had connected me to him. I'd failed to delete his number as I should have. I remembered distinctly his showing me how to do it. Maybe I was wrong about the personal feelings, maybe he simply held against me the fact that he'd taken a beating and almost gotten killed because of my failure to do my job right.

I puffed out a lungful of frustration. Giving myself credit, I felt reasonably certain that was my only mistake. Surely for a first operation that wasn't so bad.

That we'd both come so close to dying because of that mistake reminded me that one misstep was all it took.

Cecilia and Vargas had used that discovery to shift blame for the accident from them. That was why Vargas had never caught up to me and Tiff. Cecilia had called and told him they were off the hook…she had something even better to clear themselves. So Vargas hadn't bothered hunting us down. They'd told Hammond that I'd learned that Cecilia had figured out what I was up to and I'd kidnapped Tiffany in order to use her as a bargaining chip to save myself. Liars. Cecilia was in custody and, according to Adcock, was spilling her guts.

My heart ached when I thought of Tiffany and how difficult getting over this would be for her. Thankfully, Hammond had a sister in Chicago who would take care of her. According to Chief Kent the sister had stopped associating with Hammond years ago because of his chosen profession and the resulting lifestyle. Her home sounded like a good place for Tiff. I hoped I would get the opportunity to say goodbye to the little girl.

The door opened, jerking me from my troubling thoughts.

Chiefs Kent and Adcock stepped into the room. I stood in anticipation of the news.

Conrad is still in surgery. A nurse just came out and gave me an update, guarded but hopeful. As he made the statement Chief Kent looked from Barlow to me.

Everyone in the room wanted Conrad to live, only for vastly different reasons. The chiefs and Barlow, well, they wanted whatever information he could provide on

Hammond's organization. They wanted him to help pinpoint all the surviving connections.

I just wanted him to survive. Couldn't bear the thought of him dying. I blinked back the onslaught of tears.

Chief Kent touched my arm. *Adcock and I are going down for coffee, would you like something?*

I shook my head. Knew with complete certainty that my stomach could not tolerate water much less anything else.

Barlow declined anything as well. His brief glance at me spoke volumes about just how much he was holding back. It was eating at him, but he wouldn't give in.

When the chiefs had gone, leaving Barlow and me alone once more, I decided it was time to get this over with. I walked straight up to him and demanded, "Say what's on your mind, Barlow. No use beating around the bush." I was suddenly angry. Angry at myself…at him… at everything. Mainly I was hurting so fiercely I just wanted to cry but, like Barlow, I refused to surrender.

You're upset right now. This isn't a good time to talk.

I saw the concern in his battered face, but it was the other thing I saw in his eyes that wielded the most effect. Anger, bitterness, all restrained out of politeness. Now I was plain old pissed off.

"You want to know the truth?" I roared. I could tell it was a roar by the way my throat burned when I yelled it out. "Yes, he got to me. We didn't sleep together if that's what you're wondering, but he made me feel things." I moved in even closer to Barlow. "Made me feel like a woman again. And he saved my life."

There, I'd said it.

Barlow's hands dove into my hair, pulled my face to his until our lips almost touched. I felt his breath on my skin…wanted desperately for him to do this. Make me feel anything but this agony.

He drew back just far enough for me to see his lips, but he didn't release me. *Like I said before, we have unfinished business. But now isn't the time.*

I tried to pull away, but his fingers cradled my skull more tightly. *What you're feeling right now is about him.* Barlow stared at my lips a moment as if he wanted to kiss me. I wanted him to. I so wanted that escape. But he refused to give it to me. *I need it to be about us.*

I curled my fingers around his wrists and pulled his hands from my hair, held them in my own. He was right. Jesus, he was always right. A calmness fell over me and I knew he was the only one of us being objective here.

Barlow looked up and I understood that someone had walked into the room. I wheeled around and felt my heart still in my chest as I recognized one of the surgeons from the team attempting to save Conrad's life.

Fear slid through my veins.

Mr. Conrad is in Recovery now. It's a miracle he survived, he allowed, looking exhausted. *If that second bullet had been a hair's width farther right it would have nipped his heart and we wouldn't be having this discussion.*

Second bullet?

I missed part of what he said after that. What second bullet? Conrad had been hit low on the abdomen, but… images abruptly filled my head. I remembered dropping down beside him as the paramedic had ripped off his shirt. There had been two bullet holes.

But that wasn't right.

He took the shot intended for me. He flung his body over mine to protect me. Had he gotten shot again? I didn't remember seeing blood higher on his shirt when Adcock had first pulled Conrad off me.

The surgeon left the waiting room and I turned to Barlow to get what I'd missed. "Is he going to live?"

He averted his eyes as he spoke, and I knew he didn't want to see the worry in mine. *He survived surgery. If there are no complications, he should recover.*

I couldn't shake the idea that something didn't fit.

"I think I'll go for that coffee now." I looked up at Barlow. "You coming?"

He shook his head. *Someone needs to stay close by.*

I hesitated at the door. "I didn't realize he'd gotten shot twice until…" Seeing those two leaking wounds when the paramedic ripped off Conrad's shirt flashed in my mind. I shook my head. "Never mind."

I wandered to the bank of elevators and depressed the down button. Those final minutes at the Warehouse kept playing over and over in my mind. SWAT guys had been everywhere. Then the paramedics had arrived. It was all so confusing. I wondered then if I would ever be able to sleep again at night. Probably not.

In the cafeteria, I found Chiefs Kent and Adcock.

Take my chair, Merri, Kent offered. *I'll go up and keep Barlow company.*

I nodded and settled into the chair he'd vacated. I stared at the cup of coffee Adcock sipped, but I couldn't work up the enthusiasm to go for any.

Finally, when I could bear it no longer, I leaned forward, propped my arms on the table and looked directly at him. "I'm confused about something," I said bluntly. "I thought Conrad was hit only once, in the lower abdomen. Did I miss the other wound?"

The startled look in the chief's eyes took me by surprise. The question wasn't that complicated.

"I mean," I offered, "I didn't see it immediately after the ruckus had settled down." I shrugged. "Maybe I missed it. But it doesn't feel right."

Shots were flying, he reminded me. *It's a miracle you and Barlow weren't hit.*

Wasn't it, though?

Still, something wasn't right. I could feel it deep inside. "Will they run ballistics on the bullets?"

Adcock pushed up from his chair. *Really, Miss Walters, don't you think your energy would be better spent on something less trivial? He survived.*

Now I'd made him angry. Did he think I was somehow trying to blame this on him? He was the one Helen had been able to reach. I was grateful he'd gotten backup over there. He had saved Barlow and me from certain death.

"I'm sorry. I didn't mean to sound ungrateful."

His expression mellowed a little. *Look, it's been a long day for all of us. Why don't I get you a cup of coffee and we'll go back up and wait for news on Conrad's condition?*

Maybe I was being paranoid. I had been pretty damned hysterical. Shoot-outs had that affect on me.

Adcock bought my coffee and led the way back to the elevator. He jabbed the call button.

The panic that had begun to rise started to claw at me. I needed to work off some of this tension. Couldn't just sit in some waiting room any longer without dealing with this building anxiety. "I think I'll take the stairs."

Adcock shrugged. *I'll join you.*

As I trudged up the stairs, I played those final moments over and over in my mind. I had to be missing something.

Adcock suddenly stopped, grabbed me by the arms and pinned me to the railing. Several seconds ticked by before my brain assimilated what was happening.

He deserved to die, he growled, his face so near to mine I could barely read his lips.

"Oh, my God," I murmured, denial burgeoning in my chest.

Adcock hadn't tried to help Conrad. He'd tried to finish him off…that's where the second bullet to his chest had come from.

"It was *you*."

But why?

If Barlow had just let it go, but he wouldn't. He left me with no choice. I'd already made a new deal with Mathers. You were all supposed to die in there.

That was the other thing that hadn't felt right. Live hostages had been inside that antiques warehouse and still someone, Adcock I now knew, had sent in SWAT with no care as to our survival.

Whatever else Adcock said was lost on me since I hadn't taken my eyes off his. The bastard.

Fury whipped through me.

Well, that's all right. I'm sure Detective Barlow will understand that in your distraught state you merely stumbled down the stairs.

I ripped the top off my cup and dashed the hot coffee in his face.

He released me...scrubbed at his scalded eyes.

I bolted toward the next level. Only two more—

Adcock snagged the back of my shirt.

I grabbed the railing for balance, kicked backward, elbowed him, tried to knock him off balance.

One hand twisted in my hair, yanked me backward.

My fingers slid down the cold metal railing, couldn't grab on again.

I twisted...clawed...kicked.

Then I remembered what Barlow had taught me.

Surrender.

I stopped fighting so hard, let him get a firm hold on me.

He grinned hatefully at me. *This shouldn't hurt for long.*

When he would have shoved me over the rail, I grabbed onto it with one hand and slammed my full body weight into his unsuspecting frame.

For one fraction of a second he teetered, reached frantically for me, then gravity took over and he tumbled down the stairs, landing in an awkward sprawl.

Barlow was suddenly at my side, checking me for injury, then moving down to take a look at Adcock. He jerked the bastard's hands together and cuffed him, then moved back up to where I stood, paralyzed.

Can't a guy even go for coffee without running into trouble?

"Sorry you missed all the excitement," I said, my voice still wobbling.

I tried to catch up with you in the cafeteria, saw you head for the stairs when I got back to the elevator. He glanced down at Adcock. *I knew he was hiding something,* Barlow said. *I just hadn't figured out what.*

He took me into his arms and I collapsed there… didn't want to think anymore.

By early that afternoon Mason Conrad had regained consciousness. Chief Kent had taken a statement from him. Barlow and I, both looking worse for the wear, still waited to hear the rest of the story.

Adcock's broken leg and concussion had been attended to. He was under guard in another room and refusing to talk.

At least some part of this nightmare would have a decent ending, I mused. Adcock would get his. Considering how many cops as well as civilians who had died because of Luther Hammond, Adcock wouldn't be getting offered any plea bargains. Besides, Metro had an ace in the hole: Mason Conrad. He knew Luther Hammond's business inside and out.

Chief Kent entered the waiting room and both Barlow and I were on our feet. I felt reasonably certain he was as sore and achy as I was, but he didn't let on so I didn't, either.

Conrad wants to talk to you, Chief Kent said to me.

A flutter in my tummy elicited a smile on my lips. "Now?"

The chief nodded. *Just keep it brief.*

I turned back to Barlow, knowing this wouldn't sit well with him.

Give us a moment, he said to the chief.

Chief Kent relented and stepped back into the corridor.

My attention settled back on Barlow. Sometime during the course of events, he'd gotten a stitch at the corner of his lip. His jaw was still swollen and the color of recent hand-to-hand combat had set in. My heart stumbled. He'd tried so hard to protect me. Had risked his life…just like the other man down the hall. My emotions surged anew, confusing me all the more.

You did a good job, Merri.

Emotion threatened my flimsy hold on composure. Why now? Couldn't he have saved this speech for later? We'd been sitting in this stupid waiting room for hours! He had to go and make me all emotional now?

I'm very proud of you, he went on. *The city of Nashville owes you a great debt. Luther Hammond was a menace and now he's gone. Many more wrongs will be set to right with Cecilia's and Conrad's testimony. None of this would have happened without your help.*

Cecilia had fessed up a few hours ago as well. I couldn't help experiencing a little extra glee over that one.

"Thank you."

Barlow reached out, touched my cheek so gently. His own eyes looked suspiciously bright just then. *I don't want this to be the end.* He looked away a moment before letting his gaze fix firmly on mine once more. *I want to finish that business we started, but I understand you have other things to do first. I'll be waiting.*

Somehow I managed to bob my head up and down. He still wanted to see where this thing between us might go. He'd said so earlier, but our emotions had been too raw, the insanity too fresh to make sense of how we felt. There really were no words to explain how I felt at that moment. Maybe it was still too soon.

Sensing my loss for words, he left it at that and we joined the chief in the too-quiet corridor. I felt beyond numb…confused…relieved…and so damned exhausted.

This way, Chief Kent said to me.

I knew that Barlow followed, but he stayed some

distance behind us. When we reached the intensive care unit, Chief Kent hesitated.

Merri, when you've had time to come to terms with all that's happened, I want you to know that my offer still stands. Whenever you're ready there's a place in Metro for you. I'm thinking you would be most at home in our crime-scene investigation unit. If you choose to return to the archives, I can live with that as well. He patted me on the shoulder. *You think about it and let me know.*

"I will."

I barely kept my emotions at bay as I moved into the ICU and on to where the guards waited outside Mason Conrad's cubicle. The doctor was just coming out.

Don't push him, he advised sternly. *And don't keep him talking too long.*

"I'll keep it short," I assured him.

The doctor didn't look happy about it, but he let me pass.

Mason Conrad looked as pale as the sheets covering him, and a barrage of medical equipment monitored his vitals. He'd taken that bullet for me, almost paid the ultimate price for knowing too much. I owed him more than I could possibly ever hope to repay. Despite knowing what I did about who and what he was, I couldn't prevent feeling immensely grateful to him.

He watched as I moved to his bedside. "Looks like you're going to make it," I said. I felt my voice wobble, but I ushered a cheery smile into place. At least I hoped it was cheery. I tried really hard.

Looks like, he agreed. He moistened his lips. They looked dry and cracked.

A cup of water with a straw inserted into it sat on the bedside table. "Is it okay for you to have more water?"

He nodded. I put the straw to his lips and waited while he took a few sips before I set it aside.

You fooled me. The look in his eyes was definitely not what I had expected from a man reported to be a cold-hearted killer. To be honest, I hadn't known what to expect. No one was more startled than me when the chief announced that he wanted to talk to me or that he intended to cooperate fully with the police.

"I did what I had to do," I admitted.

A barely discernible nod acknowledged my statement.

I'm going to cooperate with Chief Kent, he said. *If I'm lucky maybe I'll get off a little lighter.*

"That's good." I was glad he'd decided to do the right thing. I wanted something good to come of all this.

He grimaced with the effort of reaching out and taking my hand. I didn't draw away. A ghost of a smile haunted one corner of his mouth. *You made me remember what it feels like to want someone like you. Someone sweet and innocent. Now I wish I could forget.*

My pulse fluttered, making me light-headed. I had to get back on neutral territory here. I remembered something he'd said to me my first night at Hammond's mansion. "You told me you had a sister who was blind. What happened to her?" I worked hard at keeping my respiration even, but it was not easy. My emotions were still too raw.

She died. Let the wrong kind of man take advantage of her. It was obvious that the memory still pained him.

"I'm sorry."

He squeezed my hand. *You just make sure it doesn't happen to you.*

I tried not to ask. I really did. I bit my lip. Considered just saying goodbye and getting the hell out, but I couldn't. I had to know.

"Mason…" I winced at having stepped into personal territory. I'd already let him hold my hand. Any sense of professionalism I'd ever possessed seemed to be curiously absent at the moment…or maybe being too damned curious was the problem. "Mr. Conrad—"

Mason. There was no mistaking the look in my eyes now. He remembered quite well exactly what put us on a first-name basis, beyond his insisting I call him that.

I blushed from the top of my head to the soles of my feet. "Okay. Mason. Adcock was connected to Hammond, but turned on him, is that right?"

He nodded. *He kept Hammond informed until two weeks ago. He didn't mention you. We suspected he was working with Vargas and Mathers in the end.*

It boggled my mind. How was one supposed to tell the good guys from the bad guys anymore? I sighed. That's what people like Steven Barlow were for…and maybe me, though I felt lost just now.

"Thank you…" I let him see in my eyes the sincerity of my words. "For saving my life." I blinked back the tears that crested on my lashes. "I'll check on you tomorrow," I told him. I had to get out of here. Had to clear my head of all the confusion and look at this whole situation from a more objective place. I backed away a couple of steps. "Take care."

He nodded. *You, too. Let me know if there's anything about us you can't forget.*

I turned away before I said or did something I might regret. I walked past the guards without slowing. Kent and Barlow waited outside the ICU.

"I need to go home." I walked away without waiting for a response or without even a glance at Barlow. I couldn't take any more of this. It was no longer about work. I'd begun to wonder if it ever really had been.

Ten o'clock had come and gone that night before I prepared for bed. I'd spent most of the evening with my family. Everyone was excited about Chief Kent's offer except me. I was far too exhausted, too emotionally drained, to work up any enthusiasm for anything.

Even after a long, hot bath I felt confused and torn. Torn about what I wanted to do with my future. Torn between two men who evoked very specific yet different feelings in me.

I cinched the belt of my fluffy terry-cloth robe and padded to the kitchen to make some hot chocolate. As tired as I was, sleep seemed a fleeting hope at best.

I set the kettle on the stove and turned on the flame, then dumped the cocoa mix into my cup. Might as well check out the movie offerings for tonight. My mother always said a watched pot never boiled. No use hanging around the kitchen waiting for the water to get hot.

As I shuffled into the living room, the red light above my front door flashed, warning me that someone had rung my doorbell. I looked at the clock again. Surely one of my brothers hadn't come out at this time of night to check on me. I swear. How would I ever get it through their thick skulls that I could take care of myself?

I opened the door, expecting to launch my well-cited independence tirade but quickly snapped my mouth shut when my gaze landed on Steven Barlow.

May I come in?

He still looked like hell, but he'd cleaned up. Wore another of those nice suits like the one I'd admired the first time I'd laid eyes on him. I wondered vaguely if he'd had to attend some sort of meeting, then I remembered there had been a press conference. I didn't go, Metro still wanted to keep me a secret.

"Sure. Would you like some hot chocolate?"

He thought about the question a second too long, but then surprised me with, *I'd love it.*

I supposed that guys like him generally got offered a gin and tonic or bourbon and cola. I, Merri Walters, had hot chocolate. Innocent. Naive. Yes, apparently, I was, indeed, both of those things. But not quite as much as I used to be…I'd seen and experienced too much.

When the hot chocolate steamed from our cups and we'd both taken a seat in my small but comfortable living room, he eventually got around to coming out with what he was doing here at this time of night.

Chief Kent has asked me if I'd like the chief of Homicide position.

For the first time in days I felt a genuine smile stretch across my mouth. Finally, something to celebrate. "That's great! I hope you accepted."

He held up a hand as if to slow my enthusiasm. *I did, but there are hoops we have to jump through before it's official.*

"Wow." Now, that was true justice. No one in Metro deserved the promotion more than Steven Barlow. I could vouch for that.

He braced his forearms on his knees and zeroed that piercing blue gaze in on mine. *I want you there with me, Merri. We need your kind of keen perception studying these cases. You don't have to chase down the bad guys or go undercover, just help us with the details. Nobody's better at that than you. I know Chief Kent already made you the offer, I'm asking you to seriously consider it.*

With sudden clarity I recognized exactly what I wanted to do. "You've got yourself a deal, Chief Barlow." My smile widened to a teasing grin.

That sexy, lopsided smile claimed his face before he could stop it and he winced at the pain generated by the move.

My hands flew to my mouth. "That had to hurt."

It was worth it. He reached across the table and took my hand. *You're very special, Merri.*

I sighed, but this time it had nothing to do with frustration or exhaustion. It was about satisfaction, a feeling of finally comprehending on a small level what I wanted in life. It suddenly felt very good to be me. "I'm still a little confused," I admitted, laying down the boundaries right off the bat. "I need to go slow with this personal stuff…sort out my feelings."

He searched my eyes. I saw understanding in his. *Take all the time you need. I'm not going anywhere.*

We lapsed into silence and drank our chocolate and I was okay with that. I could live with the silence. In fact, I can do most anything I choose.

Just watch me.

* * * * *

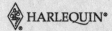
HARLEQUIN®

INTRIGUE®

Has a brand-new trilogy
to keep you
on the edge of your seat!

Better than all the rest...

THE ENFORCERS

BY

DEBRA·WEBB

JOHN DOE ON HER DOORSTEP
April

EXECUTIVE BODYGUARD
May

MAN OF HER DREAMS
June

Available wherever Harlequin Books are sold.

www.eHarlequin.com   HIMOHD

is proud to bring you
a fresh, new talent....

Don't miss
SHOW HER THE MONEY,
from new author
STEPHANIE FEAGAN
Available April 2005

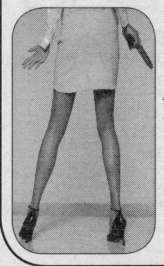

Accountant Whitney "Pink" Pearl had exposed a funny-money accounting scam by one of her firm's biggest clients— and the only evidence was locked in a box with a blow-up doll! Only Pink's feisty determination—and a little help from one savvy lawyer—could get her out of the red this time....

If you enjoyed what you just read,
then we've got an offer you can't resist!

Take 2 bestselling love stories FREE!

Plus get a FREE surprise gift!

Silhouette
BOMBSHELL™
COMING NEXT MONTH

#37 WILD WOMAN by Lindsay McKenna
Sisters of the Ark
Pilot Jessica Merrill's risk-taking actions had earned her the nickname Wild Woman. Now she'd been charged with retrieving a powerful Native American totem from the madman who would use it to gain immortality. But Jessica's doubtful partner, Mace Phillips, was less enthusiastic about the mission. It was up to her to save the tribe—and show Mace that sometimes you had to take wild chances to get what you wanted....

#38 COUNTDOWN by Ruth Wind
Athena Force
Time was running out for code breaker Kim Valenti. She had evidence that terrorists were planning to disrupt the upcoming presidential election, but when she thwarted one attack, the terrorists made her their next target. Racing to save herself, the president and his opponent, she'd have to rely on her code-breaking skills—and the help of one sympathetic member of the bomb squad—before time ran out for everyone....

#39 THE MIDAS TRAP by Sharron McClellan
Renegade archaeologist Veronica Bright knew myths were based in truth. But her professional reputation had been torn to shreds when she'd tried to prove her theories. Now the renowned Dr. Simon Owens had handed her the opportunity to fight back—on a hunt for the legendary Midas Stone. Was this finally her chance to validate years of hard work, or was it a trap?

#40 SHOW HER THE MONEY by Stephanie Feagan
Accountant Whitney "Pink" Pearl was in trouble. She'd exposed a funny money accounting scam by one for her firm's biggest clients—and the only evidence was locked in a box with a blow-up doll! Meanwhile, someone was stalking her, and when a top executive turned up dead, she realized she had been the intended victim. Only Pink's feisty determination—and the help of one savvy lawyer—could get her out of this mess!

SBCNM0305